LUNATIC

teddekker.com

DEKKER FANTASY

BOOKS OF HISTORY CHRONICLES

THE LOST BOOKS
Chosen
Infidel
Renegade
Chaos
Lunatic
Elyon

THE CIRCLE SERIES
Black
Red
White
Green (SEPTEMBER 2009)

THE PARADISE BOOKS
Showdown
Saint
Sinner

Skin
House (with FRANK PERETTI)

DEKKER MYSTERY

Kiss (WITH ERIN HEALY)
Blink of an Eye

MARTYR'S SONG SERIES
Heaven's Wager
When Heaven Weeps
Thunder of Heaven
The Martyr's Song

THE CALEB BOOKS
Blessed Child
A Man Called Blessed

DEKKER THRILLER

THR3E
Obsessed
Adam

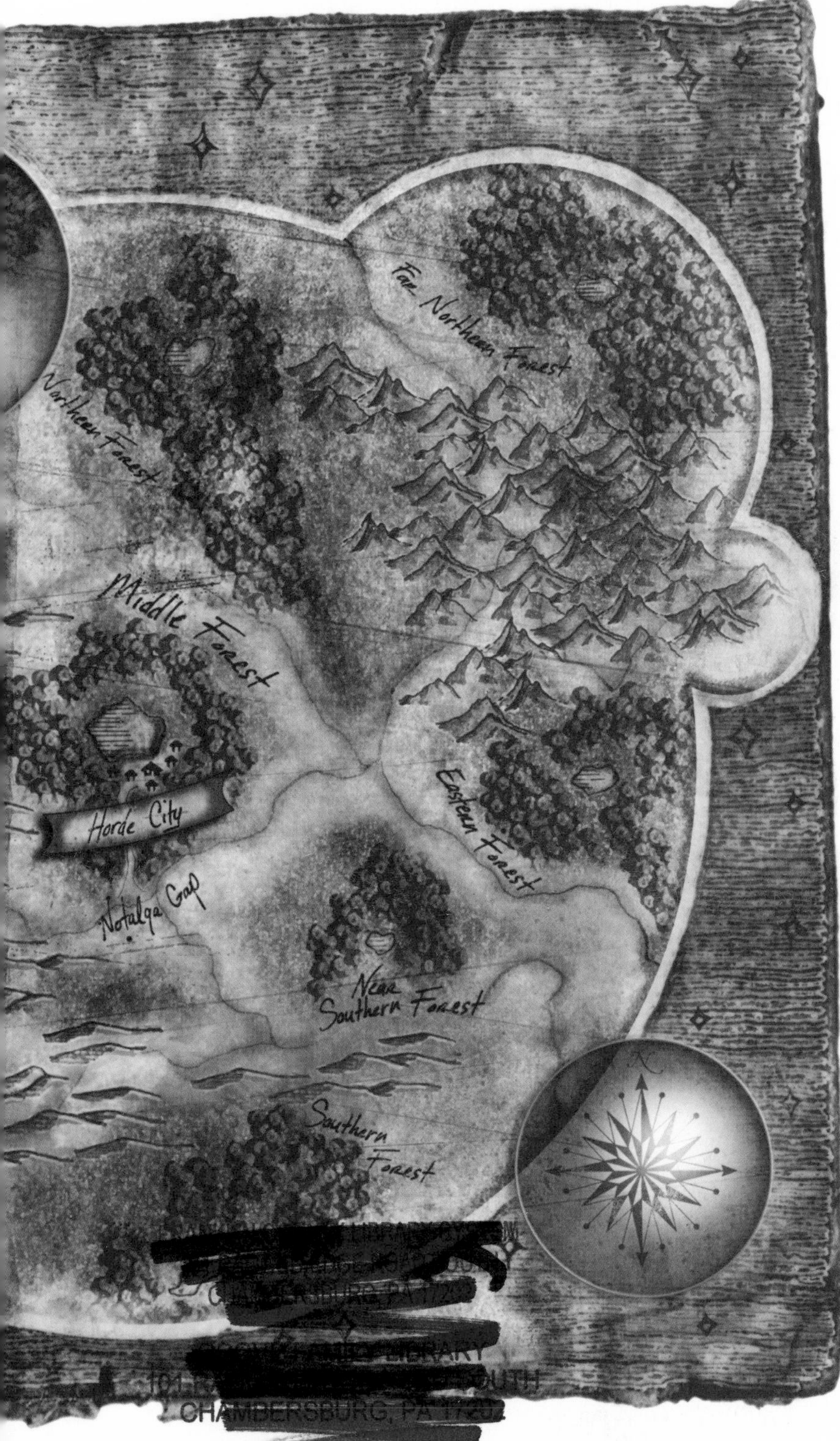
Far Northern Forest
Northern Forest
Middle Forest
Horde City
Notalga Gap
Eastern Forest
Near
Southern Forest
Southern
Forest

LUNATIC

A LOST BOOK

TED DEKKER
AND
KACI HILL

THOMAS NELSON
Since 1798

NASHVILLE DALLAS MEXICO CITY RIO DE JANEIRO BEIJING

Published in Nashville, Tennessee, by Thomas Nelson. Thomas Nelson is a registered trademark of Thomas Nelson, Inc.

Published in association with Thomas Nelson and Creative Trust, 5141 Virginia Way, Suite 320, Brentwood, TN, 37027.

Thomas Nelson books may be purchased in bulk for educational, business, fund-raising, or sales promotional use. For information, please e-mail SpecialMarkets@ThomasNelson.com.

Page design by Casey Hooper
Map design by Chris Ward

Library of Congress Cataloging-in-Publication Data

Dekker, Ted, 1962-
Lunatic / Ted Dekker and Kaci Hill.
p. cm. -- (Lost books ; bk. 5)
"A Lost Book."
Summary: Five years after leaving home, Johnis, Silvie, and Darsal return to find that the Horde has taken over Middle, Thomas and the rest of the Forest Guard have gone into hiding, and a strange new force has begun challenging everything they thought they knew.
ISBN 978-1-59554-373-8 (hardcover)
[1. Fantasy. 2. Christian life--Fiction.] I. Hill, Kaci. II. Title.
PZ7.D3684Lun 2009
[Fic]--dc22

2009007882ta

Printed in the United States of America
09 10 11 12 QW 6 5 4 3 2 1

beginnings

Our story begins in a world totally like our own, yet completely different. What once happened seems to be repeating itself two thousand years later.

But this time the future belongs to the young, to the warriors, to the lovers. To those who can follow hidden clues and find a great treasure, which will unlock the mysteries of life and wealth.

Twenty years have passed since the lush, colored forests were turned into desert by Teeleh, enemy of Elyon and vilest of all creatures. Evil now rules the land and shows itself as a painful, scaly disease that covers the flesh of the Horde living in the wasteland.

The powerful green waters, once precious to Elyon, with the exception of seven small lakes surrounded by seven small forests, have vanished from the earth. Those few who have chosen to follow the ways of Elyon are now called Forest Dwellers, bathing once daily in the powerful waters to cleanse their skin of the scabbing disease.

For thirteen years, the number of their sworn enemy, the Horde, grew, and the Forest Guard was severely diminished by war, forcing Thomas, supreme commander, to lower the army's recruitment age to sixteen. A thousand young recruits showed themselves worthy and now serve in the Forest Guard.

From among the thousand, four young fighters—Johnis, Silvie, Billos, and Darsal—were handpicked by Thomas to lead.

Unbeknownst to Thomas and those in the forests, our four heroes have also been chosen by the legendary white Roush, guardians of all that is good, for a far greater mission, and they are forbidden to tell a soul. Braving terrible battles, crushing defeat, capture, death, and betrayal, they pursued their quest to find the seven original Books of History, a mission that took them from one reality into another.

From their world to the histories, two thousand years into their past.

Into a city known as Las Vegas.

And now we join our heroes deep in the mountains of Romania on the day after their great victory, having secured all seven books, thereby foiling the plans of the Dark One, who would use the books to destroy humankind. They will now leave our world and return to Thomas and the Forest Guard, two thousand years from now.

But five years have passed since they left their home in the distant future. The world they once knew there has changed. If you are Horde, sworn enemy of Thomas and the Forest Guard, you will undoubtedly think very favorably about the change.

Unfortunately Johnis, Silvie, and Darsal are not Horde.

one

Almost a day had passed. Twilight now fell over the horizon. Curling smoke still wafted heavenward, blocking the stars. A cool breeze drove the lingering stench of burning debris away from them.

Darsal sat across from Silvie, knees to her chest. Before her were the seven books, neatly lined up in a row between the girls. Two black ones were stacked on top of each other. Beside them, the green. Next, purple. Red. And then the blue and brown stacked together.

The seven Books of History. Recovered at last.

Her face was still damp, tears mixing with soot.

"Are you ready?" Johnis's soft voice came from behind Darsal. Then his hand touched her shoulder, and he crouched between her and Silvie.

He pocketed two books, placed a third in front of him, and drew his knife. "Darsal, it's time to go home. To Middle." He smiled. "It's over. You'll see. No more books. We won."

The last time he'd asked her to slit her finger, they'd been stolen away by seven accursed bundles of paper and leather, bound with twine. Sucked through time into a world of cars and airplanes and vampires and terrible betrayal.

Of nightmare and sorrow.

Of misery and cruel sacrifice.

"It feels more a reckoning than triumph."

"We saved the world, Darsal," Johnis said. "We did it. *You* did it."

"Mission accomplished." Darsal tried to scoff but couldn't. She couldn't help staring at the books. "Back. Back to what?"

Johnis and Silvie kept quiet. Let her talk.

"It's been a long time for me," she said, aware of the tension in her voice. "A bit unnerving."

They both watched her. Waiting. For hours. Johnis refused to touch the books until she was ready. And they'd been far beyond patient.

It was long past time.

"We'll be with you, Darsal," Silvie said. "We'll return heroes."

Darsal nodded. She picked up one of the books, eased it into her waistband, and set another in front of her. Silvie did the same.

Now all three knelt with a single book before them.

Darsal slit her index finger with her blade. Johnis and Silvie cut theirs in unison. Johnis drew a loud breath. Grinned.

"You'll come to the wedding, Darsal, won't you?"

A forced smile. "I wouldn't miss it."

He winked at her and traded an amused look with Silvie, then held his finger a fraction of an inch off the leathery cover of his book. Silvie's hand snaked over his a second behind.

"For Elyon," he said.

Darsal's hand shot out and pressed against the cover of her book. "For Elyon."

two

"I'm growing weary of your incompetence, Marak." Qurong stormed around the perimeter of the conference room, gray eyes ablaze. Long dreadlocks and black and red robes flapped about the supreme commander's tall, powerful frame. Morst—a white paste meant to soothe the painful burning, mute the stench, and conceal the lesions covering his skin—was beginning to crack with his temper.

"With respect, my lord, this situation was unceremoniously dumped in my lap. It's taken eighteen months to undo the mistakes of my predecessor with regards to Eram, and in the meantime I've spent eight months putting together plans to annihilate the albinos, plans that merely await my final transcription and your approval."

Marak stood with his hands at the small of his back, impatient for his commander to complete his tirade. He wanted out of the conference room, with its pungent mix of morst, sweat, and curling smoke.

"Tell me something: what would General Martyn have thought of your pitiful excuses?" Qurong demanded. Martyn had been a longtime general under Qurong, a turncoat from among the albinos years ago. He'd been cunning enough to put Thomas Hunter's skills to the test.

But that was five years and five generals ago.

"Respectfully, sir, General Martyn would not have approved the complete elimination of the albinos at all."

"His only vice. Regardless, your inefficiency would have met with his severe displeasure. My generals remain on the downslide. Unfortunately for you, my patience is thin. So enough of these pathetic, cowardly attempts to dodge responsibility. I highly doubt the escape of fifty albinos was the result of a dead man. Perhaps I will require another torch."

Marak momentarily froze. The last general Qurong had "demoted" had burned. Marak eyed the two lit torches mounted on six-foot poles and tried not to think too long about what might have taken place. Nor what the priest Sucrow had done before dragging the corpse to his thrall to use for his black arts. Marak had never cared to ask for any of the details.

"What do you think, General?"

He looked past Qurong, past the two narrow steps leading to a small landing that contained Qurong's chair, past the dark wood and thick purple cushion, and through the open window that overlooked Middle Lake, toward Sucrow's thrall.

"I don't think that will be necessary, my lord."

"Just as you've not found it necessary to execute the vermin when I tell you to?"

Marak balked. Two weeks ago they had rounded up fifty albinos, among them his sister-in-law and his grandfather. His captain had suggested setting up a trap to catch Jordan of Southern, who happened to be Marak's brother.

Jordan had come running for his wife. Most of the prisoners had escaped. Marak's family had been recaptured.

"With respect, sir, they may have informa—"

"You've had more than enough time to interrogate and execute the mongrels. Sucrow, tell me, how difficult is it to kill an albino, his wench, and an old man?"

"Killing them is swift and simple." Sucrow stood tall and thin in his black cowl and pointed hood. "It's keeping them alive that's the art form." Sucrow cackled. Narrow, piercing gray eyes drilled Marak with a malignant glower.

Marak's eyes narrowed. "Priest . . ."

"Go on," Qurong prompted. He received twisted pleasure from stirring up the rivalry between his general and his priest.

"Perhaps there is something the general does not wish us to know."

"Enlighten me, Priest," Qurong said.

"The general can't seem to remember that a dead relative is a dead relative," Sucrow taunted.

Marak curled his fist.

"Though I am enjoying the exclusive use of them in our ceremonies," Sucrow finished. "And Teeleh is well pleased with the woman."

The priest's hatred of albinos ran deeper than any tie to kin. He would kill relatives who accumulated the disease. Slowly.

And what he could do to an albino would make anyone's insides curdle.

"Is that so?" Qurong asked, leering.

Marak fought to keep control of his temper. He had no desire to execute his own blood. But even though Qurong himself had once hesitated on a matter of family, he didn't expect the supreme commander to consider this the same situation.

Hesitation never boded well.

And he had hesitated too long.

"It seems the priest is better suited for this than the general. Tell me something, Marak," Qurong continued. "Is it that you are incapable of catching albinos or that you are unwilling to catch albinos?"

"My lord, the Desecration will eliminate all of the albinos, including the prisoners wasting dungeon space." Marak cut himself off before he could add that ultimate loyalty to his supreme commander held his brother, sister-in-law, and grandfather in a dungeon.

Qurong waved him to silence. "Whatever you're doing blustering around in an office in Middle obviously isn't working. I don't understand the difficulty of a few diseased, smooth-skinned rats."

Marak bit his tongue. Thomas Hunter's Circle were diseased, not simpletons. Quite the opposite, in fact, they were a crafty lot who retained all the brilliance they'd possessed before the Horde had defeated them and pushed all who refused to join them into the desert. They were called "albinos" because of their smooth skin, not for any lack of intelligence.

"You said you trained under Martyn. Was that a lie?"

Marak refused to react to Qurong's baiting. "Certainly not, my lord."

"Did Martyn fail to teach you adequately? Was he too lenient on you? Or did he teach you to love albinos?" Qurong spat, lip curling into a sneer.

"General Martyn was more than adequate during my training with him, Commander."

"Then why are you wasting both my time and Sucrow's men? You've been using his serpent warriors for ten months and now you hesitate like a coward."

Serpent warriors. Sucrow's own private army, a religious faction with fangs. Most called them "throaters," a term incorporated almost two years ago that referred to warriors who kept tally of their kills and reveled in bloodlust and glory.

Eighteen months of penance for his predecessors' idiocy.

Eight months of working on a plan to systematically finish off the enemy.

Naught but accusations of treachery and cowardice for his reward.

Marak held his tongue. A lesser man than Qurong would find a blade in his gut. "I find albinos as distasteful as you do, sir."

"Then what exactly is your current strategy? As far as I can tell, it is nothing but throaters and warriors chasing shadows in the south desert, pretending to do their duties and making a mockery of you. Is it that, Marak? Can you not control your own men? Do the servants of a priest terrify you? Or do you plan on undermining me?"

Sucrow's serpent warriors were brutal.

Efficient and precise, though.

"The men are under my control, sir. I've spent months completing plans to bring to you for approval. Our plans for bringing Eram in without a fight have been tabled upon your request."

Qurong had no business pretending to know what went on in the field. The old man hadn't fought in battle in years and left men like Marak to do the grunt work.

"Well, then," Qurong taunted. "Let's hear your plan, General."

Marak bit back his proud smile. Shortly after Martyn's departure, Marak had come across his war journal. The details had proven fascinating. He'd devoted himself to study, and by the time he had been made general, he had learned enough to know a few new tricks to killing albinos more efficiently.

His brother had once said the Circle would never crack, nor be desecrated—his words verbatim. Marak had chosen the mission's name from his younger brother's declaration.

"There are two stages to Desecration, my lord. My men have studied their movements and place them in the northwest desert. I have hunters out there as we speak, searching out the vermin."

He'd followed his little brother closely enough to put them in the northwest desert. Knew they were somewhere in canyons or mountains. Knew as soon as he found a red lake, the albinos were only days from discovery. From annihilation.

Time. All he needed was time.

And if Jordan didn't break down and tell them where the Circle was, Marak would simply orchestrate his "escape" and let his little brother lead the scouts directly to them. Cruel, but necessary.

"Phase one is almost complete," Marak explained. "We've spent the last few months developing a poison that will only affect those with the disease. It causes open sores on their skins, an infection that spreads like fire over dried grass. The albinos have something in their skin that the poison attacks. We are immune to it. It's only a matter of days before we find the exact location of the Circle. We've also managed to make it available in several forms. Any exposure is lethal. I—"

"Enough." Qurong paced away from Marak, fist knotting around his sword. "I want results, Marak. You began with a thousand. And yet, despite your attempts, they keep taking our people and forcing them into these rites of theirs. Despite your assurances and your talk of victory, you have, in fact, only captured two hundred and some. Not even half of the estimated number."

"My lord—" Marak bit back a curse. Would Qurong ever let him finish?

"And this last incident alone should be enough to order your execution. Fifty albinos don't just waltz out of their cages and disappear. I'd love to hear how you managed that one. Or do you intend to blame the rebels?"

His brother had somehow set them free. Marak still wasn't sure how Jordan had pulled it off. The youth had knowingly walked into a trap, freed fifty men, women—including his own wife—and children, and been captured only because he wouldn't leave his wife behind, and their grandfather wouldn't leave Jordan behind.

Marak would never confess that, though.

"The culprit is being interrogated and dealt with as we speak, Commander. I assure you—"

"I will be assured of *nothing,* Marak!" Qurong spun around to face him, finger jabbing at him. "Martyn assured me he would kill the albinos, and his assurance was but hollow boasting! Woref assured me he would rout out the mongrels, and it amounted to nothing! When that failed, Rowen came, assuring me he would starve them out, and he was dead within two months! And now you think you and Sucrow's pack of throaters can round them up and systematically kill them when they're nowhere to be found?"

"Commander, it will take time, but I insist—"

Qurong struck Marak to the ground with the flat of his sword. Marak hit hard, landing on elbows and palms, surprised at the strength the much older man still possessed.

"I've lost one child to this devilish sorcery, Marak, and I will *not* lose another!"

Marak got up, fire rising in his chest. Still, he kept his voice even, considered his words before speaking. "Many have lost loved ones to the albinos, Commander, respectfully. But know that our best efforts are going into this. Mind, body, soul, our highest priority is Desecration."

Qurong closed the distance between them in two long strides, grabbed Marak by the collar, and pulled their faces close. "I want those albinos dead. All of them, no excuses. And since you can't seem to do the job yourself, not only will you be taking Sucrow's help, you will report to him."

Marak bit back something rash. Sucrow was listening with his silent gloating, his eternal sneer plastered on his face, and it drove Marak mad. Over his dead body would he take orders from a priest.

"My lord, there is no need—"

"Do you require further penalty, General?"

Marak braced himself, swallowed his pride. "No, my lord."

"You had better hope not, General."

three

Darsal's eyes flew open. She lay half on her back, half on her left shoulder. Silvie whispered to her, strong hand shaking her to consciousness.

"You hit your head." Silvie's voice was breathy, barely audible. Right in Darsal's ear.

A crack of light penetrated through a hole in the floor and one window. Dim yellow beams revealed a low, slanted ceiling. Outside the window were spindly brown tree branches, filtering down to two large trunks.

Dust filled her nostrils. An attic.

The rank morning breath of someone's ragged, heavy breathing sounded in her ears. Johnis, his face only inches from hers, peered through a crack. He was shaking, face white and taut, lip firmly clenched between his teeth. The light shone across his straining brown eye, making it gleam like a fish's, huge and round.

Darsal smelled the familiar stench of rotting meat. She gasped and rolled into a crouch.

"Shh!" One of Silvie's hands clamped on her shoulder, the other over her mouth, trembling. The slender blonde pulled Darsal backward and forced her onto what felt like a wooden crate against her legs and beneath her rump.

Silvie was cold and stiff. With one hand she still clutched Darsal's shoulder. With the other she now covered her nose and mouth. "We're—we're here." She stifled a sneeze, red faced and looking somewhat sick, as if allergic to something in their little prison.

Darsal was glad she had not returned alone. But knowing that didn't alleviate the tension. Even ten years hadn't spoiled that smell. Horde. The Horde stench was making Silvie nauseated.

"Where is *here*?" Darsal tried to take in the attic space. She'd hoped they would arrive in Middle, where Johnis grew up. Where Thomas Hunter lived and where they were heroes among the Forest Guard, just like Silvie and Johnis promised.

Instead they were in an attic just above a pack of Scabs.

The space was only about eight feet wide, with an uneven ceiling possibly seven feet high at the zenith and as short as five feet at its lowest point. Dust particles drifted along in the light. Brooms, boxes, and rope littered the small workspace.

Johnis didn't budge from the hole in the floor. Half-panicked.

"Johnis," Darsal hissed. When he didn't move, she shoved him aside and peered through the hole.

She saw what looked like an odd-shaped war room. The top of an old Scab's head shone white and round beneath them. He was screaming at a young officer who wore tan and reddish yellow. Desert colors. The officer looked dirty, as if he'd just come from a fight, from what Darsal could see.

A third stood near a torch, covered by a pointed black hood.

She nearly bolted through the ceiling.

"Qurong!" Johnis reeled back. "Qurong. And I—I know . . . I know where we are."

Qurong and his new priest and his new general all in one place.

A knot formed in Darsal's throat. *Elyon. Why are we less than ten feet from Scabs? Is this your idea of a joke?* "Then that means—"

Johnis darted for the window, kicking up attic debris. Silvie snatched at him, wild-eyed herself. He fought her, bent on the window.

"Johnis!" Silvie hissed, pinning one arm. "Quiet!"

Below them, all conversation stopped. Darsal imagined them gawking at the ceiling, eyes fixed on the small hole above them.

Johnis, Silvie, and Darsal didn't dare breathe.

"What's that sound?" Qurong asked.

Pause.

"General, continue."

And Darsal knew. Knew from Johnis's reaction to the mere

layout of the room beneath them. Still, she had to *see* it to believe it. She climbed toward the window, on tiptoe so she wouldn't make any sound, and peered out. Her heart sank into her boots.

From this vantage point she could see where the Gatherings in Middle used to be, the expansive gardens and tree groves, and the lake.

The lake, once pristine and clear.

Now muddy and brown.

Scab children played along the banks, and Scab warriors guarded the lush terrain.

Silvie pushed up beside her, ducked her head low so no one looking up would see.

Darsal's gaze roved beyond the muddy banks, along the bridge that spanned the now-muddy Middle Lake, and to the opposite shore.

Fan-shaped, narrow steps rose out of the water and up to a portico that led to a pair of brass-overlaid doors with two entwined, winged serpents and an incense altar. The doors opened into a dome-topped temple.

Sucrow's thrall.

"Desecration is finally coming into play, my lord. We're putting out a sizable reward for any albino brought in. None dare set foot outside the desert."

"I remain unimpressed."

Choking back bile, Darsal motioned Johnis to come up beside her to look at Middle Forest, once beautiful and glorious with vibrant-colored flowers and a crystalline lake. Where night after night the warriors danced and celebrated life, where unions and passings were held with gusto, and where food and wine came in generous proportion.

Her beckoning wasn't too different from asking him to identify a loved one's corpse. Johnis's soft brown eyes turned on her. Trembling, he obeyed in slow motion and came up on her left.

"With all due respect, sir, I'm fully capa—"

"I didn't ask your opinion, Marak."

"My house used to be there." Johnis pointed down the road as far as they could see, northward. He clearly wasn't hearing the conversation below.

Darsal gave Silvie a worried look.

"Johnis . . ." Silvie reached around Darsal and grabbed him by the collar, pulling him between them. "It's . . ."

"Middle."

CASSAK GALLOPED UP THE DUST-COVERED WESTERN ROAD. His foam-flecked horse trembled beneath him, anxious to stop. Marak wanted him keeping close watch on Eram's forces. The half-breeds.

Sucrow wanted him checking in with the albino hunting parties.

And thanks to being forced to do both, he was late to Warryn's interrogation.

Disloyalty to Sucrow meant disloyalty to Qurong.

Disloyalty to Sucrow was the price of his loyalty to General Marak.

But even Marak couldn't argue against the fact that it was more important to handle Eram and the hunting parties, to protect everyone from the albino disease, than it was to try to protect Marak's little brother.

Maybe.

Albinos were already dead.

Marak needed to remember that.

The temple was directly ahead. Cassak rode up and swung down almost before the beast beneath him came to a complete halt.

His servant snatched the reins. His scout knelt before him, then stood in salute.

"Report," Cassak ordered. "Make it quick."

"The throater took him over an hour ago," his scout reported, referring to Warryn, chief of the "serpent warriors," the throaters, and the albino prisoner Jordan of Southern, Marak's younger brother.

Cassak started marching, forcing the scout to run to catch up.

He and Sucrow had a deal. Sucrow got the woman for his rituals. The throaters got to practice their skills on all three.

And Marak didn't have to execute the three.

Yet.

Marak would likely change his mind if he knew what Sucrow was doing.

"Over an hour?" Cassak snapped. He turned on the scout. "And you're only now telling me this?"

"You were occupied, Captain, I didn't want to intrude—"

"When I tell you to inform me of a throater's dealings," Cassak growled, "it is always first priority! Do you understand me?"

The scout drew up on himself but didn't cower. Oh no, he wouldn't cower. But he knew well that Cassak had punished warriors severely for less.

"I'll deal with you later. Finish the report before I change my mind."

"Qurong's furious over the albinos. He's forcing the general to report to the priest."

Cassak swore. He had half a mind to go run the priest through just for spite. Could too.

Loyalty. His general's mantra.

Loyalty to his supreme commander before all else.

Loyalty to his general second.

He carried no loyalty toward the priest.

"Captain . . ."

"Water the horse. I've a throater to kill."

four

"We need to think," Darsal whispered. She climbed down. Silvie followed, but neither she nor Johnis answered. Johnis looked about ready to jump out the window and take off in a suicide run.

Thus far they'd gone unheard. Lucky.

But luck never liked to be pushed.

Darsal motioned to Silvie and grabbed a crate on one end. Silvie joined her and picked up the other end. They hoisted the box and lowered it over the hole that opened the attic floor to the room below. It slipped.

They steadied the crate until it rested quietly in place. The dim light snuffed out, save the window. Johnis turned to stare.

Silvie found a long cloth and drew it over the window, stuffing the corners along the edges of the frame to hold it up.

The room grew dark.

"Qurong is in Middle? Now?" Silvie again. "The Guard . . . The Horde—"

"Stop!" Johnis's voice, though soft, fell like glass among them, and Silvie flinched. "Five years," Johnis rasped. "Five years and . . . Middle is . . ."

"Where is Thomas?" Darsal dared ask.

They'd been told five years would pass in Middle between their leaving and their returning. But no one had said anything about this atrocity.

Darsal felt tricked. Betrayed. "If Qurong is here and their new general is here, then the Scabs have . . ."

No one answered.

Thomas gone. The others probably dead. Middle infested with Scabs, with that abomination called the Dark Priest.

But . . . *how*?

"Dead." Silvie's blue eyes narrowed to slits and fixed on the floor, groping at knives that weren't there. The girl's parents had been killed by Scabs. One blade was all Silvie of Southern needed to fulfill her vow of revenge.

"Or Scab." Darsal felt like the walls of the storage room were closing in, threatening to crush all three of them. The floor seemed to warp.

Maybe it would collapse. Expose them to the enemy.

"They've killed the entire Guard," Silvie said. "They'd have to. No one defeats the Guard. Unless the traitor . . ."

Darsal drew a sharp breath and blinked. "*This* is what we saved those bloody books for? *This?* After—"

"Stop!" Johnis struck her. Darsal staggered back, more startled he'd hit her than actually hurt.

Silvie caught Darsal before she could fall to the ground and righted her. "Johnis, keep it down." Thank Elyon, Qurong was shouting too loudly to hear them.

Darsal pushed off. "I am not turning Horde, and I am not going to die like a rat in a cage."

Johnis wasn't seeing Silvie or Darsal. "No, no . . ." He darted back toward the crates and scaled up toward the window.

Silvie tugged at his ankle.

He shook her off. "Kiella, my parents. My *mother* . . ." His voice caught in his throat and lodged there.

Rosa. Darsal groaned. *Oh no. Not again.*

"Johnis, come down," Silvie whispered. "We'll have to find them. They didn't kill all of them. We'll just have to find the Guard and warn them."

He was already pushing up the window, scooting something around to make more room. He kicked loose of Silvie and swung his leg up.

Darsal grabbed him and jerked him down. She and Silvie both caught his flailing form and lowered his struggling, writhing mass to the ground before he hit. Darsal clamped a hand over his mouth. He kicked at her.

Silvie planted her knee against his throat and chest, leaned close, then whispered something Darsal couldn't hear. Johnis stopped fighting and grew still.

Qurong's voice wafted up from the conference room below. Sucrow hissed a reply, and then the general spoke.

"How much time do you need?"

"Six, maybe eight months," Marak said. "Sucrow's throaters have their uses. Eight months at the most."

"Do it in three."

"My lord—"

"Three months, General."

"So they aren't all dead," Silvie whispered, her face only inches from Johnis's. "They can't be." She let Johnis up, and the three of them scooted closer to the hole to listen.

"They could be Scabs." Darsal shuddered.

Succumbing to the skin scabbing disease that plagued the Horde—that cracked the skin and turned it white and flaky, that itched and burned like fire and robbed their minds of the capacity to even see their diseased condition—was worse than death.

All three of them had felt it before.

None wished to feel it again.

Silvie scratched the back of her neck. "Don't think like that."

Johnis hushed them, riveted once more to the crack in the floor. He was still shaking and wiping his eyes, but now his expression had changed.

Darsal envisioned his mind beginning to work its magic, that insane part of him that could concoct wild schemes only Elyon could actually execute while keeping all three of them alive.

"When does the clock start for us?" Darsal asked. "It's been five years here. I haven't bathed in the lakes in ten—"

"Please don't talk." Johnis groaned.

They listened.

The Horde had run the Guard and the Forest's inhabitants into the desert and taken over Middle. The Guard had gone deep. Thomas Hunter had been unheard of and unseen for two years.

Qurong unleashed once more on his general, this time about a band of rebels gathering outside the forest.

Darsal had heard enough.

"We need to get out of here," she whispered.

"We're trapped." Silvie perched on a crate, features now obscured by shadows. "I don't believe this."

None of them were truly still. Silvie fidgeted. Johnis had come out of his shock and begun pacing, hands ruffling his hair. And Darsal felt herself shivering down in her marrow.

"Never mind what you believe. We need a plan," she said. "Johnis, what building is this? I can't tell from up here."

Darsal and Silvie had only been in Middle a few weeks, but Johnis had spent sixteen years here. Even if things had changed, it shouldn't take his memory long to reorient itself.

Johnis spoke. "This is where the council used to meet. Remember that big building with the amphitheater on one side?"

She nodded. They'd been there several times. Usually for a

formal reprimand. "The amphitheater runs up against the lake. We're on the same side, opposite end, then."

"Right," Johnis murmured.

"We could use the books." Silvie withdrew one of her Books of History and put it between them. For a second what remained of the light caught her eyes and lit them like a cat's. "Touch them with blood and go someplace else. Someplace safe."

"No." Johnis and Darsal spoke at the same time.

"Get that away from me." Darsal withdrew her book and tossed it. The leather thumped on the ground.

They froze as the muffled voices below grew quiet. For a full minute neither the three young Forest Guards trapped in the attic nor the Scabs below said a word.

"What was that?"

"Rats."

"Find out. We're finished here."

five

Cassak stormed into the back of Sucrow's interrogation room. Warryn hadn't noticed yet, but the throater would get an earful the second he stopped for a moment's rest.

"Bloody snake," Cassak growled.

Warryn ignored him. He was deep in his interrogation at this point.

Or rather, his torture.

"Your orders were to wait."

The throater smirked, still intent on the albino they had finally captured. For eighteen months Jordan of Southern had wreaked havoc on Middle, raiding the town and stirring up trouble in the ranks.

"Silence while I'm on the supreme commander's business," the throater taunted.

"His or the priest's?"

No answer.

Cassak folded his arms, watching in silence.

The flames burned through Jordan's skin. The albino grimaced, teeth ground together. With his body stretched out across the altar and laid bare, he could do little else. His smooth, golden brown skin shone with sweat, marred black and red where the throaters had applied the lit torch.

Warryn, the throater performing the torture, knew his work well. Marak had hesitated on rounding up his own brother for execution, but Qurong had had enough, and it was time to bring the albino raider to justice.

If they could catch him.

Warryn's capture of Jordan's wife marked the end for the wily albino. Marak hadn't liked the idea, but Cassak knew no surer way to ensnare him. After days of arguing he'd convinced Marak of his loyalties and the inevitability of the mess.

Teeleh help him if Marak learned the whole of it.

"Burn him," Warryn ordered his men. "We'll loosen his tongue."

"Not . . ." Jordan gasped. "Betray . . ."

Warryn's face twisted into a cruel grin. "Scream for me."

The albino set his jaw and braced himself. Cassak could see the muscles in his limbs tighten. Bullheaded adolescent, just like his brother Marak. Neither readily showed pain.

"You saw the trap, fool," Cassak muttered. "All you had to do was run." Loyalty, Marak's mantra. Jordan's mantra. This "interrogation" was pointless.

The albino's quivering turned to thrashing. He'd held out longer than most, but even he had his limitations. The boy screamed in pain.

"Withdraw." Waving his assistant away, Warryn stepped around to the albino's side and yanked his head up by the hair with a gloved hand. "This can end, wretch. I can kill you quickly or slowly, but that is up to you. Where are the rest of the vermin?"

The albino said nothing. Warryn motioned for the wire and a long, thin knife. The albino tried to kick, but the shackles on his ankles prevented him from succeeding. The real screaming started.

"Where, wretch?" Warryn roared over the albino's cries. "How did you get in? How did the others escape?" Question after question with no real pause to let the albino respond.

Warryn was going to kill the wretch.

"Enough. Question him again later."

The throater cursed. "He's close."

"Start on the woman, then."

"WHAT'S IN THE CRATE?" JOHNIS ASKED. HIS EXPRESSION was grim.

Silvie opened it. "Blankets, boxes of dry goods, morst."

Johnis reached down and picked Darsal's book off the floor. "Give me the other." She did, glad to be done with the business.

Then realized what he was doing. "You're going to leave them? Here?"

He looked somewhat torn. "I don't want to be caught with them. We'll decide how to come back and what to do with them later."

Johnis lay all of the books at the bottom of the crate and covered them carefully before closing the lid and setting another crate atop. Seemed to adjust something behind him. Straightened his shirt.

Now this was a bizarre turn.

"Is that you or the scabbing disease talking?"

He scowled at her. "It's me, Darsal. If we try to leave, and we're caught, the Scabs have the books."

"And if we escape, they still have the books." Darsal returned his hard look. "You really want to leave them?"

"No." He wouldn't look at her. "They won't find the crate." Johnis sucked a breath.

"Fuzzy white bat tell you that?"

Johnis's fist knotted and came off the crate. He squeezed hard, then brought his fist back down in a very controlled manner.

"What'd you put in your waistband?"

He furrowed a brow. Didn't answer the question. Instead he said, "If we can get out unnoticed, they won't know to look."

Darsal frowned. A Book of History. He'd thought not to keep all seven in one place.

Good.

She chided herself for not thinking of that first. Glanced over. "Silvie?"

"Leaving them is a bad idea," Silvie said slowly. By the look on her face, she knew too. "But I agree with Johnis. Getting caught with them is worse. How do we plan to come back?"

Johnis hesitated. "We'll figure it out. First we find Thomas."

Instinctively Darsal glanced at her tanned skin. "First we bathe."

"First we get out of here."

"From one hell to another," Darsal muttered. "We need to bathe before we—"

"I *know*." Johnis still looked as though he might jump out the window and do something that would get them all killed.

Silvie ran her tongue over her mouth. She was scared and trapped and itchy for a fight. "I say we just duck out and try not to be seen."

"With what weapons? We weren't armed when we used the books."

Darsal looked away. That was her fault, and they all knew it. She'd disarmed them herself.

Johnis glanced at her. "I didn't mean anything by that."

She nodded.

He dropped to both knees and lifted the crate to listen through the crack in the floor. "Okay, if this is the old council hall, then the attic's a series of storage rooms, and we're in the one above the main hall. You remember?"

"Yes." Darsal dropped beside him, caught her breath. She hadn't forgotten the basic layout. Johnis's mind was working again.

That mattered.

Impulsive Johnis only burned them, and only the mercies of Elyon ever got them out mostly unscathed.

Mostly.

"The amphitheater's on the south side, and the Gatherings were about a half mile east."

"Right." Johnis got up and made another round along his invisible track. His boot scuffed against the wood.

"What's the best way out of here?" Darsal asked. "Preferably without drawing attention to ourselves."

"I've only been up here a couple times, both to hide. The door dumps out into a narrow corridor that runs into a series of hallways. The rooms are small, but the halls run all over the attic space. Assuming they haven't changed much."

Johnis glanced up at the window, probably still considering the jump, then continued. "There are ladders. We'll have to find one, but the only one I know might not drop us where we want to be. I don't know what it is now. It could put us on top of Sucrow for all I know."

"I certainly won't mind crushing him." Silvie shifted closer to Johnis. "What if we got Horde clothing again? That could work."

"We'd have to take out a few Scabs barehanded without drawing attention," Darsal said. "We'll never make it if we all leave at once. Johnis knows Middle far better than we do. So what if . . . ?"

Darsal hesitated and started over. "One of us needs to distract the guards. The other two can slip by during the diversion. Then we—"

"I don't want to split up."

"But you know it's our best option. Divide them. We'll meet up at the lake, bathe, and find Thomas."

He pursed his lips, clearly unhappy at the suggestion. They didn't have time for this! Guards were probably approaching now to see what the Horde leaders had heard above them.

Darsal spun to Silvie. "Talk to him."

"I prefer a fight to running," the blonde fired back. "But she's right—we have to get out first."

Silence as they all contemplated the plan. "What happens to the distracter?" Johnis asked.

Darsal didn't want to think about that. "Let's just get to the Middle pool and bathe. I'll find you."

"You're going to do it?" Johnis turned on his heels back toward her. His face had gone pale again. Was he really so concerned? She was still the better fighter. "Darsal . . . no . . ."

"Yes. You two let me go down first and create a diversion."

"You should let me, Darsal. I grew up here."

"Here isn't home anymore, Johnis. And your growing up here is why it has to be me. You two need stealth. I just need speed. I'll—"

"Shh!" Silvie's hand flew up. "Someone's coming."

Darsal lowered her voice. "I'll go down first. After I get out, I may have to hide out for an hour or two."

"Let me go," Johnis insisted. "I know this place best."

She shook her head. "No. We meet at the far side of the lake. Bathe. Find Thomas."

"Hurry!" Silvie snapped.

Johnis gave his begrudging consent. "Don't wait too long or you'll start to turn." He shoved out his fist. Darsal and Silvie put their hands over his. "For Elyon."

"For Elyon."

A key jangled in the lock. Silvie dove behind the door. Darsal ducked behind the book box. Johnis vanished behind something with a tarp over it. The doorknob turned. Darsal's heart was a giant throbbing knot in her throat. Slowly the door opened. A dark figure inched inside. He smelled awful.

Silvie lashed out, grabbed the Scab in a headlock, and twisted sharply. The Scab nearly fell on top of her much smaller frame.

Johnis closed the door. "Key!" Silvie tossed it to him. Darsal came out and reached Silvie just as the girl drew the Scab's sword and gave it to her. Silvie took his knife.

More footsteps.

"Darsal!" Johnis plastered his back against the door, hand on the knob. He threw her a look.

She nodded and took a ragged breath. After ten years the blade was familiar in her hand, but after Earth, the sword also sickened her. She wasn't sure she could kill again, not even to save her life.

She'd done more in her ten-year life in the other world than even these two knew.

Darsal passed Johnis the sword. "Bathe. Then Thomas."

He accepted with little more than eye contact, then swung the door open. Darsal sprang out into the narrow hallway.

Six

"Halt!"

Darsal raced the opposite way, ignoring the guard's shouts. She tore down the narrow passages and banked a sharp left, then right, praying to Elyon she wouldn't run into a dead end. The hallway was even narrower than Johnis had told her. The Scab Silvie killed had to have bent at an awkward angle just to fit through.

"Stop her. We have a runner!"

At the next three-way in the passage, she saw the left shaft was smaller than the right and chose it. The Scab couldn't follow where he couldn't fit.

She threw herself down the passage and was forced to her hands and knees, sweating and crawling as fast as she could, feeling the rough, uneven beams.

But she'd been wrong about the Scab not fitting; his loud grunts close behind made that clear enough. A hand latched onto her foot. Darsal curled into a ball, kicked into the Scab's belly, and kept going, free for the moment.

She was on wooden beams that crossed over a large room, a catwalk of sorts. But the beams were spaced too far apart for comfort, and they bowed under her weight.

"Get back here, you little wench! I'll slit your throat!"

Darsal wobbled precariously, latched on with one hand, and pressed her foot against a beam to hold her weight. She grabbed with the other hand and resumed crawling. The shakes came so hard she could barely make her hands and feet hold on.

The Scab grabbed her by the calf and pulled hard. She kicked and tried to keep going. But he had her like a fish dangling from a hook and wouldn't let go. He jerked her toward him.

She released her grip and flew backward into him.

The beams bowed, then broke under their combined weight, and they both fell, grappling for control.

Darsal threw her weight sideways and grabbed his tunic, pulling her body close to his torso and curling her legs under her. He hit the ground with a heavy thud, flat on his back, unconscious. Heartbeat still skyrocketing, Darsal grabbed his sword and knife and sprang up. Turned. Where was she?

A large, fan-shaped room. Council hall, but completely redesigned: wood floors, blue rug across the middle and down aisles on either side of three sections of silky cushions, picture on the wall.

Shouts and running down the hall. More swearing. A voice that sounded like Silvie screeched from beyond the door.

"Dear Elyon."

Four Scabs poured into the room.

Among them the one called Marak.

Darsal scanned the room for another exit. One more, but it was on the same wall as the one the Scabs raced from, on the other end.

She ran for it.

The smallest of the Scabs sped toward her. She lunged forward, blade extended. The two swords scraped together, and his nearly took her hand off. She blocked, then took a swipe at his head, using her sword as a club.

Even now the thought of killing this Scab struck her as offensive.

She cursed herself.

His blade slapped her sideways, then down. Almost cut her in half. Darsal rolled and raised her sword in time to block a third swing.

Sweat trickled down her neck. Sticky morst from her assailant dripped down on her forehead. She grimaced.

She could easily grab her knife and run him through the stomach . . .

Instead, Darsal swept his feet from under him, rolled to her feet, and fled for the door.

The second and third corralled her, swords drawn. She couldn't see the general. Pivoting on her heel, she twirled away from the door, ran up the wall and along it, then sprang off and clubbed the nearest Scab in the head.

He went sprawling.

Blood oozed from a wound to her upper arm she hadn't noticed before. Now the gash throbbed with irritating pain.

Two more to go, if the general was gone. One on either side. Darsal feinted for the door, then banked right and darted around the taller, older Scab.

"Teeleh's fangs, stop her, you fools!"

A rope snapped tight around her throat and yanked her flat on her back, sword flying. Darsal's yelp cut short when she hit the floor. She twisted, scrambling to her knees as the Scab dragged her toward him.

Her nose rammed against large, heavy boots.

He picked her up by the collar, hefted her a few inches off the ground, stared at her for a moment, then set her down.

A pair of hands grabbed each of her arms and jerked them behind her back. Blood oozed down her arm. The throbbing pain returned. She struggled out of sheer bullheadedness as they held her wrists together and bound them.

Hopeless.

Elyon help Johnis and Silvie, or her own demise would be pointless.

Now she could see her captor: tall, lean, dreadlocks over his shoulders and down his chest. Gray eyes dull and cold. Morst splitting apart and gumming where his white skin had started to flake.

He wore leather battle gear and his sword strapped across his back, two throwing knives on each thigh as Silvie would have worn them.

General Marak.

He stared at her. Then his face cracked into a stern, humorless smile as he motioned to the two youths behind him. "Take her away."

JOHNIS AND SILVIE REACTED AS ONE AS SOON AS DARSAL was down the hall with the Scab calling after her.

Silvie flung the dead Scab's cloak over Johnis and tucked her knife into her waistband, out of sight.

Time to play Scab thug and albino prisoner.

They found a ladder and shimmied down.

Something crashed from Darsal's direction far behind them now. A Scab thundered curses.

"Elyon help her," he whispered, pressing the stolen sword against Silvie's throat. "Move for the atrium. Right."

He guided Silvie toward the atrium. Checked his waistband, just to be satisfied. The book was still there.

Johnis swept his gaze from side to side down the hall. Winged serpents guarded each doorway, lonely silver and black opal sentinels with leering red-glass eyes. The one outside the main room was larger and stood above a kind of incense altar. Pungent aroma wafted after them.

Polished wooden floors with blue carpets lined the hallways.

He saw Teeleh's winged serpent image, hangmen dangling from bowl-shaped torch stands blazing on the walls, and crossed Horde swords above Horde shields and crests.

The hall looked like a private sanctuary for Teeleh. A palace chapel.

"You're cutting me," Silvie whispered through clenched teeth.

He loosened his grip. Her light skin had reddened where he'd grabbed too tightly, and a thin cut lacerated her neck.

Two Scab acolytes in white rounded the corner and marched abreast down the hall toward them, swinging incense. Behind them stormed a priest in a pointed hood.

Sucrow!

He froze. Then bolted to his right, dragging Silvie with him.

"Get them!" Sucrow screamed.

He released Silvie's wrist and fled out the front door, down the whitewashed temple steps. Side by side they vaulted a low railing and sprinted down a hard-packed dirt road.

"Which way?" Silvie asked from his side.

"Alley!"

He cut to his right between two mud huts. The sounds of barking dogs chased them south. Barracks ahead on the left, with the lake to his right—west.

"This way," he panted, cutting right again.

He leaped over a box lying in the street. Past Horde children playing with a vine jump rope. The children's mothers shrieked and called them away from the crazy albinos racing past.

On past wood-and-reed frame houses, then mud-brick ones. Out of the cleaner, prettier part of the city. Deeper into the trees. Past weeds that overran yards, swallowing the little huts alive. Enormous tree roots sometimes grew straight through the sides of the buildings. No fences between the yards.

Mud squished where hard-packed dirt had been.

The muddy lake lay directly ahead.

"We've lost them!" Silvie cast a look over her shoulder as she ran for the lake by his side.

"Into the water!"

Johnis cut through a yard and down the steep bank. Tossed the Book of History into the grass. Leaped off the ledge like he used to when he was a boy and dove into warm, murky water.

No burning, tingling sensation.

No healing powers of Elyon's water.

He swam deeper, submerged, feeling nothing.

Then surfaced twenty yards from shore, sputtering and coughing. Johnis looked down. Silvie came up immediately after.

The water was so brown he couldn't even see the two of them in it. Muddy droplets made rivulets down Silvie's light skin.

Why?

"It's not working," Silvie cried, eyes wide on him. "Now what?"

Johnis set his jaw and started for the shore to his right. At least they were free of the guards. For the moment.

"Johnis . . ."

"What?"

Silvie eyed him. "I didn't say anything."

"Johnis . . ."

Her mouth had not moved. Johnis shrugged it off. Retrieved the book and pocketed it.

"Where now?"

An image formed in his mind of something he'd forgotten. A pool, near the edge of the forest.

"Drink . . ."

"Johnis?"

"Nothing. Just an odd sensation. We can't stay here."

"And Darsal?"

Darsal. She would come looking soon. "Give me your knife."

He carved a simple sign into the tree closest to him, then returned the knife.

"Old hiding place of mine." Johnis's throat was even more parched now that he'd swallowed mud. "The bank winds around, and then a path heads south. Follow me!"

Seven

The cage door clanged shut. Darsal broke her fall with her palms. Her shackles clanked together and thumped against the hard-packed dirt floor.

"Fool albino," muttered the guard. He turned the lock and left her, torchlight retreating with him. A second door thudded closed.

A thin tendril of pale light came down the corridor. Dimly she noted her immediate surroundings. A six-by-six cell, probably not over six feet high.

For a long time she merely lay there, drifting in and out of restless half-sleep. Her body slowly numbed itself to the beating, and the tears dried on her face. The metal bands around her wrists and ankles were cool against her skin.

Elyon save me.

She rolled to one side. More time elapsed, her limbs stiffening, joints beginning to ache. Her left side went numb from lying on it so long.

"Elyon . . ."

Darsal wrapped her arms around her knees, pressing them against her chest. Then flinched back when her hand touched an open wound on her right arm.

But the pain cleared her head. She bit her lip.

Had Johnis and Silvie made it? If not, this had all been for nothing.

Darsal hadn't fought her way out of a storage closet to wind up as Scab target practice.

She jumped up, slamming her head against the back corner of the cage, and grabbed the bars. Darsal winced, then ran her fingers along the lock and tried to pick it with her fingernail.

"I don't imagine that will aid you."

Darsal turned. "Who's there?"

An itch. She scratched the back of her head.

Past hers, rows of large iron cages lay mostly empty, desolate save the occasional bone or scrap of clothing. In the cell next to her own lay a gray-bearded man with an eye patch and a lined face. The remaining eye regarded her with a piercing gaze—the kind difficult to break free of.

In the cell on his other side was a youth—a blond boy of about sixteen or seventeen whose bare back was scarred from old whiplashes and raw and bleeding from a fresh scoring, his body burned and beaten.

And in a cell beyond him a woman lay shrouded in shadows. Her face wasn't visible, only her outline and long hair.

All three were watching her closely.

Forest Dwellers. Albinos.

Darsal released her breath and felt most of the tension leave her corded muscles. This could still be a dream. All a dream.

"My name is Xedan." The old man smiled in the hazy gloom. Several teeth were missing. His leathered face was bruised and battered; he cradled his right arm in a makeshift sling crafted from what appeared to be a shirtsleeve. He scooted forward and extended a three-fingered, nail-less hand through the bars.

A full thirty seconds passed.

Finally she remembered the old Forest Guard greeting.

They clasped forearms.

"Elyon's strength. That rascal is my grandson Jordan. The woman is his wife, Rona." Xedan motioned to the young couple.

Jordan lifted his hand in a greeting. Rona remained unmoving.

Darsal rocked back, trying to make sense of it.

Another itch behind her neck.

"Elyon's strength. We've got to get out of here before we turn Scab."

Jordan quirked a brow and muttered something unintelligible. "There's no need to panic. From here there is no shadow of turning."

Darsal scowled. "What do you mean, we won't turn? Of course we will. It just hasn't started yet. Unless this itch I've got counts."

"You're just scared. You're safe. Never mind the itching skin.

It's only that." He rose up on his knees and faced her, gripping the bars. "You can't turn. You can't. They can become like us, but we can't go back to being like them."

"You're lying." She looked them over. Their skin was smooth, mottled only by the Scabs' abuse. "How long have you been down here?"

"We're not sure, actually. Many days. Time passes differently down here. But you'll see. You'll see, I promise."

"Don't mock me," she said. "You know full well in three days, maybe four, we'll be completely Horde. You can't have been here more than a day. You've lost your sense of time. Is this what they do? Lock us up until we turn and then kill us?"

Jordan's shoulders sagged. He glanced back at his brutalized wife, rested his forehead against the metal. "Well, they *will* kill us."

Xedan held up his hand, silencing his grandson. He motioned for Darsal to come closer. She leaned up against the bars, felt her slick, sweaty flesh against the warm metal.

The grandfather reached his fingers between the bars and brushed back her dark hair from her face. A certain sadness was in his eyes, the kind an adult reserved for a frightened child who had no reason to be.

His finger traced the scar on her cheek. "What's your name?"

"Darsal. My name is Darsal, and we have to get out of here before we turn Horde."

Xedan passed a tattered cloak through the bars. "Here. Try to rest."

"What in the name of Elyon have they done to you?" she asked.

"I might ask the same of you. Do you think Elyon so fickle?"

"It's something in the food, isn't it? The water, the food, the air, something."

This was a nightmare. She'd been driven into a hellish sleep from which she could never wake.

"Look, we want out as badly as you do," Jordan said. "I don't want to die or see my wife die. But we aren't deceived. Look at me. Do I look deceived? Does Grandfather sound crazy?"

It made such shocking sense. She could almost believe it . . . only it wasn't true. This was Shataiki talk. *So this is how Teeleh seduced Tanis. I want to believe them, but I don't dare. Dear Elyon, I've traded one hell for another.*

The dungeon doors clanged open. They fell quiet. Jordan stood, defiant despite the torture. Two purple and black–robed men entered behind the guard, who moved for Rona's cell.

Jordan grabbed the bars on his cage, confidence abruptly replaced by deep anguish. "Please . . . Don't . . . You have no right!"

But Darsal suspected these Horde weren't interested in rights.

One of the men went into Rona's cell and dragged her out. She was barely conscious and other than a groan offered no resistance. The other went into Jordan's cell and struck him three times with a cane. The man left Jordan in a heap, slammed the cage door shut, and locked it. Then they were gone.

None spoke for several minutes.

Darsal broke the tension.

"There has to be a way out of here."

"I've already tried." Jordan twisted slowly to face her, anguish bared. Tears gathered in his eyes, a few slid down his cheeks. His chest heaved. "It should have worked. It should have worked."

Darsal searched her cage for any sign the iron had corroded enough to let her break out. She tested the bars one by one.

But each proved stronger than her.

If she couldn't get out, maybe there was a way to lure one of the guards in. The four Scabs had taken her easily enough, in large part because of her reluctance to use lethal force, but against a single guard . . .

She was sure she could easily handle one of these Scabs.

Elyon, Elyon, did you save me only to cast me back into hell?

Johnis had promised her she was forgiven—and that mattered. It also mattered that she'd undone the damage she'd created. Stopped the storm she'd unleashed these last ten years.

Ended the chaos.

This was her penance. This captivity in hell. But no penance would ever soothe her remorse. Not even this dungeon.

"Darsal?" Xedan's voice whispered. That soft voice so gentle she *wanted* to believe his insanity.

She fell forward onto her face and wept quietly into the ground.

"THE NEXT TIME YOU DEFY MY ORDERS TO WAIT, I'LL SEE you hanged," Cassak snapped.

"On whose authority?" Warryn taunted.

Cassak cracked a knuckle. The throater had defied him because he now had his loophole. The serpent warriors were running the army.

Priests commanding generals.

Abominable.

"Your priest has the upper hand at the moment," Cassak warned. "But Qurong himself will want to know why you're prolonging the lives of diseased albinos."

They were still in the interrogation room. Without Jordan's screams the chamber was far too quiet.

Warryn sneered. He finished relighting the incense and cleaned up the blood and skin from his last effort. He enjoyed his newfound power.

"The problem with military men is that they see things too simply," the throater commented. "You fail to appreciate the true nature of such a threat."

"The true nature of the threat is that the albinos are diseased and it's spreading. We have an epidemic and potential civil war on our hands."

Warryn sneered at him.

Cassak drew his weapon and brought up the arc. His blade clashed against Warryn's. Metal grated. The swords twisted free. Again they clanged.

Warryn feinted and thrust sideways. Cassak blocked, twisted. More singing steel. Cassak disarmed the throater and forced him against the wall, sword point beneath his opponent's chin.

For a long minute they glared at each other. Point made.

"Well, finish it," Warryn goaded.

Cassak growled. Cut Warryn's skin.

A scout knocked in the doorway.

Cassak snorted and sheathed the blade. Marak didn't need any more trouble. He stepped back and allowed Warryn to stand. Didn't turn his back on the throater.

"Come." Cassak extended his hand without looking at the man. A scroll fit in his palm. He unrolled the note. Scanned it.

Movement in the northwest desert. Eram was up to something. Eram, the half-breed general, holed up in the desert. He'd lured about a third of their people—all half-breeds themselves—into the northwest desert shortly after the drowning incident, two years and two generals ago.

The Eramites were smaller in number, but entirely made up of half-breeds, former Forest Dwellers.

Two guards arrived behind the scout, carrying a woman between them by the armpits. Albino. Barely conscious.

Albino wretch.

What was left, anyway.

Warryn kept her in an induced stupor. Tormenting the woman had nothing to do with interrogation and everything to do with breaking down the husband.

Rona was half-dragged to the altar and placed prone on top. Wrists and ankles restrained.

Warryn took a long dreg of wine and motioned for his assistant to begin. The assistant picked up a shaft of wood about a foot long with a thick knot on one end the size of Cassak's fist.

The tortures began. The albino didn't have the strength to scream. Only a pathetic whimper as the small club struck her knee. As Warryn progressed, Cassak grew uneasy.

Marak didn't deserve this.

Cassak narrowed his eyes. He'd seen enough. And there was Eram to deal with. "I'm going to attend to real business."

"Such as?"

"A rebellion in the desert." Cassak started for the door. "A word of warning: don't harm the woman more than you must."

He left before Warryn could respond.

Time to give the priest a little visit.

"Johnis . . ." The alluring female voice came into his mind again.

He stopped at the edge of the hard-packed path and listened. Quiet singing drifted along the wind. Memories of Natalga Gap entered his mind.

"Silvie, are you sure you didn't . . ."

"I haven't said a word, Johnis, just like last time." She glanced back at him, shielding her eyes from the waning sun. Smoky yellow cloud cover wafted.

"A gift-giver in the south . . ."

Johnis looked at Silvie, her blue eyes narrowed. Frustrated. But the longer he looked at her the less she looked like Silvie. Before him Silvie transformed. She grew tall, her fair skin translucent and smooth, so delicate he could see her veins. Flawless. One blue eye carried a sliver of red, the other turned purple with the same red glint. Her short hair grew long and looked of white gold.

"Aid me, Chosen One . . ."

"What are you looking at?" Silvie asked.

The vision fled.

Johnis gaped. "I saw a beautiful woman. She wanted my help."

Silvie looked over her shoulder, then glared at him. "Flattering, but I don't need your help."

"No, no, it wasn't you. It was . . ."

"There's no one there."

"She was white. Really white."

"A Roush?" She meant the furry, green-eyed white bats, enemies of Shataiki and servants of Elyon, who had aided them. The same kind who got them into this mess.

"No. Not a Roush. A . . . woman."

"Come to think of it," Silvie continued, not really listening, "we've seen neither Roush nor Shataiki since we returned. You'd think Shataiki would be swarming a Horde city."

"True." Johnis gladly accepted the change of subject. But he could still see the multicolored gaze in his mind's eye, still feel a pull toward the hidden pool at the edge of the forest.

"Aid me, Chosen One . . ."

Johnis spun, sword ready. No one. "Okay, who's there? Come out where we can see you!"

"There's no one here yet, and I want it to stay that way."

A woman wandering in the desert, faint from thirst. A man imprisoned by an enemy closing in.

"Chosen One . . ."

"She wants our help, Silvie," he protested. "I can't ignore her. She's . . ."

"She's what?" Silvie's brow went up. The vision receded. "I don't like this talk of another woman."

"It isn't like that. She's just . . ."

He described the woman and her voice. But the more he dwelled on her, the stronger her song became. He could hear her voice in his head.

Cool air breezed over his skin.

"We are not chasing the woman in your head," Silvie pronounced. "Forget it. You are not going lunatic on me again. Ever."

The reddish, purple-blue eyes fixed on him. Swelled, opened wider and wider, until all he could see was what they reflected. Stark, endless white desert. Orange-red sunlight fading. Purple shadows.

She was surrounded by enemies. Being devoured by darkness.

His heart yearned for the desert.

"Johnis." Silvie snapped her fingers in front of his face.

His arms fell loose at his sides. Johnis took several steps toward the desert.

Silvie grabbed his shoulder. "Where are you going?"

"To help her."

"No. You're taking me to that hidden pool of yours. We are not wandering out into the desert because you think you heard someone calling you."

"I saw Roush once, remember? No one else did." His feet begged forward. Only Silvie's hand restrained him.

"So you did. But I don't hear voices, and I'm not going. Nor are you."

"Silvie . . ."

More visions. The eyes showed him the canyons, Natalga Gap, and beyond. South. He had to go south.

Silvie pulled him east. "You said it was this way. The pool."

"That woman . . ."

"There is no woman. There's you and me. Darsal somewhere, and we need to bathe before we turn Scab. I personally can't stand the itchy skin, and the flaking is gross. So come on." She pulled. "Show me the pool."

"Silvie, wait. What if it's a vision from Elyon? Wouldn't it be wrong to ignore it? My heart says to go."

That quieted her.

"Elyon wants you to bathe," she said.

"But Silvie . . ."

The southern desert. The woman.

"Johnis." Silvie's sweaty, slender hand pulled him back. East off the path, just like he'd told her earlier.

"Johnis, we're in the open. We can't stay here."

He lingered. Silvie was distracting him, cutting off the troubled woman. Every time Silvie spoke, he could no longer hear the beautiful woman in the desert.

"Your heart is with me. With Elyon. Now come. No more talk of imaginary women."

She had a point.

Johnis started to follow. But the draw toward the desert intensified with each step. His feet were heavy and sluggish.

"Aid me, Chosen One. Aid me . . ."

"We can't stay, Johnis."

He'd stopped again.

"I'll admit you'll smell better." Silvie smiled at him. "And I'm all the woman you need, don't you think?"

South. He had to go south, not east.

He had to bathe too.

Why didn't Silvie want to help this woman? The scabbing disease, maybe. No, too soon.

Johnis nodded. "East it is."

They went on, but the siren song wouldn't leave.

"I await you, Johnisss . . ."

eight

What cause did you have to torture them, Priest?" Marak demanded.

"We needed information out of the boy. I merely did the nasty business of interrogating your *little brother* for you." Sucrow's slate-gray eyes, covered in a milky film, drilled Marak with a hard stare. A bony finger with a massive brass-and-gold ring jabbed toward his face. The gaudy snakelike bangles that adorned the dark priest's arms jingled at the movement.

They stood at the bottom of the steps of Qurong's palace, now with its own private sanctuary built onto the northwest side, directly across the lake from Sucrow's thrall.

The step gave way to a hard-packed dirt road that spanned wide enough for four horses to walk abreast, and it split in three forks: one north, one south, and one toward the bridge.

Sucrow jeered. Fingered the serpent pendant around his neck. "You know, sometimes I think you care more about the albino than you care about our cause. Maybe you should have been betrothed to him."

The knot in Marak's chest tightened.

"She moans like a coward when we bleed her. And whenever Teeleh comes she screams. She knows well the tickle of his claws. Didn't baby brother tell you, General?"

Marak snugged the hilt of his sword in his right palm, in part as a message to the white-faced priest, in part because he wished to use it.

The priest cackled. "Now that will serve you well: a dead priest to go alongside all your other failures. Besides, I don't think Qurong will appreciate you killing your superior. Treasonous, don't you think?"

He turned his back on the priest. "Get out of my sight."

"Your family's turned into the enemy, General."

Marak marched away from Sucrow before he could decide to follow through on his impulse to take the man's head off.

Three subordinates waited for Marak, all save one were on horseback. The last offered Marak the reins to his own mount.

Marak accepted. "Go interrogate her. We'll find the other two. Then tell the commanders to meet me at the lake an hour before first light. We'll ride at dawn. Anyone who's late will face penalties."

The men obeyed. Marak went for the atrium. He glimpsed Cassak, his captain, headed from the interrogation chambers.

Where Warryn was torturing his brother.

The captain was almost past him. Marak had to know.

He caught his friend's arm. "What's the word?"

Cassak stopped. Marak saw the scroll in the captain's hand and tore it from him. He skimmed.

"Cassak . . . tell me."

Hesitation.

"Don't let Sucrow get to you," the captain said.

Marak growled. "Take a troop into the desert and find me those albinos. Then I want you personally to report Eram's whereabouts."

Cassak frowned. "Marak."

So much for pretense.

He straightened and looked at his friend. "How bad was it?"

Cassak shook his head. "You shouldn't ask me questions, Marak. Just trust me." Marak raised a brow. Something was bothering his captain. He threw him a questioning look, eyes narrow.

Cassak scowled. "When it comes, it comes."

"What?"

His friend spoke slowly. "They've taken Rona again."

Marak worked his fist.

"General, end it. Don't wait for Sucrow to force you or to use them against you. Do the right thing and execute them."

"They're already dead." The general turned his back and stormed out. He had an albino hunt to lead.

SUCROW WAITED UNTIL MARAK WAS GONE BEFORE RE-treating into his temple. The foolish general needed to learn to leave religious matters to priests and worry only about his precious plan to eliminate the albinos. His Desecration. A fitting mission name.

Marak also needed to learn his newfound place in the world. A world in which he was subject to Qurong's priest.

Sucrow crossed through the atrium and the outer court into a side chamber, intent on a hidden passage to the library.

Someone pressed the sharp tip of a dagger between his shoulder blades.

He paused, then reached for a concealed knife within his robes. "Who is there?"

Cassak stepped into the light. Kept his dagger where Sucrow could see it.

Coming to fulfill his duty to Marak and make certain Warryn didn't get too carried away with his torture. The leech.

Sucrow stilled but let a sneer spread across his face. "I could order you executed for treason, Captain. Enter."

The man closed the door and entered the room. Twirled his dagger.

Sucrow lit a candle and sat against the small wooden table.

Cassak sat. Long braids fell heavy over his shoulders. The man stank of desert, blood, and sweat.

"Now, what is it you want, Captain?" It was almost comical, this notion that a mere captain would try to sway Teeleh's priest on his general's behalf.

"Don't tempt him too far, Priest."

"You are not in a position to make demands. Did you not hear? Qurong has granted all military authority to myself and my serpent warriors." Sucrow waved a dismissive hand and moved to a seat across from Cassak. "Why are you here?"

"You're torturing my general's brother."

"Now isn't the time for second thoughts on trapping Jordan of Southern, Captain."

"The plan was simply to capture and execute them."

"Patience." Sucrow began to wish he were speaking with Marak instead. Marak was much more reasonable. Cassak, though, better appreciated Sucrow's position.

"First of all, I believe it is Marak prolonging the inevitable. I merely provided him an outlet—all he had to do was leave them at my full disposal. Sec—"

"Priest—"

"And second, Qurong wanted my serpent warriors dealing with these albinos because Marak won't be able to do what's necessary to break them. He's too close. Third, and most important, I am now your general's ranking officer. To question me is treason."

Cassak's expression turned dark. "Execute them and be done."

The man was tenacious, that much was certain. If it wasn't enough that Marak himself was clinging to Sucrow's arm and crying like a baby, it was worse with his captain nagging him.

"What do you care about three albinos, anyway?"

"I don't. But I don't torture them."

"Spoken like a warrior."

"Spoken like a man."

The two drilled each other with hard stares. Sucrow lost. He stood and waved a dismissive hand. "Go. I have things to do."

"Priest—"

"Be gone."

"Priest, do not dismiss me."

Sucrow turned back. "Answer me this: do you think your own general is losing his edge?"

The captain grew silent, white-faced, as if he hadn't considered what his demands were implying.

Sucrow let that thought sink deep into Cassak's mind. He sneered. "Either the capture of his albino brother is making him unfit to lead an army, Captain, or your claims are but ill-founded woman's speak. Now, which is it?"

Cassak's expression changed with the epiphany that his concern would undermine his general. He growled and stalked out.

Sucrow turned back to his work. Such idiots.

Even as Johnis parted moss and vines and crouched next to the hidden pool, the strange woman's haunting plea stayed with him. He hadn't heard her voice again, but the impulse to run into the desert increased.

"Still seeing invisible women?" Silvie asked. By now the moon was overhead and the stars were out, and he couldn't see her very well.

"No. Not in two hours, since last time."

"But . . ."

"But I still think we need to go into the desert." He splashed water on his face, expecting it to sting a little.

"It doesn't sting." Johnis stared. As he stared, an image shimmered along the surface of the water. A woman's pale face and shimmering, white-blonde hair. One eye blue, one purple. Both with red slivers.

Her mouth moved. *"Aid me, Chosen One . . ."*

"Johnis." Silvie touched his back.

The image faded.

Silvie stared down at him as if he'd grown a thousand limbs, like the grove of spider trees they hid in.

His gaze drifted to the grove. Spider trees were enormous bushes that grew to about ten feet. Runners spreading up to fifteen feet.

Beneath this tentlike canopy was the hidden pool.

Johnis looked back at the dark surface of the water, just to be sure.

Nothing.

"Silvie, something isn't . . ."

She sank down next to him and cupped the liquid with her hand. "It's . . ."

"I saw something. In the water."

"Your imaginary friend?"

"Well . . . Yes. I saw her reflection in the water. Something's wrong. It should burn like mad, and I swear I saw something."

Silvie scoffed. "There's nothing in it."

"I want a better look."

Johnis wiped the dirt off his palms until they were clean and scooped with both hands. Again, no stinging sensation. No healing power.

"This isn't . . . Why doesn't it work?"

"Maybe we have to give it more time."

"No. No, they've defiled it." Johnis raked long fingers through wet, muddy hair. Dirt flaked out. "But I thought they didn't know about this one."

"It's been five years here. Maybe . . . maybe they found it."

"Johnisss . . ."

Johnis stared at the pool, merely a dark, glassy spot here in the shadows. The woman's image surfaced, willowy across the rippling water. Her transparent skin seemed to glow.

The desert.

Her image receded.

Johnis sucked a breath. "I don't think they found it . . ."

He had to know.

He scooped a double handful and walked out into the sand and the moonlight. The light glinted at an angle.

A reddish tint colored the dark liquid.

He dropped the water.

"Johnis?" Silvie's footsteps fell toward him.

The water was red. Bloodred.

He shook his hands.

The desert. Something in the desert.

Silvie caught him by the tunic and tugged. Johnis tried to breathe. But she wouldn't believe him, so there was no point.

"Darsal, Johnis." Silvie pulled him back into the grove. "Darsal, water, Thomas. No shenanigans, no lunatic ideas."

He nodded. Forced his legs to move. "We'll have to wait for morning. We need to rest anyway. Although I don't know if Darsal will know to look for us here."

"She said she'd find us, remember? And you left her a sign." She grinned. "Though she might kill you for carving a Book of History."

Johnis half-smiled. The desert still plagued him.

The woman's song soothed his soul. She wanted him to come. Needed him to come.

"Johnis."

He shook himself back to reality.

"She'll know it was us . . ." Johnis rubbed his ear. "We didn't really count on being chased out. She wasn't at the lake . . ."

"We didn't exactly have time to wait for her. She's buried herself somewhere; we'll find her in the morning."

"She's good at hiding." His mind slipped back into the past.

Then grew cloudy, eclipsed by those strange eyes.

"Aid me, Chosen One. I await in the desert. Aid me."

"Snap out of it, Johnis."

He pivoted on his heels. Grumbled at his own foolishness. "Right. Darsal we'll look for in the morning. There's water in the desert, Silvie. Remember?"

"I'm not traipsing across the desert again, love. Sorry. I've followed you to hell and back enough times. And we had Roush to thank last time. No such luck now."

"Maybe, maybe not."

His heart screamed to go south, out into open desert.

Not this time.

Johnis wrenched his mind to his own will. *Please, Elyon. This is not a good time for this.* "If Thomas is in the desert, we'll have no choice. And Thomas will go where there's water."

"Darsal would go to the lake."

So much time lost.

Each second one closer to turning Horde.

The desert.

If they turned Horde before reaching Thomas, it was all over.

"It's a risk we have to take," he said finally.

Silvie didn't answer. They were both torn between Darsal, the safety of the Forest Guard, and Elyon's healing waters.

"I'll take first watch."

Long pause.

"Wake me in two hours," Silvie finally said. "We leave at dawn."

nine

Darsal pulled Xedan's cloak over her body and vanished beneath it, nightmares of treachery and swarming bats and cold shackles flooding her. Desert and death. All her past sins swept over her, the carnage consumed her.

In the dream she died by fire, in an inferno she deserved.

"Elyon! Elyon . . . !"

"Darsal. Darsal, wake up!"

Darsal's eyes flew open beneath the dark canopy of a tattered cloak. She flung back the cloak. Her joints were stiff and cramped.

Night consumed her. "Elyon?"

A single soft laugh. "No, dear. I am Xedan. You were having a frightful dream, dear girl."

"Grandfather is hardly the Maker." Jordan gave an uneasy chuckle. "You aren't still afraid of turning to Horde, are you?"

She slumped along the bars.

An itch started down the back of her neck and worked its way along her spine.

I'm trapped. Trapped in hell and turning Scab while these insane Forest Dwellers try to convince me the inevitable won't happen.

"Darsal?" Jordan repeated.

Elyon remained silent, the elusive wellspring just beyond her reach, mocking her while dark bats hunted her down like a rodent to devour her alive.

Elyon, have I overly angered you? Will mercy never be granted me?

Her dry, parched throat felt like cotton. She rose to her knees and rattled the bars. "Guard," she rasped. "Guard!"

A minute later the Scab came, scowling at her and grumbling for rousing him out of sleep or whatever mindless thing he was doing. "What?"

"Could I have some water? Please." Darsal rubbed her throat and chest. Over her breastbone it ached a little. "And is it day or night?"

He studied her, then grunted. "Midmorning. I'll see about the water."

Darsal sank back down. "Do any of you feel it yet?" She massaged her elbow.

Not even Elyon could stop the scabbing disease without water.

"Darsal, it's going to be all right," Jordan said. "There's nothing to fear. Calm down." He spoke sternly, eyes riddled with concern. "No, I don't feel anything. What happened to you to make you think this way?"

"Nothing!" she snapped, then softened. "It's the way it is, which is why we have to get out of here. We have to find Thomas."

"Thomas?" Xedan gave a short laugh. "I wouldn't worry about him. He's probably buried so deep no one will ever find him until he's ready to be found."

"You know where he is, then?" Xedan was making sense again—either that or she just didn't have the strength or will to retaliate against his seductive lies.

"Well, no. No, I don't. But that's my point, love. You see . . ."

The guard's boots thumped lightly on the dirt floor. Torchlight momentarily blinded her. He shoved a tumbler of water between the bars. "Here, wench."

Darsal started forward and snatched it from his hand. She poured a little into her palm, thinking maybe, just maybe . . .

Nothing.

She sighed and drank to the bottom, then returned it. "Thank you."

No water. No Middle Forest.

No Thomas. No Johnis and Silvie and Billos.

No bats.

Nothing but Scabs and their bloody skin disease.

Her bloody skin disease.

"Now," Xedan said softly after the Scab stomped off. "Tell me what's made you think you're in such desperate need to bathe once you've already done so?"

Darsal tensed. "I've been gone awhile. The last time I was

here was before the Scabs took over Middle. I haven't bathed in . . ."

Technically she hadn't bathed in over a decade. How much faster would the disease progress? Did she start on day one here or day two or three?

Maybe she was already Horde and didn't know it yet.

This is a nightmare concocted by Teeleh himself. He knows what I want most. And he's offering it on a silver platter.

"For the love of Elyon, what's happened these past five years?" she asked.

Jordan answered. "What happened is a drowning that turned the lakes red. You really don't remember? The Horde. The blood. The . . ."

Haunted eyes looked into the distance, relived some horrific memory.

He sucked a breath. "Don't you remember any of this?"

"As I said, I've been gone a long time. My friends and I returned to this . . . this place . . ." Darsal trailed off at the thought of what had befallen in their absence. "But you say the water turned to blood. How did you keep the disease away?"

"We found something greater than the lakes." Xedan continued to study her, transfixed at the idea she was unaware of such important events.

"Sacrilege." She stiffened. *Now I know this is all a ruse of Teeleh, a final temptation. The devil's invitation.*

"No, love. Who is greater: the lakes or Elyon?"

Darsal cleared her throat. "I don't think you understand . . ."

"Understand what, love?"

Seconds ticked on.

"Everything."

The Books of History. Six in an attic storage space well out of reach.

Thank Elyon, Johnis had taken one.

Assuming he didn't turn Scab.

Darsal tensed.

They had found the books. Then left them.

If they all turned Scab . . .

No. She didn't care.

The books were history.

The others were waiting on an answer.

Darsal had held her tongue for a decade. Held it for so long, and then everything came crashing in. And there had been no point in trying to say it to her two lovebird partners in crime.

They wouldn't understand, anyway.

But Xedan looked as if he might.

And if he didn't, he would pretend.

So Darsal told them about the other world.

All of it.

"Another world. Another life. And for me it was much longer than five measly years. A world with more darkness and less hope than I care to remember. Bleak and starless, full of diseased men. It's inside them there. In some ways it makes it worse. You don't know who's diseased and who isn't. You don't know when you've become a Scab."

CASSAK SWUNG OFF HIS HORSE AND LET HIS BOOTS THUMP. Dust from the hot desert floor swirled up and clung to his nose.

He turned to meet his men and the twelve albinos they'd captured. Four youths, the rest adults. Three female. All bound and forced to their knees.

"They were headed for the city," his lieutenant said. "Likely a rescue party for the three the general's got."

Cassak looked the prisoners over. He preferred to take his own tallies, the only reason these twelve required his presence before execution. Their faces were set—even the youngest. Pendants dangled from their throats.

"Which one's the leader?" he asked.

"They're not saying."

Cassak frowned. Not that it would have spared any of them. "Start with the youngest."

His man drew his sword and went to the smallest of the youths. Drew back.

Hooves pounded the desert. Cassak turned. Warryn and two others approached. Cassak turned back to the albinos.

Warryn's boots thumped against the ground. He'd swung down off his horse. "This is the priest's territory."

"My orders come from Marak."

"And Marak no longer has the authority to execute albinos."

"I am on an errand regarding Eram."

"These are not Eram," Warryn reminded, a sneer ever fixed on his face. "My orders are to ensure protocol is followed."

"General's orders," Cassak snapped. He gave the command to execute the albinos. This time the blade fell. Soon the albinos lay dead in a row. Twelve less to worry about.

"Now," Cassak continued, "you may come with me to see to this scouting party of Eram's or you may return, but do not interfere where it is not your concern."

Warryn's eyes narrowed. "Remember your place."

"It is you who forgets."

Cassak remounted and summoned his men. "Hiya!"

DREAMS PLAGUED JOHNIS THROUGHOUT THE NIGHT. THE desert summoned him. The woman's eyes wouldn't leave him. Blue, purple, red.

He woke stiff jointed and thirsty. Muddy grass and a dark hollow swallowing him. A soft body shifted against his back. He bolted upright. His foot and lower leg fell into water.

He jumped away from it. A shaft of light broke between mossy spider trees. He sighed. "Silvie . . ." She breathed steadily and deeply at his side.

He could now feel the onset of the disease in his joints and on his skin. If they didn't find water, they could be half-Scab by the end of the day.

Johnis rubbed his face and stared into the crimson water. Bloodred. Not just tinged red, but thick, jewel-colored liquid so still it looked like glass.

"Johnis . . ."

His brow furrowed. The voice was coming from the water.

"Johnis . . ."

Her eyes. The perfect skin, the multicolored gaze that beckoned him from afar . . .

Silvie shifted in her sleep, mumbling. She rolled closer to where Johnis had just been lying and seemed to reach for him. Her arm struck air, though, and flopped to the ground.

Silvie turned back on her side, massaging her face and squinting in the pale light.

"Johnis?"

"You still don't hear her, do you?"

The red pool seemed to mock him, a round gaping hole fixed in a menace, a malignant gloating, laughing at his helpless plight.

Red water.

Siren song from the deep.

"No, I don't." Silvie stirred and sat up. "Why does she want you—"

"I don't know what she wants."

Impulsively he eased the book out of his waistband and set it to the side.

"Maybe she tainted the water."

"No . . ."

The pull intensified. He could see her reflection again. She invited him in, wanted him to come. She needed him.

His whole body screamed for Elyon's water.

Johnis stepped toward it.

"Something's wrong." Silvie's voice briefly pulled him out of the trance. "It's tainted. The voice proves it."

"She's real," he insisted. His heart raced. "This water was Elyon's, I know."

"You could . . ."

It was worth the risk.

"Johnis."

"The Horde might have done something. Look at it, red as Shataiki eyes. For all you know Teeleh—"

"If it kills me you can still find another lake. Find a lake. Find Darsal. Find Thomas."

"Swim with me, Johnis . . ."

Water.

She grabbed his pant leg. "I don't want you to—"

"Die? Becoming Horde is worse." His foot reached the edge of the water.

He flinched.

Nothing.

Cold crimson liquid rushed over his toes. His foot slipped off the ledge. Johnis plunged beneath the surface.

His feet couldn't find the bottom. Purplish-red bubbled from the depths.

Light flickered.

Flashed purple.

"Swim to me, Chosen One . . ."

Long, satin tendrils of white-blonde hair swirled around him. The woman! Her transparent skin turned the same color as the light reflected in the water. Vibrant eyes glowed up at him.

Then she darted for the bottom. Bubbles surrounded him.

Johnis swam deeper. His lungs burned.

He ignored it. She had to surface sometime. Sometime soon. If he was running out of air, so was she.

Maybe.

"Shataiki swarm this half of the world . . . the rest banished, banished, banished, banished. Feed and kill, feed and kill . . ."

He sucked in water, startled at the image in his head. What was that?

A sharp yelp, like a wounded wolf.

"Aid me . . ."

Johnis's lungs rebelled.

Surface!

He came back up sputtering, both hands on the ledge. Mud stirred into the cold water, washing off his skin and clothes and hair.

A strong hand hauled him over the edge and dumped him. Silvie struck his back to help him choke out the water.

Air. Johnis coughed out the last of it and glanced at his hands.

Still turning Scab.

"Silvie, did you see her?" He got his feet under him, looked around.

In the desert.

In the water.

Hostage to Shataiki.

The woman in the pool . . .

"The point of an imaginary friend is that no one else can see her." Silvie folded her arms. "I've half a mind to throw you back in there."

"She had to have come up first, Silvie. Didn't you see her?"

Silvie's icy glare was answer enough.

His throat stung.

Water.

Johnis crouched and took a greedy drink, letting it fill his mouth. A coppery taste flooded against his palate, between his teeth, under his tongue. Coppery and sweet. His cheeks puffed out.

The woman. She'd almost killed him. Or had she saved him?

Then he swallowed. Cool water slid down his throat and into his stomach.

Silvie looked on in silent horror, with wide blue eyes and pallid skin.

Johnis shivered. By Elyon, the water was cold. He shook his head like a dog, slinging droplets all over Silvie.

"Johnis!" She jumped up. A hitch in her hip stopped her

movement, though. She rubbed at the joint. "So now what? We sit here and wait to see if it kills you?"

"It won't take more than a few minutes, I should think." He drank again. Despite his teasing, he knew the pool could still be poisoned. Could still kill him. And even if Scabs didn't do it, Shataiki could.

Or time could have simply soured the pool. Natural contamination. Was that even possible?

Anything is possible. Anything.

Johnis scooped more water into his palm and drank. Whatever was done was done. He stripped off his shirt and wrung it out. "We'll know in a few minutes. For now we wait. And decide. Last night we said we'd go after Darsal. Stick with the plan? Or find water and Thomas first?"

"We don't know of a lake close enough." Silvie curled up on herself and continued to gawk at him. "We'd have to strike out across open desert. Maybe try to make it to one of the other forests."

Johnis shook his head. "Thomas wouldn't take to the desert unless he had to. If he's in the desert, the forests fell to the Horde."

Silvie didn't comment.

"And if Darsal's been caught, she's got less of a chance than we do."

"She'd kill us if we didn't go to Thomas. He has to have scouts, spies, something to keep him on top of the Horde. We find them, we find the Horde."

"Agreed." Johnis mulled over what they had overheard the day before. Not much, but enough to chill the bones. "Well, we could always follow the Horde."

"Excuse me?"

"You heard. They're on a search-and-destroy mission. The Guard's gone deep. We want to find Thomas; we could follow the hunters."

"Or wait for Thomas to attack."

"It doesn't sound like he's been doing much of that." He paused. "Of course, there is the woman. She might . . ."

"I am not interested in some imaginary woman of yours."

"You weren't interested in Roush, either," Johnis snapped. "But they were there all the same!"

Silvie ground her teeth.

"Shataiki all around, where the eyes cannot tell . . . the River, the River, and all between, echoes with things unseen . . ."

A soft punch. Silvie.

The desert.

All the answers were in the desert.

"What if she needs help? What if she's trying to help us? 'Aid me,' she keeps saying. 'In the desert.' And Thomas is in the desert."

"We can find Thomas without your beautiful woman."

Beat.

Johnis let his head clear before speaking. He hated yelling at her, but sometimes she just wouldn't listen.

"I'm not sure Thomas wants to be found." He paced. "I think

we have to assume we're on our own. Thomas likely thinks we've either defected or died out there anyway by now."

That thought made him stop pacing. And reminded him of the strange woman's pleas to join her in the desert.

"So we really are alone," Silvie spoke slowly.

"You and me. And Darsal."

Wordless, he slipped off, out of the circle of spider trees and over the threshold into the desert.

Male voices caught his attention. He ducked behind some brush and waited to see if they'd heard him. There were three, all Scabs in Scab uniform. Dogs sniffed for Johnis's scent.

"Think it was albinos or Eramites?" one asked.

"Eram isn't that stupid." This was the taller Scab. He seemed older, more experienced. The other two flitted around him like horseflies.

Johnis settled and listened further. Who was Eram?

"Stupid enough to cross Marak," the third said.

"Marak waits when he should swing and swings when he should wait," the first said. "And provokes the priest too often."

"The priest," the second scoffed.

"Where'd the bloody albinos go?" another protested. "They're ghosts, the lot of them."

"They aren't ghosts, and they have nowhere to go. Be patient."

Johnis backed away and snuck over to Silvie.

She was waiting for him, glaring. "So they've finally split forces. Something to remember."

"We need to find Darsal." He borrowed her knife and carved another Book of History into the soft bark of one of the spider trees.

It was a long shot she'd ever find this place, but better than nothing.

"If Darsal managed to escape and make it to the lake, she'll know by now it doesn't work. Hopefully she'll find your mark. And not kill you for carving another book."

"But she'd hide out and circle back. And a Book of History makes sense to us and not to anyone else. She'll get over it." He retrieved his book from the ground. Brushed off the dirt. Tucked it back in his waistband.

"If she's not there?"

"Then we go into the desert. It's our only option. The Horde's too familiar with Natalga Gap. I'd take my chances north if I were him."

"No, we find water," Silvie said. "*That* is our only option."

Johnis wrung the rest of the water out of his shirt and shook it out. More water slung on Silvie.

She flinched back and made a face. "Just put it on already."

The urge to sling it at her again came over him, but Johnis dismissed it. They didn't have the time for that.

He donned his shirt, chilly against his skin.

The woman's reflection rippled across the surface of the pool.

Silvie scooted forward and knelt, lapping like a dog and scooping with both hands, gorging herself.

The face vanished.

He blinked.

She sat up and wiped her chin. "No more fantasy women."

"I'm telling you, she's real." He dropped beside her. Looked into the pool. Nothing. Just red water.

His mind drifted for a moment, tried to refocus. Another early sign of the disease.

"Seek me in the desert, Chosen One . . ."

"Do we really have time to return to the lake?" Silvie asked, staring at the forest to their right.

Darsal. Darsal was waiting, one way or another.

His mind's eye saw fruit and wine and brilliant eyes like glittering jewels. A warm, exotic presence flooded his soul, spilled into him like waterfalls.

"It's two hours just to Middle," Silvie was saying. "And that's if we run."

Both of them were losing it.

"Are you arguing for or against the desert?" he asked her. "You aren't making sense."

"I'm arguing for finding water and ignoring this newfound fantasy of yours. And for leaving Darsal to find us. She's good at that, you recall."

"That was a little low."

His mind drifted again, from the pool with the woman's face to her haunting, seductive voice. Then caught up to Silvie's insinuation.

Darsal *was* really good at this game of hide-and-seek. And the betrayal nigh broke her. She had been so hopeless before . . .

What if she hadn't really planned on joining back up with them? Jumping out of an attic into a roomful of Horde unarmed was suicidal.

And not any different than what Billos had done for her.

"We can't abandon Darsal."

She faced him. "What good are we to Darsal if we're Horde? Honestly, do you think we can make it? Get back to Middle, find Darsal, rescue her if she's captive, then go in search of water, all before the disease turns us stupid?"

"You have a point," Johnis conceded.

But the notion of leaving Darsal behind sat like a brick in his gut. Assuming Darsal was anywhere near Middle.

Unlikely.

Unless she was captive.

The brick started to rot. Acidic poison worked its way into his chest and throat.

He had to get to the desert.

He had to get to Darsal.

His heart was tearing in two.

"We have to find water before we—"

"We have to keep our word first," Johnis snapped. "Then we go for the desert." *Into the desert.* "And we find out if this woman is for real or not."

"You mean 'water.' You're not using your head."

"No, I'm following my heart." Johnis stood. "We go back and we look. Then . . . then we find water."

ten

You don't know if you're a Scab?" Jordan spoke after another hour or so. His tears had dried. Her story had at least temporarily distracted him from whatever the Scabs were doing to his wife. His voice was stronger.

The increasing pain to her joints and skin and the stiffness served as a haunting reminder of her predicament. So far no cracks, but the agony brutalized her.

"It's too difficult to explain." She tucked herself back under the cloak, her only solace from the chafing disease. "I don't understand any of this. Where is everyone? Why are the Scabs ruling Middle? What happened to everyone? Where is Thomas? And this nonsense about not turning?"

Xedan drew a breath. "The Horde took over Middle a long

time ago. We don't know where the others are. We were separated from them ourselves."

"Grandfather and I drowned with Thomas. Rona, a few months later. Things got out of control. The Horde had gone on an albino hunting spree. The Circle split into groups to keep from being annihilated and went deep. Very, very deep . . ."

Darsal nodded. "If you were caught, you couldn't reveal the others."

Pain flashed across Jordan's face.

"No," he said. "We couldn't. We have a rendezvous point in the . . ." He hesitated and glanced toward the guard, then looked at Darsal. "That is, Jordan of Southern is far from home. And if the sun kisses the sky he'll meet Jordan last."

Darsal thought the riddle out. The sun kissed the sky in the east . . .

"Our band was small," Xedan offered. "And close to Middle."

"Strategically placed," Jordan reminded him.

"You weren't with the others," Darsal noted.

Jordan's expression turned grim. "I was leading a smaller group. A decoy to keep the Horde away from the main body of the Circle." He fell quiet, then continued. "A month ago we were routed. Fifty of ours were taken, Rona included. Grandfather, three others, and I helped them escape. Only Rona was recaptured," Jordan said, eyes flashing. His normally amiable expression turned wicked. "I couldn't leave her." He shook, struggling not to lose composure.

Xedan's gaze returned to Darsal. "We all have our price, so it seems."

"Drowning," Darsal repeated.

The pain from the disease was like many teeth and claws chewing all over her body, ravenous predators tearing and fighting over her flesh. She'd seen a pack of hyenas do that once, and the picture resurfaced now.

"Your wounds bother you?" Xedan asked. "You've taken quite a beating—two in less than twenty-four hours."

The gash on her arm from fighting the Scab. She'd almost forgotten. It did hurt, but now she'd never notice.

A dry, humorless laugh snorted out of her. She winced. "Elyon's angry with me."

Her voice was raspy, dry. She coughed.

"The Horde's taken over, you say. The others . . . dead or hiding? Or Scab?"

"No." Jordan's voice came out small and weak, so he cleared it and started over. "No. But listen to me, Darsal. Listen to me. I'll tell you what happened if you promise to listen. The Circle, those who drowned in the red lakes, followers of Elyon, are hunted by the Horde. We drown to find life and spend it as outcasts. Your choice in this world is to live as Horde or die as followers of Elyon."

He paused.

"And let me tell you, dying is the better choice by far."

The Books of History hadn't killed her.

So now the disease would.

Or the very water that Elyon once used to heal them.

A door rattled open and torchlight poured into the hall. Darsal squeezed her eyes shut and risked the pain to curl up tighter. Her body screamed in protest, making her whimper.

"Stand up," the guard ordered. The others started shuffling. Darsal didn't move. The Scab rattled her cage door. "Stand up!"

She stirred, quivering. The gash on her arm throbbed and a vein pounded against her temple. She staggered to her feet, ignoring the onslaught of pain and what felt like at least three broken ribs.

Xedan and Jordan were already on their feet.

Darsal grabbed a bar and pulled herself the rest of the way up. Dry blood crackled on her lip and nose.

Her right knee popped, caving on her.

Cursing, she gripped the metal tighter, holding herself upright. Her whole body felt swollen twice its normal size and incredibly heavy. Her skull outweighed an elephant.

This wasn't the guard. He was a little older than Jordan and had an officer's insignia. General.

Marak.

The Scab gave them each a chunk of bread, a piece of fruit, and water in a skin.

"What do you want?" she asked.

But he wasn't interested in her. He went to Jordan's cage and stopped in front of him. The two men regarded each other. Darsal sensed a history there. Enemies of long standing, equally matched in strength and cunning, and a high respect and knowledge of the other.

Jordan kept his arms loose, refusing to pull on the shackles, fists knotting. Shoulders back, chin level with the guard's. It wasn't anger or even hate in his eyes, though.

It was sorrow. An unyielding, broken grief, oppressing the whole room.

Marak's gaze, however, had nothing but bitterness and scorn. And perhaps the kind of pity that comes when you think a person is hopelessly deceived and there's nothing left to be done about it.

And now Darsal could see the men's resemblance to one another. Marak's scaly white skin made it difficult, but he and the old man and Jordan had similar builds, similar expressions.

They looked related.

Jordan drew his lips tightly together. "I won't change my mind."

"This can end." Marak put his hands up on the bars. His chalky gray eyes stared at the slightly smaller, younger prisoner. His voice was low, deep. "Just tell me where they are."

"It could end if you would allow it." Jordan's chin lowered, then rose again to Marak. "Don't let Qurong turn you into a coward."

"You're the coward."

Jordan flinched. He looked once more at Marak. "If you say so."

"Sucrow is forcing my hand."

"Sucrow. Are you blind, Marak?" Jordan's fists knotted. "I hope you're enjoying this." He thrust a finger at Rona. "Open your eyes."

Marak scowled and wouldn't look down at the woman. "I won't enjoy watching you die." But he glanced toward the door, afraid the guard might overhear.

"But you'll be there. You'll do nothing and stand there while we're—"

A sharp look from Xedan cut him off.

"It's better than watching the disease take you," Marak whispered at last. He glanced at Xedan, then Rona, and back to Jordan. "Now *that* I can't watch."

"Why are you here?" Jordan repeated.

"It won't be much longer. Qurong is putting Sucrow over my head."

Silence. Jordan's lips pressed tight.

Marak caught Darsal's stare and returned it for a long beat, then he broke away and walked into the darkness. The door clanged shut.

"DEFINITELY HEADED SOUTH," CASSAK MUSED. HE AND Warryn lay on their stomachs on an overhang, observing through a spyglass the ten men they knew to be the Eramite half-breeds. All on horseback. All armed.

"Order your men to attack now."

"Patience. The priest may be in command, but you are not him. We don't need a second front."

Admittedly, the temptation to take out the rebels while they were so close and unaware was strong.

But his orders were to keep the peace.

"Bloody rabble-rouser," Warryn muttered.

Eram had lured about a third of their people into the northwest desert shortly after the drowning incident, two years and two generals ago.

"There's a reason he was demoted."

The renegade general's rebellion started as mere disagreement. To him, the albinos, in their pacifist state, were more a distraction than a threat. Insult to injury, Eram was sick of the many restrictions half-breeds endured.

"He's a traitor."

"Not to many."

"Irrelevant."

Marak had warned Qurong not to push the matter and had warned Eram not to do anything rash, but neither had listened. Eram simply packed up his followers and his belongings and left Middle. Every last one of them former Forest Guard, with Guard training and knowledge.

Both sides had exchanged words and idle threats, but neither was ready to move to war. Eram was outnumbered, but he was a force with which to be reckoned.

Marak had neither time nor patience for any of it. Neither did Cassak, for that matter.

Eram's men continued their march, unaware.

"What do the scouts say?"

Warryn didn't respond.

"What do—"

The throater had remounted and was starting down the hill-side toward the rebels. Cassak swore. "Bloody fool . . ."

He hurried after Warryn and cut him off, breaking between the throater and the startled rebel scouts.

"Let them pass," Cassak warned, sword half-drawn.

Warryn snarled. "Do not—"

Cassak's sword rang out. He pressed the tip at Warryn's neck. "I will cut you down now if you detain them."

Long pause.

"You," Cassak ordered the rebels, "take a message to your general. Tell him this man was in dereliction of duty and that we do not wish a fight. Now go."

He released Warryn. "Marak will be waiting."

eleven

"I thought you said this was a shortcut."

"It is," Johnis protested. They had taken the shortest route to the east side of Middle Lake, around the edge of the forest, winding their way through the trees like phantoms.

"It's almost noon," Silvie said. "You realize how far back we have to retrace before—"

"I know."

Each step toward the city was a step that would have to be retraced before they found precious healing water.

But this was a matter of principle.

So they stared down death.

"Look at this place, Johnis."

Most of the forest houses had been crushed. The place looked like a war zone, as if someone had uprooted most of the trees and flung them into homes and another had come along and rebuilt Scab huts in their place.

As they neared, the ever-watchful spire of the thrall glared at them from the horizon, looming over the trees like a sentinel god. Silvie shielded her eyes from the late-morning sun and studied the temple for a minute.

"Don't." Johnis took her hand and led her on, unwilling to dwell on the hellish monument to Teeleh. "We can't stop."

"We're wasting our time." Silvie started to say more, then closed her mouth and looked away.

They stole deeper into the trees, ignoring the steady onset of stiffness and pain brought on by the Horde disease.

Until they found water, they were as good as Scabs.

Elyon help them.

"Still have the book?" Silvie asked.

"Yes. Once we get Darsal we need to retrieve the others."

"Bathe first."

Right. Bathe.

Not go traipsing through the desert for beautiful women.

Johnis took her through some old hiking trails and over an outcropping of rock in a narrow ravine. The rotten-meat smell of the disease was already on the wind.

Inviting . . .

What? Since when had the disease ever smelled inviting? He didn't think that. He never would, even if he became one.

They came up on a house from the south side, with a small

yard and two or three Scab children playing in it. He pulled Silvie behind a tree, and they watched the youngsters for a minute.

"What are we doing?" she demanded. "The lake's right there. Let's get down there, collect Darsal, and get out of here."

"We need to fit in. Clothes. And morst. Wait here."

He gave her his sword and stole around to the north side of the house, keeping to the fence and below the tall grass. The kids were too busy playing to notice him, and he hoped he wouldn't encounter anyone in the house. His stomach turned over, but he forced back the jitters and made his way to the small porch area, ducked down behind a tall plant. So far, so good.

The sound of movement inside. His heart sped up. He'd have to wait. Not good—each passing moment the stiffness in his joints worsened and the subtle pain grew more pronounced.

He glanced at his hands and arms.

No cracks yet.

But how long? When had day one started for them—in the other world or here? Maybe Silvie had been right.

Maybe coming back for Darsal before finding a lake was so much foolishness.

At last the sounds beyond the wall stilled. Johnis tried the door. Open. He ducked behind a couch made of reeds and wood, down cushion and blanket thrown over it. Wiped his palms and darted across the open hallway into the room on the left and behind the door, waiting. Window on the far wall. Three small grass mats were on the ground—beds. A few toys strewn about. A large trunk holding their possessions.

The next room had to be the mother and father's, judging by the large bed made of bark.

A trunk rested on the far side of the bed. Of course. What woman in her right mind would put it near the window where some strange albino could take clothes out of it?

Silvie was waiting. He looked around, then crossed the room and lifted the lid. Horde clothes.

No time to be choosy. He grabbed two tunics, two pairs of pants, and a cloak similar to what the woman had been wearing. Different color, though. Rummaging, he found a jar of morst and stuffed it in his pocket.

He closed the trunk, heart pounding.

Thomas had trained them for this.

Well, probably not *this*.

Johnis wrapped the two sets of clothing and the morst into the cloak and tucked the whole thing under his own cloak, then slipped back toward the window. He climbed out and ducked down. Clothing in hand, he made his way back around the house and into the woods.

"Hurry up already."

Johnis spun around to see that Silvie had gone on her own mission and returned with a sack. She eyed him and dropped the bag. "Some passable food, drinking water, a couple small blades."

Johnis nodded, though he found himself oddly irritated at her for running off when he'd told her to wait. Still, she'd spared them valuable time.

"Good," he said. "We need to change. The cloak is yours." He untied the bundle and tossed her the smaller set of clothes and the cloak.

They quickly changed into the hooded cloaks, then put morst over their exposed skin and into their hair. Silvie pocketed the jar. "Avoid eye contact."

"Why?"

"Are your eyes white?"

She was being a bit sassy, wasn't she?

"Fine. Try to keep up."

twelve

Marak stood outside the door leading to the war room for a minute, composing himself, unwilling to let his mind linger too long on Jordan's eyes. Finally he took a long breath and pushed open the door. The officers were already inside, waiting.

He scowled at Cassak when he entered the officer's war room. "You're useless."

"I told you that you didn't want to know," the captain replied. "You shouldn't have gone into that dungeon."

He had needed to see for himself. Had to look his brother in the face and know what he'd sentenced them to. But nothing could have prepared him to see Rona so completely brutalized and his brother so violently angry. His anger and remorse had nearly ruled him.

It was well he left the cell, before Jordan's gaze could divide soul and spirit and plant seeds of treason in his heart.

Teeleh, what have I agreed to do to them?

"Fine. Is everyone here?" He scanned the room, knowing the answer. Two throaters—their chief, Warryn, included—were present. Warryn had a smirk on his face when Marak entered.

Marak gave the man a long, cold stare that silenced the room. Warryn returned it, but broke off first. Marak leaned on one knee. He motioned his second. "Tell me something worth hearing. First, the escapees from the palace."

"Our scouts are all over the place," the second replied. "The gates are sealed off. We started with the city, then moved around the lake. They can't have gotten far. And we're searching the desert."

"Bring them alive."

Warryn's smug looked returned. His long mustache twitched. "If that's what you prefer."

Subhuman waste like him rounded up vermin indiscriminately, locked them up, often terrorized them, then slaughtered them like chattel. At least Marak had the decency to make death come quickly.

Except when his kid brother and sister-in-law were concerned.

"Bring them in for questioning, but behave yourselves. I need them to talk. I want to know how three albinos breached temple security. You've searched the palace and the thrall?"

Nods.

"What did you find?"

"No sign of forced entry, and no one saw them come in."

Sucrow was right. This didn't bode well. Marak listened to the rest of the report and soon grew weary of hearing the long version of *We learned nothing in fourteen hours.*

Finally, the excuses became simply nauseating. Marak shook his head and raised his hand, stopping his commander mid-speech. "Just find me the albinos. I don't care how you do it or what did and didn't work. Bring them in and find out how they escaped us. And don't allow for any mistakes, or heads will roll. Cassak, Warryn—the rebel scouts?"

"Moving south," Cassak and Warryn spoke at the same time. The pair traded hard scowls.

"Moving—" Again, neither outspoke the other.

Marak pointed. "Cassak."

"But—" Warryn started to protest.

"Silence. Captain?"

"They're moving food and water, but their camp is still intact. And they seem considerably close to where we've placed the albinos."

Curious. Marak stopped listening, musing while his men considered the ramifications. Finally he dismissed them.

Warryn lingered. "General."

Marak fumed. His hand longed for his hilt, but he refrained. Sucrow didn't need much of an excuse.

"I'm not interested, Warryn."

"I'm only here to offer a word of advice."

"I take my own counsel."

Warryn's hand closed around Marak's arm. Marak half-drew

his sword, but remembered Sucrow had his family. "Just don't be foolish."

"SHE ISN'T HERE." SILVIE FINISHED CARVING ANOTHER Book of History into a broad-leafed tree and knelt beside Johnis on a steep bank overlooking the muddy waters of Middle Lake.

She scratched her sides, then her arms, with a reddish piece of bark.

Broad leaves of burnt orange and gold partially obscured them from the road.

"She has to be here." Johnis fought the urge to scream for Darsal.

But he knew better.

Darsal would have been right where he'd carved into the bark at daybreak.

A day wasted.

Maybe Darsal *had* gone suicidal.

Or she'd been caught.

"We've been all the way around the lake. Either she didn't find your Book of History sign funny, or she was never here to be mad about it." Silvie straightened the oversized garments that swallowed her slender frame.

With braids in her short hair, she looked surprisingly Scab.

"It wasn't supposed to be funny," Johnis snapped, suddenly frustrated with her. "She's supposed to be here."

"Well, obviously something's happened."

"That isn't good enough." Heat rose in his chest. Johnis wanted to strangle one or both women. As soon as he found the missing one.

"Would you get a grip?" Silvie scowled. "You're acting like an idiot."

"I am not. The disease is getting to you."

"Getting to me, is it?" She quirked a brow. "Seen any more women in the lake this morning, Chosen One?" Her voice dripped sarcasm.

Johnis's mind drifted from Silvie's voice. Away from the little cluster of trees that sheltered them. Away from the bridge over Middle Lake and Sucrow's temple.

Into the desert, where a beautiful woman with her low, silky voice and her mesmerizing gaze awaited their help.

A fog billowed up in his mind, seeped deep inside of him. The woman's face appeared before him, the desert reflected in her eyes. She smiled at him with perfect lips.

"Make haste, my mighty Chosen One. Render me aid, in the wilderness where those of the Guard dwell . . ."

"Elyon, you're beautiful," Johnis breathed.

"A little random," Silvie replied with a smile, snapping his focus back. "But thank you." Her cheeks flushed.

Heat flooded Johnis's face. He didn't dare tell her he hadn't meant to say that out loud, much less that he'd said it to a woman only he could see. Instead, he merely said, "Seemed the simplest way to end a fight."

"Aren't you a charmer?" Her voice went deadpan. She knew.

Perspiration slid down his spine. He fought the urge to scratch, forced himself to focus. Much longer and they wouldn't require deception. The fog dissipated.

No Darsal, no water, no Forest Guard.

Just this cursed disease nibbling away at their flesh.

Motion from the road.

Six Scabs on horseback headed toward them. Among them General Marak.

"Silvie."

She gripped his shoulder with a firm hand, breath against his neck.

"You! Get up here!"

For a moment neither moved, held fast by unseen chains. The general called them out again. Silvie's hand tightened into a fist at his back, a small growth on his shoulder blade.

Of course, at this distance Marak couldn't possibly know their identity. Although if there was a split among the Horde, looking like a Scab might not aid them, after all.

A third command, gruff and impatient. The general likely would not suffer a fourth. And at this point there was only one thing left to do: behave like a Scab.

Johnis straightened and started up the bridge where the general waited. Ten feet away he stopped and bowed. Silvie followed him, hood low.

"Forgive the delay, sir," he said. "What does the general require of us?"

Marak's gray eyes scrutinized Johnis and Silvie from head to toe and back. "What are you doing down there?"

"Looking for albinos, sir. We were told some escaped last night and that a reward was out for their recapture. Naturally, my wife and I were more than eager to help you be rid of the vermin."

Marak studied them closer, eyes narrow. "Is that so? I don't believe that knowledge was public yet."

"I understand that, General. But you see, the ruckus last night had my attention, and there was this guard—"

Marak's face hardened instantly, his anger creasing his skin until it cracked through the morst and began to flake. "Which guard?"

Inside Johnis was reeling, fighting the urge to whip around and run back toward the trees where no one would find him.

The desert. The desert was always safe.

"Johnis . . ."

He shook the presence off. Not now. "I'm afraid I failed to ask his name, sir. Please, my intention isn't to get anyone in trouble. I only meant to help."

"Really. How thoughtful of you."

The endless itching, like ravenous wolves gnawing on bones, tormented him. His hand instinctively went to scratch, but he caught himself, unwilling to show his arms.

Marak snorted. "All right, move along, then. And if you do happen across those albinos . . . Tell them I'm going to make them wish they were dead."

The desert, the desert, the desert . . .

"Aid me, Chosen One . . ."

Focus already, Johnis!

"We will, General." He bowed again and left with Silvie in tow.

She looped her arm around his and leaned close. "He's watching."

"Keep walking," he whispered back.

Her weight pressed against him. Under her cloak, her hand was probably already on a knife, half-drawn and ready to unleash on whoever threatened them.

"Still watching?"

"He's not, but his second is." She hesitated, then spoke. "We have to find water, Johnis."

"The desert, Johnis . . . Come to the desert and aid me . . ."

"Out in the desert where Thomas is, not here in this blasted forest!" She was getting impatient. They needed water, soon.

No more resisting. Too many women involved.

He wanted to hit something.

"Fine," he responded.

"We can come back for her," Silvie argued. Elyon alive, what was she arguing for? "But we have to leave now."

"Fine."

"Seriously, if I don't get to water, I will be hunting albinos in the service of the Horde myself! You know the disease will ruin our minds."

"I said fine!" he snapped. He strode faster, off the beaten path and into the forest. Once they were out of sight of the general and his men, they lost the urge to keep quiet.

"You don't have to be so . . ."

His mind drifted.

The strange woman's voice flooded his mind. *"Come, Johnis . . . between the southern gap and forest wander I . . . Render me aid, mighty Chosen One . . . chosen for appointed tasks none else may bear . . ."*

"Are you even listening to me?"

"You keep saying the same things over and over again. Let me see your knife."

She glowered at him. He was being demanding, but at the moment he didn't care.

They were leaving Darsal to the disease. To the Horde.

Johnis carved another Book of History into yet another sacrificial tree. Seven books, seven trees.

Below this one he added a catalina cactus.

An image of the canyons between Natalga Gap and the southern edge of Middle came into mind. They'd been there many times. Their first mission together they'd gone in search of catalina cacti.

What could possibly be different now?

"'Chosen for appointed tasks none else may bear,'" he muttered, trying to work out the meaning.

"Excuse me?"

"Nothing. You think she'd understand we went south?"

"Who said we were going south?" Silvie sheathed her knife he'd borrowed.

"I did." He didn't want to tell her about the beautiful woman again. It would only irritate her.

"Well, I disagree. You're forgetting you already said Thomas most likely would go north. You're right. The Horde is too familiar with the canyons and Natalga Gap. And there's a Horde city out that way. Assuming it's still there after five years."

"The Horde has the forests. They no longer need a desert dwelling."

Silvie conceded. "Why south?"

He started walking. She really needed to learn to trust him. "If we move fast we can make the north edge of the Natalga Gap before dark."

She grabbed him. "Why south?" Her gray eyes narrowed. "That woman of yours. She told you to go out there."

Johnis shrugged free. "We're going into the desert because we're out of time to try finding Darsal."

"That wasn't my question. I know that already. That woman's gotten to you, hasn't she?"

Johnis went south, fully expecting her to follow.

"What if it's a trap?"

He laughed. "Silvie, what possible reason could a woman I've never met have to trap me? The disease is messing with you. You're the one begging me for water. Are we going or not?"

She scowled. Then started after him. "Fine."

thirteen

Xedan tried twice—well, twice that Darsal could remember—to offer her some solace, but she would have none.

Futile.

Beneath the cocoon of a tattered, borrowed cloak, her skin began to turn brittle. The pain in her joints made her moan on the floor of her tiny cell.

"Darsal," Jordan said, "you must eat."

"Do you believe me yet?" she asked from beneath her cloak.

Hesitation.

"I believe you're in a lot of pain. Sit up and eat something. Drink the water they left you. It'll help."

Darsal stretched her limbs and back and pushed back the cloak. Her cellmates gasped. She rubbed her eyes and sat up, then felt her skin slough off.

She yelped and held her hands where she could see.

Long cracks covered her body and split into flakes like dried mud baking in the sunlight. Tanned skin and dark hair had turned grayish white.

Sign of the living dead.

"Now do you believe?" she demanded. "I'm turning to Horde. Elyon's forsaken me. I begged him. I wanted to believe you. I really did."

Jordan's eyes were wide, and his face had gone completely white. Instinctively he looked at his hands, then pulled up his sleeves, just to be certain.

"How are you only now beginning to turn?" Xedan drew back.

"It's complicated." Darsal scratched, further deflated when flakes of dried skin sloughed off. "I don't understand how it works. But I'm trapped in here, and it's over. I'm as good as dead."

"Drink something," Xedan said. "Drink the water. It'll clear your—"

"Forget the water! It doesn't matter! It doesn't matter!" Darsal curled into a ball and whipped the cloak back over her again.

Her skin hurt and itched.

Her bones and joints were stiff and aching.

She had no way out.

"Darsal." She heard Jordan raise up on his knees and shuffle around, could imagine his hands on the bars and face pressed against the slimy metal. "Darsal, remember what you asked my grandfather?"

She clenched her teeth and gave him silence.

More movement. "Here," Jordan said, "Give this to her."

"I don't want it."

"Take it, Darsal," Jordan insisted. Xedan pressed something round in her hand. His leather pendant.

"I can't take this from you."

"You'll want it when you catch the Circle." Jordan looked down, frowning. "We don't have much longer anyway."

She brought her hand back under the cloak and pressed it to her chest. Still she didn't speak. Jordan, however, was undeterred. "Darsal, listen to me. You know it's going to affect your mind soon. You've been gone a long time, and there's much to say and little time. Are you listening to me?"

Silence. Xedan's three fingers gently took hold of her foot and squeezed. "Elyon hasn't forsaken you, dear."

"Darsal, you need to drown. You need to find a red lake and drown. You have to get out—"

"I know I need to bathe!"

"No, you don't need to bathe. You need to drown!" Jordan yelled. A corrective look from Xedan settled him a little. He took a breath, worked his fists. "All of Elyon's lakes are red now. But you can't just take a swim. Elyon changed the rules. You have to dive into the water and drown. You understand?"

"I'm going Scab, so you're plotting my death?"

"Darsal!" Jordan bellowed her name with the force of one in authority, a man rebuking a child.

She went quiet.

Jordan softened his voice. "I am not trying to kill you, girl. I'm trying to help save you. Do you want to become a Scab?"

"No."

"So listen to me. There's a hidden pool the Guard used to use. It's right near the southern edge of the forest. The Horde never found it, but it's red. It's not very wide, but it's very deep. I want you to escape here and find—"

"A hidden pool."

"A hidden pool I'm going to tell you how to find. Grandfather doesn't even know where this one is. And then you can make your way around—"

The dungeon door clanked open. Torchlight poured into the hall. Darsal pulled Xedan's cloak further over her head and faked sleep.

"What do you want now?" Despair flooded Jordan's voice. His wife. They must have come for Rona again. *Oh, Jordan . . .*

How much could one man take?

Shuffling feet. Darsal heard a scuffle and Jordan's desperate pleas not to take Rona. She heard him fall, heard the sound of a boot striking human flesh with a dull thud.

Then a new guard spoke. "Is she alive or dead?"

"She's ill," Xedan replied, stricken. "There was no cause for that."

"You're all ill."

"Elyon, don't take her," Jordan pleaded, presumably from the ground. His voice was shaky from the brief—but sound—beating. He groaned.

The guard didn't respond. Darsal heard the woman being dragged away.

"Could you bring her another blanket?" Xedan asked. "And perhaps some more fruit? It'll help."

The guard scoffed. "She's going to die down here regardless." He left, shadows creeping in his wake. The lock creaked into place.

"HE'S TAKING HER AGAIN?" CASSAK ASKED HIS SCOUT. HE'D left the council and gone to take care of some leftover business with the rebels.

The scout nodded sharply.

He had to keep an eye on the throater.

And he had to keep Eram's men and Marak's men separated.

"When?" he snapped.

"Just now. Right after the general left his brother."

Cassak swore. "Marak went down there?" Of all the stupid things to do.

"Yes, sir."

"Fine. Send word to Commander Reyan. I'll be an hour late. No one is to disturb the rebels."

"Captain, the commander is—"

"I said go," he snapped. His scout looked perplexed. Cassak

was only a captain, and he answered to Reyan. The apparent defiance stunned the scout.

"Tell him it's for Marak," Cassak supplied. "General's orders come first."

fourteen

Johnis's legs hurt. Both calves and thighs felt like someone was filleting him with knives. With every step and with each painful motion the realization that his journey really was over sank in further. Life as he knew it was dead. Over. Gone.

"Aid me, Johnis . . . Come to the desert, where I may be found . . ."

The desert. Endless, blinding western sun.

He'd failed Darsal.

"I have water, my Johnisss . . ."

"Water. Water, Silvie. She says she has water . . ." He squinted and bowed his head. His flaking skin grew hotter and tears streamed down his face.

Elyon, help us . . .

Nothing.

"We'll see."

Johnis felt his mind drift. The inviting, invisible presence he vaguely understood as an unsettling power, a gentle tug of his will by a very powerful woman he couldn't see.

"Follow your heart."

His heart said he was going mad. That this was all futile. There was no woman in the desert, just like there were no Forest Dwellers in the forests, only Horde.

All he had was this thin, dwindling hope that maybe, just maybe, he could help this woman stranded in the desert and that she would help them survive.

"Johnis." Silvie squeezed his shoulder. He'd sunk to his knees. Now he groaned.

"He won."

"Don't say . . . Don't say that, Johnis." Her hand gripped the back of his neck.

Her hand. Her cracking, flaking skin. White, dried-out hair and dull eyes. The pain in their joints and muscles made quick movement impossible.

Johnis struggled to refocus. A task growing in difficulty.

"They're all gone. It's over. Teeleh and the Shataiki won, and it's over. 'Save the world.' Save the world from what? We may have saved Las Vegas from Alucard, but the search for the books was a fool's errand! Elyon has abandoned this world to the Horde, and now us with it."

"That's only the scabbing disease talking."

He knew she was right, but already he wasn't as sure as he had been a few hours ago. A few more hours and he wouldn't even care that they'd abandoned Darsal. Wouldn't care that they'd lost the books they'd nearly died to retrieve. Wouldn't care that everyone was gone. Wouldn't care a rat's behind about anything he'd once loved.

"Curse those blasted books," he muttered.

She slapped him hard across the face. He fell backward, caught himself with his palms, stunned.

"Stop talking like this!"

He jumped to his feet and flung wide his arms. "What am I supposed to say? You want water, Silvie? I can get it for you, just like before, only now it doesn't even work! Even if we find water, it's useless!"

"I didn't follow you out here to listen to you shrivel up and die!"

"What do you want me to do, Silvie? The last time there was always water to be found, a lake back in Middle waiting for us to bathe in. Now what? Nothing but muddy water. Even the clear water has no power."

Power. This woman who could speak to him across a desert had immeasurable power. He could feel it, even from the city. And the closer he came . . .

"At least we'll be able to drink it." Silvie's hands went to her hips. "At least we can drink it."

"Johnis . . ."

"Not now!" he screamed at the woman in his head. Silvie

stared at him. His senses sharpened, well aware of even the tiniest perceptions.

He raked his hands through his hair.

White flakes fell out.

Silvie made a face at him and stepped back.

"We can't escape the Scabs if we've become Scabs, Silvie. Only a handful of people knew about that pool."

"What's gotten into you? You never talk like this."

"My family is dead," he snapped.

"So is mine. For a whole lot longer." Her lackluster gray eyes drilled him hard, set like flint.

A last flash of sunlight blitzed across the sky, then fell into night. From somewhere in the canyon came soft insect chirping. Still farther away a coyote howled.

"I'm sorry, Silvie," he said at last. "I didn't mean . . . It's just that I don't like this helpless feeling. And this woman wants my . . ."

"Johnis . . ."

Cloud cover rolled in and with it more mist. The air cooled and fog thickened. No stars, moonlight veiled with fingerlike, wispy tendrils of silver and gray shadow.

Johnis closed his eyes and drank in the chilly air. It was like water to his thick, parched tongue. "Silvie? Tell me you see this . . ."

"See what?"

"The fog. The cool air, I can almost taste—"

"Come to me, Johniss . . . Seek that which may be found."

Before him was the woman's multicolored gaze, the strange

eyes he could lose himself in. In her eyes he saw through the mist to a river half a mile wide with hot springs on both sides, cold water rushing over falls and across the desert.

Water.

Johnis trudged forward, aching for the river the woman showed him, wondering where it was. Maybe Thomas and the others were there.

A great tree spanned the river, enormous leaves concealing fruit the size of both his fists. On the far side of the river was a forest like none he'd ever seen.

"Beautiful . . ."

"Johnis, there's nothing there."

His eyes widened. "You don't see . . ."

Silvie put one hand on each shoulder and forced eye contact. "I see nothing but empty desert and your eyes turning gray, Johnis."

"There's a river and fruit trees and . . ."

"Aid me, Johnis . . . Come, come quickly, while the cool of evening lingers . . ."

Silvie's arms wrapped around him. She kissed him full on the mouth.

His mind refocused. Johnis cradled her head. The musty Scab scent was already settling in, but it wasn't as bad as he remembered.

She pulled back. Cupped his cheek. Her eyes were glassy. Skin slick with sweat. "There is you and me, and the desert."

"Johnis . . ."

Silvie tipped his chin up. Traced the curve of his mouth. "You and me."

He blinked. "Yes. Yes, of course."

"You understand that? The disease isn't making you forget?"

Her hand slid into his.

The river and the trees disappeared.

Silence fell over them.

"I'm not going to lose you, Johnis of Ramos."

He headed for the Gap. "You won't, Silvie. It's just the disease talking."

"You're sure?"

"Of course. Come on."

They started the final leg for Natalga Gap. Silvie had to be right. Johnis was just seeing mirages. The desert and the scabbing disease was getting to him.

"You are nigh, my Chosen One . . . Come to me, Johnis . . ."

"DROWN, DARSAL," THEY KEPT INSISTING. EVEN IN HER FITful slumber she could hear the insistent voices. *"Elyon doesn't require constant bathing anymore,"* Jordan repeated. "*Escape, Darsal. Escape and find water. Find Elyon.*"

Darsal turned. *Elyon doesn't want me. It doesn't hurt so much now. Penance. My penance is to be Scab. Death.*

"What is this?" A gruff male voice interrupted her drifting thoughts. "What is the meaning of this?"

Rotten-egg smell assaulted her. Her eyes opened. Darkness greeted her.

"What have you done with the albino prisoner?"

A guard stood beyond the iron bars, glaring in at her. What he could possibly mean, she had no clue. Her mind swam with the scabbing disease.

Darsal pushed herself up to her seat. "Excuse me?"

The Scab's white eyes were round and confused. "You . . . What's the meaning of this?"

She glanced down at her hand, and his meaning hit her at once. The disease had taken most of her skin, turning her to Scab as she slept.

The guard had evidently never seen an albino turn to Scab before.

Which could only mean . . .

Dear Elyon! It was true then? These albinos really didn't turn back to Scab?

She looked at the other cages and saw that she was alone. Rona was gone. Jordan and Xedan appeared to be sleeping.

From the fog in her mind came a most obvious course.

She forced her aching muscles to respond, pushing herself to her feet. "Where is the woman?"

"She was taken for questioning. But you . . . You're . . . You're not albino?"

"Do I look like an albino to you, fool?" Darsal strode angrily for the door. "That cursed prisoner tricked me and escaped. Get me out of here!"

The guard stood still, confused. "Who are you? You're no guard I've seen. How did she—"

"Get me out of here, you fool! I was sent on personal orders of General Marak, if you must know. I came here, and this wench managed to reach through the cage and knock me out. And if you breathe a word of it, I'll slit your throat. Now unlock this blasted door. I have to track her down or it'll be my hide!"

He walked up to the door, withdrawing his keys. A slight smile curved his mouth as the pieces fell into place for him, however misguided they were. Darsal's heart thumped loudly. It was actually working. In the dim light he mistook her for a Scab.

Because she *was* one.

The latch fell open. "I would make haste," the guard said. "If Sucrow finds out, you'll pay."

Darsal stepped out of her cell. "Sucrow? Not Marak?"

The Scab hesitated, then turned away. "You know what they say."

"No, I don't know what they say."

But the guard just walked away, clearly not eager to expound.

Jordan and Xedan were still imprisoned. She heard them stirring. But Rona wasn't here. Jordan would never leave Rona.

She'd have to come back.

"Hey, give me your overcloak, I can't be seen in these clothes."

He turned back, offered a grin and a chuckle, then pulled off his hooded cloak. "Next time Marak might be better off sending a man to do his bidding." He tossed the garment to her.

"What's your name? I'll tell him what you think."

His grin softened. "I didn't mean it like that."

"No? Then I'll keep the cloak, if you don't mind."

He grunted at the veiled threat. "It's yours."

"And your sword."

He frowned, looked about to say something, then thought better of it and handed it over.

"Thank you," Darsal said. "Now leave me before I decide to test it."

The Scab guard left her alone in the dungeon, free from her cage.

She stood still for a long minute, trying to contemplate the meaning of her sudden fortune, grasping at the tendrils of a plan that might lead to her survival. She looked at the back of her hand again.

Jordan went up on his knees. "Go."

"Jordan—"

"Go now!" He pointed at the door. *"Now!"*

He wanted her to leave them. To what?

She had no key. If she took out the guard, she'd draw attention.

There were two possible paths ahead of her.

One led to this drowning the albinos had filled her mind with.

One led to life as a Scab among the Horde.

Both were death.

She was as well off in the cage behind her.

Unless . . . unless the drowning really did lead to a new kind of life, as they had insisted. But even that life would likely lead to death because the Horde now ruled Other Earth. Albinos were nothing more than hunted animals.

And yet . . . the idea of living as a Scab . . .

She let her mind wander. Maybe it wasn't so bad. Maybe she could be happy as a Scab. Within a day she wouldn't know the difference. The disease would take her mind and make her believe the Horde was right and the albinos were wrong.

She would be utterly deceived.

But what was so wrong about that, if you no longer realized that you were deceived?

As they said back on the other Earth, ignorance is bliss.

"Don't give in, Darsal," Jordan warned. His voice was tight. His eyes . . . "Get out of here."

Darsal grunted. No, she would not give in to the scabbing disease, not yet.

"I'll come back," she promised.

Jordan didn't comment.

"I promise."

"Drown, Darsal. That's all that matters." His voice was firm. Jaw set. Eyes expressionless and resolute.

What was he not saying?

She would flee this putrid Horde city, find the red pool they'd told her about.

And then . . .

She shrugged into the oversized cloak and pulled up the hood.

And then she would decide.

"I'll come back," she repeated. "I promise. I'll get you out of here. All of you."

Quiet. Darsal started out.

"Elyon's strength," he called after her.

Elyon, what was she doing?

She tightened her grip on the sword. She would not desert them.

Small consolation.

It took her only a few minutes to navigate her way through several halls, up a long flight of stone steps leading to the surface, past the iron gate, and into the Horde city.

Night shrouded her. And no one paid her the slightest attention. Thankfully a good moon showed her the way.

Her feet and legs ached with each step and her skin felt like it was on fire, but she didn't slow to ease the pain or pause to satisfy her thirst. She walked with her head down, mind fixed only on getting out now, before she lost the last reserves of urgency to do so.

Get out into the forest; find the water. Drink. Wash.

Drown?

She couldn't imagine anything so foolish. But faced by the certainty of death at any rate, she might even just drown.

Stay south, Jordan had told her. *Stay south and don't be seen. You're following the road, but not really. And don't let anyone find you. You'll eventually go through a ditch. It'll take an hour or so to get there, maybe more if you have to hide out awhile. Look for the spider trees and the marsh. If you reach the desert, you've missed it.*

She reached the forest and picked up her pace. The place where wood and desert meet, just like her dreams. She surveyed the trees in search of beady, red eyes.

None showed themselves.

She tripped, her sore, stiff muscles screaming. Stifled a yelp and pressed south in search of a red pool not even Thomas Hunter had known about on the word of a condemned man who claimed she had to drown.

Don't think about that. Not yet. Not yet.

The trees rustled, unseen wings beating against whispering leaves. She glimpsed a shadow of what might have been an oversized bird. Or bat.

First to find the pool.

fifteen

An hour passed before Darsal had gone far enough to escape all traces, sights, sounds, and smells of Horde in the forest. Except for those that traveled with her, on her flesh, in her hair and nostrils and mind.

She had to fight the urge to scratch off her own skin.

But did it really matter anymore?

She fumbled over a stump and kept going, pressing into the unknown.

Here in the dark the trees were full of mangy fur, beady red eyes, and long, razorlike fangs. Sweat oozed down her neck and spine, mixing with the tingly, invisible sensation of an icy claw raking along the tender skin and slicing her to ribbons.

Darsal could almost feel the Shataikis' breath at her ear and neck, smell the horrid stench like sulfur and ash.

A dark laughter echoed through the forest. Darsal spun around, tried to see her tormentors. Laughter and wings.

"Stay away!" Her fists knotted around her sword, body coiled in a half crouch. "I killed one of your queens," she warned. "You are nothing to me! Nothing!"

Shallow breathing, pulsing hearts.

Madness, girl. You're going mad. Is this real or not? Darsal didn't know anymore. In the dungeon it was dreams. *What am I doing?*

Rustling wings, a high-pitched squeal. Where were they? How many?

Darsal ran, one arm over her head. Invisible bats breezed past her ear and shrieked. She suspected that it was all in her mind, part of her turning Horde . . .

Maybe.

Darsal still slapped at the beasts, which were always out of reach. More bats circled through the leaves, rattling branches and herding her like a wayward cow. She couldn't see them. Couldn't see them, but they were there, in her mind, bent on consuming her alive.

It took her another hour to find Jordan's grove of spider trees, and she'd carelessly rushed over a ledge, slipped down a muddy slope, rolled sideways, and struck shoulder first against a rock among the trees.

Silence.

She groaned, rubbed her eyes. Spider trees dripped down over her face and blotted out the moon. Mud caked her skin, cooling it. She crawled on all fours, then rose up on her knees.

She'd landed in what looked like a marsh or swamp. Fog and cloud cover obscured her vision, but enough moonlight escaped to let her glimpse her surroundings.

Darsal pulled a twig free of her hair and brought one foot under her, pushed up, and stood. Her eyes immediately searched the swampy floor west. Gradually grass and mud and tree mingled with reddish sand and desert wheat.

Her heart thrilled. Close. So close. She sucked a long, ragged breath.

"Look for the grove of spider trees. You'll find a cluster of them that looks like a tent or a canopy of sorts, with a small gap somewhat like a door. It'll be a good place to hide. Drown, Darsal. Drown and live!"

A cruel joke? The ramblings of a madman? But she'd seen his eyes. Soft, mournful eyes that bore no hate.

Then again, if Jordan was sick, he might truly believe the same as the general about albinos: better dead than diseased.

Hadn't Darsal once said as much herself?

She turned full circle and tried to gain her bearings. Ledge. Rocks. Desert meeting forest on the western side. Spider trees forming a kind of refuge. But where?

Darsal kept south. Jordan had implied that the grove of spider trees wasn't big, merely well concealed, and therefore she wouldn't have trouble finding the pool.

But did she really want to find this red pool, submerge herself, inhale water, and drown? Feet squishing over black mud, she still had the nagging thought that the enemy was somehow trying to trick her into killing herself.

Jordan and Xedan could have tricked her. They could be Shataiki disguised as Forest Guard. Or the whole thing could be a sadistic pretense meant to fool her into betraying the Guard. Betraying Thomas. Betraying Elyon.

She had meant to ask more, so much more. How did the lakes turn red? Why? Why would Elyon change the rules he himself had put into place? Furthermore, why would Elyon expect her to die?

But the prospect of her turning had preoccupied her with a self-loathing that had left no room for hope or even the means of hope.

"There is much to say and little time. Trust me, Darsal. Just trust me, if nothing else. You have to drown in a red lake. You must. Elyon will be with you. Do so and never turn Horde again."

The woods threatened to swallow her. A thick grove of spider trees closed in from the forest, blocking out the border. She stopped.

The overgrown runner plants grew up about four feet, trunks in a half-moon shape, runners and leaves fashioning a kind of dome. A hut, almost.

Moonlight flickered, then vanished, behind cloud cover. A gentle breeze kissed her skin, ruffling her hair, and mist wafted up from the ground.

There wasn't much time. The Scabs would be hunting her now. They would find her soon enough. She took a deep breath and entered the little cavern, heart driving blood through her chest like ranchers driving a thousand cattle across open plain.

The space inside was warm, musty, and dry. It was about twelve feet across. In the dark she couldn't tell the color of the pool, but it looked about ten feet across and glimmered up at her. Beckoning. Mocking.

Darsal froze at the mere sight of the water. Itching and burning and flaking aside, she could only gawk and hold her breath. She knew its color, even if she couldn't see very well. She'd followed Jordan's instructions and Xedan's promptings to the letter, and everything thus far had been exactly as they had said.

There were no more pristine lakes of Elyon.

There were muddy, useless lakes.

There were these defiled, blood-infested red lakes that were also useless to her.

Unless she drowned in such.

So said the condemned.

Darsal took a few steps forward and merely stared. She circled the pool, crouched beside it, then stood and resumed her anxious pacing. Her heart rate soared, if that were possible at this point.

She wondered briefly about Johnis and Silvie. They had either turned Horde or died. Left her to turn Horde or die. Or they'd drowned and were alive, which sounded very much like a contradiction to her.

Darsal slid to her knees, face pressed against the sand. She curled into a ball, all hope of this whole mess being merely a nightmare shattered. "Elyon, I can't do this. I can't do this. This is madness, and I can't."

He had yet to hear her. Yet to answer her. Xedan had come. Jordan had come. But Elyon had not. And even they were only temporary solace, with all their madness about drowning.

She scratched hard at a place on her shoulder blade, but it was just out of reach and she could only twist uncomfortably.

She sat up, staring at the clouds that concealed the lesser lights of star and moon. Lesser but no less glorious.

Behind her the red pool still summoned her, still called. Still dared her to jump and see for herself if Jordan and Xedan were telling the truth.

At worst, they were liars and she would die and be rid of the scabbing disease for good.

She snorted. Yes, either way Jordan would be right, wouldn't he? Either she would drown and the water would somehow revive her without the disease, or she would drown and be forever without the disease in whatever afterlife awaited her.

Of course, maybe Elyon's idea of hell was eternity with a skin disease that drove you mad and a million Shataiki scraping away your flesh. It would work.

Blood roared in her ears. Her muscles tensed and she completely lost track of time. The sky grew darker. Time passed. She clutched Jordan's necklace.

At last she could bring herself to move. No other recourse presented itself.

She would die.

Darsal stood and went back to the spider trees, her feet swishing over sand, then squishing through mud.

Muggy air hit her when she came back into the refuge. Once more she faced the pool. Circled it, sizing the water up the same way she would a Scab.

She removed her boots and placed them to one side. Then her clothes.

She put her right toe into the water, flinched back.

Nothing.

She sighed. No, nothing would happen yet. Of course.

Darsal stepped into the cold, thick water and slipped, gasped. Then managed a short laugh. Evidently the pool had a sharp ledge and she'd stepped off it. She started to tread in the deep, deep water.

So Jordan was right. The water would not work this way anymore, for reasons unknown to her.

Hot tears streamed down her face alongside cold red.

Dripped down off her chin.

Blood and water.

Never taint the water with blood. Never.

Darsal drew a deep breath and plunged under.

Sixteen

Darsal stroked with her arms and kicked, swimming quickly so she couldn't change her mind. Deeper, deeper. Gradually the water became warm. It occurred to her that the pool could be fed by an underground river.

If she swam deep enough she might be sucked in.

It also occurred to her that she hadn't exactly seen for certain the water's color. Furthermore, if Elyon truly had condemned her, he had no reason to allow her to test him in this nonsensical and blasphemous way.

But beneath the surface the water was dark.

She swam deeper.

This was something Johnis would do and as a result would probably kill her.

Her lungs started to burn.

Darsal let herself float for a moment, eyes closed, adrenaline racing and mind reeling. This was a mistake, a gross mistake.

She couldn't make herself swallow water. She couldn't! Even if she tried, her body would rebel. Her mind rebelled at the mere thought.

And then she was out of air.

On instinct she exhaled, then inhaled.

The mouthful of water made her sputter. Sparks filled her vision and she clutched her throat, kicking toward what she thought was the surface then realized wasn't.

Darsal sucked in another breath to scream. Choking on water, she now knew she'd never make it. This cursed pool was determined to have her and would take her straight into its gullet.

Death had come. So be it.

She breathed out, pursed her lips, and glared into the dark.

Then opened her mouth and took in a long, gluttonous breath.

Water scraped down her lungs like Shataiki claws, and yellow, red, and blue tinged her sight. She didn't fight it.

Against all urge to struggle, Darsal curled her limbs together and took another defiant drag of killing water.

The last ten years for nothing. The ordeal with the books all ended in being cut off, left to rot in a prison cell, and now suicide by drowning. Absolutely nothing.

All went black.

Her heart stopped, her lungs no longer cried for air and begged her to relieve them of water. Her limbs did not move. She did not blink. She was suspended in the water in a dead man's float.

Red light filtered up from below, where she'd expected to find a muddy black floor and come to rest against other idiots who had come to drown.

Someone's horrific screams flooded her mind, penetrated the water, and invaded every pore of her being until she, too, wanted to scream but could not.

The sound of cracking whips overpowered the voice, even though the louder they came the louder the wretched voice shrieked.

So loud Darsal thought her bones would shatter into a million pieces.

I never abandoned you, Darsal. I've heard you, and I am here.

And then her heart began to pump. Blood filled her veins and circulated on its course. Her mind cleared, and red light swarmed her. She was surfacing, fast, and a tingling sensation made her quiver. Dizzying.

Darsal, Darsal, Darsal. Don't you know I love you and I made you and I love the way I made you?

She looked around for the voice in the water. "I'm a traitor. I've done—"

I am not yet done with you.

"I will do whatever you ask of me."

Then return to the Horde and love them for me. For Johnis.

Suspended beneath the surface, having died and come back to

life, Darsal didn't, for a single breath of the living water, question Elyon's request.

"I will. I will, I will!"

And then the water was silent and she was rising quickly.

Darsal's eyes widened when she broke the face of the water, lungs still heavy. She clambered over the ledge and pulled herself out. Fell forward and vomited water. Lots of water. Multiple liters of water.

She sputtered and coughed up the rest, then started to laugh and cry at the same time. Pale light glowed through the gap in the spider trees and lit the pool bloodred. She looked down at her smooth, tanned skin.

Her eyes widened.

She'd really breathed Elyon's water.

She'd swum with him, heard his voice, felt the disease melt away from her riddled body.

She had died and come to life!

The words echoed through her mind.

Return to the Horde and love them for me. For Johnis.

Heart still pounding, Darsal dressed, pants, tunic, boots. Horde cloak. Then reached for the sword. She hesitated, then held the weapon in both hands. She'd told Johnis she wasn't ready. Not after the carnage she'd caused.

Not after the innocents she'd killed.

She drew her blade from its scabbard, studied it a minute, then pushed it back into its leather covering and tied the sheath to her back.

Something caught her attention. One of the trees. In the dim light she couldn't make it out.

Darsal came closer. Something was carved in the wood. Curious in a hiding place so closely guarded.

Then she saw it: a crudely carved book. Not just any book.

A Book of History.

"I'm going to beat him."

But her initial irritation turned to a broad grin. She couldn't help it. Johnis and Silvie were alive! And they'd found the pool. Had they drowned?

No, they wouldn't know about Elyon's waters turning red.

Elyon's command took on new meaning. Darsal's mind reeled with the implications.

Jordan indicated the Circle was in the northwest desert.

If she could rescue Jordan and the other two, maybe they could all find Johnis and Silvie and make sure they drowned. Then they could find the Guard.

Return to the Horde and love them for me. For Johnis.

Jordan. Johnis. Forest Guard. Then she would find out what loving the Horde could possibly mean.

"GO ON, MARAK," CASSAK SAID QUIETLY. "I'LL HANDLE the cleanup."

His general said nothing.

"Go home," Cassak persisted.

Marak wouldn't look at him. He gave a brief nod and mounted his horse. Started back toward the city. Those last moments had been quiet.

The albinos had finally stopped screaming.

In the end they clenched their teeth and died in silent defiance.

Cassak sat on a rock, slowly wiping blood off his sword. Marak's Desecration test proved a success. The three albinos were dead.

A shame the fourth escaped.

His men carried off the bodies to be destroyed.

"Nicely done, eh?" Warryn sneered beside him.

Cassak raised his head, scowling, and followed the throater's gaze to Marak's shrinking form.

"Now maybe his head's cleared," the throater continued. "Our orders are to round up the rest."

"Your orders. Mine are elsewhere."

"Eram comes second to the albinos."

Cassak's eyes narrowed. "We will see."

DARSAL SKIDDED TO A STOP AT THE TOP OF A HILL OVERlooking the city of Middle. The sun blazed overhead. Far below and to her left, out several hundred feet, was the edge of Middle Lake, murky and brown, with the bridge crossing over to the ominous thrall. Directly across and on her right was the palace and the Horde's dungeon.

The whole place crawled with Scabs.

Return to the Horde and love them for me. For Johnis.

Now she was here with the disgusting smell and sights and wondering what in the world Elyon had meant. Maybe 'them' meant Jordan and his wife and grandfather.

She could love them.

For a second the despair that had overwhelmed her tickled the back of her mind, crept up with steel claws, and caressed her spine and neck. She swallowed and shook her head.

She wasn't alone.

Jordan had told her the truth.

Now she needed to sneak back in, brave his "I told you so," and get all of them out of this place.

They would escape into the desert.

To whatever refuge Elyon had planned for them.

Darsal climbed back down the hillside and pondered her next move. She would rely on stealth. Less was more.

She soon found the dungeons, as bleak on the outside as they were on the inside.

Her courage wavered only a moment.

Darting in, Darsal slipped past the guard and into the darkness. Several torches lit the way. She took one and came down the staircase into the long hall, past several corridors, and into what used to be the cells she shared with the others.

She tried the door. Unlocked. Breathless, she burst inside and called out softly. "Jordan!" She raced to their cells, imagining their faces. "Thank Elyon you were . . ."

No one answered.

Darsal nearly fell into the bars.

Rona's cage was empty. So were Jordan's and Xedan's.

Blood stained the back wall and the dirt floor.

Her brow furrowed, arms limp at her sides, mind refusing to understand.

"Jordan?"

Maybe it was the wrong cell. She'd gone the wrong way, chased an empty room.

The dungeon ran cold. Every ounce of excitement crashed out of her body. Her limbs felt stiff and icy.

No, this was the right room. Their blankets and Xedan's tattered cloak were still within the empty prison cells.

"Dead," came a rich, gruff voice from behind. Only now did she notice that atrocious Scab scent. "Jordan of Southern is dead."

The torch fell from her hand, landed on hard-packed dirt, and snuffed out in an instant. Darsal felt her balance start to give. She put her hand on the iron bar. There was no way she would collapse like a child in front of this Scab.

She continued to stare at the empty cages.

"As you will be," the voice finished. Shuffling feet told Darsal that more were with him. The scuffling and short whispers fell very still.

She turned to face her captor, unslung her sword.

General Marak's tall, lean frame filled the doorway. His scaly, battle-scarred face was set, jaw clenched. Gray eyes overcast and dark. Brow creased in an emotion Darsal couldn't place. He wore tans and browns, two knives on each thigh, and a sword across his back. Behind him was a commander.

But why was he here?

For a long minute they merely regarded each other with penetrating stares. His hand was on the hilt of his sword. He hadn't drawn it. He shouldn't have been able to walk up on her. She should be wiping his blood off her blade.

Return to the Horde and love them for me. For Johnis.

She could still fight her way out. This general hadn't expected anyone alive, much less free and armed, down here. She couldn't love her three cellmates if they were dead. Maybe Marak was hiding them somewhere.

No, Darsal. Love this *one.*

This *Scab*?

Bile rose in her throat. Never.

The commander grabbed at her wrists. Darsal slammed her fist into his nose, then her elbow. He went backward. She raised her sword to swing it, then paused midstroke.

That cost her. The commander recovered, slapped her sword away, and shoved her to her knees. Her sword clattered to the floor. Marak picked it up.

Darsal struggled. Only at Elyon's quiet prompting did she fall still. *You want me to love this Scab?*

The silent affirmative unnerved her.

Marak was still staring. Darsal swallowed her pride. Whatever Elyon meant, fine. She would try. But her cellmates . . .

"They're really dead?" she asked.

Marak's eyes had a soft cast to them that hadn't been there before. What color would his eyes be, beneath the disease that slowly rotted him through?

Stop this nonsense. He's a Scab. Why should I care?

Elyon's words still echoed.

"You want me to kill her, sir?"

Marak held up his hand. "Why are you here?"

Once more Jordan's expression came to mind. None of them had hated her. None of them.

Return to the Horde and love them, Elyon had said. But what was it he wanted? She couldn't save the three Forest Guard if they were already dead. And she couldn't escape now to help Johnis and find the others.

"Their executions were moved up because they helped you escape," the general said.

"But they didn't . . ." Darsal tried to rise but was forced back down. Her knees slammed into the ground. Jordan's necklace bounced off her chin.

"I see their effort was in vain." Marak pushed past her, past Rona's cage, and entered Jordan's. Why was he so concerned over this particular albino?

Old memories came back, something Johnis once said. His compassion for a Scab had gotten them in a world of trouble once. He'd looked at one the same way Jordan had this one.

"I came for them," Darsal said. "I was coming to help them escape."

She watched Marak search for something, not find it, and swear softly. He balled his fists. "You knew he would die."

"I didn't." Her mind struggled to understand him and couldn't. There was nothing to understand. He blamed her needlessly for executing three albinos.

"Kill her," Marak ordered.

No! Elyon wasn't done with her! An impulse nibbled at her mind, chewing in the back and daring her.

She fought it, digging her elbows at the Scab again.

The commander's rough hand forced her head down. Her nose struck the floor. Darsal sprang half up before the sword touched her neck.

Love him.

The sword was coming down. How to . . .

"Let me serve you." The words were out before she realized it, barely audible. But her mind caught up, and she knew there was no bluff.

There would be no heroic rescue, no escape.

But maybe, maybe there was still a point to all of this.

Maybe the mission with the books had been only the prologue for something more—something greater.

Greater than saving the world?

Maybe Elyon was doing something else.

The sword did not fall.

She stared up at Marak. At the gray eyes and repulsive skin. Yes. Maybe she *could* live among Scabs. Her mission would be to love them.

To serve this one. Love *this one.* This beast of a man who would sooner take her head than look at her.

Penance. She'd stolen life in her bitterness over Billos's death. Now maybe she could save life.

"I will serve you." Her voice was confident this time. Whatever loving a Scab was, that was her mission and her penance.

His commander cuffed her head. He repositioned his sword.

Marak lifted his hand to stop the man.

"Sir?"

"Let her finish," he growled. He was looking at her again with that unreadable expression.

The commander silenced. Marak waited.

"Let me be your slave." Elyon help her, she was begging a Scab for her life. Thomas wouldn't be pleased. Billos would call her a baby. Maybe she was.

She didn't know what else to say. That he had stayed his commander said he was at least considering the idea. And if he was even considering, for whatever reason ran through his head, that meant maybe Elyon had put the otherwise repulsive notion of being a slave—worse, slave to a Scab—in her head.

Darsal waited. Jordan's necklace swung on her neck. A beat.

"General?" the commander asked.

Marak was staring at her, at the dangling necklace. Her heart skipped a few beats. She looked him in the eyes. Refused to look away.

The general forced her head back by a tuft of hair. She stared up into Marak's unyielding gaze. He shoved her forward. "Get her in chains."

Seventeen

The disease was settling in. Johnis walked faster to ignore his stiff joints and sore muscles, but that was no longer helping.

He could smell carrion birds in the distance. Smell something salty that tasted of copper. Feel the smallest of hairs move on his arm. And he could see the desert with hawk's eyes.

His arms and legs were completely white and scaly, flaking in coin-sized pieces. As were his stomach, sides, and chest.

"Anything from your invisible lady?" Silvie's dry voice was low and husky. Long cracks flaked along the creases in her face, now fixed in a constant frown. Her lip had split, and dried blood caked the corner of her mouth.

"No." Johnis tasted salt on his lips. He stopped, wiping away sweat that wasn't there. "We'll get to Natalga Gap and find help. Maybe find her. Maybe she can . . ."

"I don't want the help of some imaginary woman." Silvie retreated beneath an overhang and pressed against a rock formation to rest. She slid down along the wall, slumped over. "It's over."

"It can't be over. We didn't do all of this just to keel over dead in the desert."

"We have no water, Johnis!" she snapped at him, gray eyes narrowed. Gray eyes with a sick, yellow cast to them. She scraped at her flesh. "We're dying."

"I didn't come out here to die!"

"They're dead."

Johnis clenched his teeth and tore at his hair. Hot tears stung his eyes. He'd saved them. He'd never hurt any of them.

But you did, didn't you, Johnis? You did hurt them, and you justified it. You'd do it again if you could.

"We won't find water in time, even if it's there to find. Assuming Darsal's alive, she's Horde too. We can't touch her. And if the others are there, we can't hope to find them. We're Horde. They'll kill us."

The sun dipped low in the horizon and churned the canyon's sparkling colors. Once more the clouds were rolling in, taming the brilliant colors to solemn shadows. Even a trace or two of yellowish-green. A warm, stale breeze picked up, sharp and biting at first.

"Johnis . . ."

He froze. Realized where he was. "The woman. She said she would be out here. Somewhere." His thoughts or the woman's? "We should . . ."

"No, Johnis. No beautiful women. Just me."

He frowned at her. Offered his hand. "Come on. It'll be better with the sun gone." She accepted, then followed him west—or, rather, what he thought was west.

"This way . . ."

The wind at their backs shifted head-on and forced them to turn aside. Fog dampened his cheeks. His limbs turned cold.

He couldn't see.

Johnis drew a sharp breath. "Silvie . . . Remember what I told you?"

Even the dry sand turned to mud.

The desert was eerily quiet. No insects. No jackals, no coyotes howling. Out toward the horizon, across the dunes, and nestled in a canyon, the ground seemed to ripple, to shimmer.

"Silvie, are you seeing this?"

Deep blue flickered, rocked up and down, swirled like waves lapping a shore.

A river?

Silvie trembled, stepped forward. "Y-yes. Your visions . . . ?"

He nodded dumbly.

Her arms went limp at her sides. Johnis found his legs and stumbled toward the river like a drunk. "We need water . . ."

"Hello, mighty Chosen One . . . Is this what you seek?"

Yes, they needed water. They would die without water, and then there would be no one left. No one but Scabs and Shataiki. But the Shataiki hadn't been so bad, had they? Oversized black bats, no trouble, no worries. And Scabs. Yes, he did have a scab, right on his left knee where he'd skinned it earlier. Minor things.

"Do you hear her now?"

Johnis could only bob his head. The woman's siren song floated toward him. Summoned him. This time he had no choice.

She was close. Very, very close.

The river seemed to move, ever beyond their grasp. It taunted him.

"We should run," Silvie said.

He forced his feet forward. "Yes, we should."

But neither increased speed. The energy required simply wasn't there, and the water constantly retreated from them.

He could see the woman in the surface of the water, just like before. Her white-blonde hair rippled. Her eyes, blue and purple flecked with red, swallowed him. Promised pleasure and power and life.

Colder. Darker.

Minutes passed.

A white fog settled over them, curling over desert shrub and rock like elongated fingers.

The dark haze swelled until he could see nothing.

Nothing, including Silvie.

He stopped and turned a tight circle without actually leaving the place where he stood. "Silvie?"

No answer. But she'd been right beside him, up until . . .

His heart sank like lead into his boots when he realized he didn't know exactly when Silvie had gotten away from him. He neither saw nor heard her now.

"Silvie, don't do this to me."

Not this. Not now. Not after Middle and the Scabs and losing his parents and sister. And Darsal.

Alone.

No family to hound and scold him.

No supreme commander to kick his butt and put him back to work.

No Darsal to call him an idealistic fool.

No Silvie to slap him around.

Just absolute solitude and darkness.

"Silvie? Where are you?" Johnis took several tentative steps, listening, straining to see or hear any sign of her.

Silence.

He called out again, ignoring the way his voice broke, that he sounded like a child and should be embarrassed for it.

Not Silvie. Not her too.

He dropped to his knees and groaned.

"Fear not, my Chosen One. Raise up your head."

He obeyed without hesitation, half-aware the woman's voice was outside his head.

Silvie. Prone. On the sand.

Johnis started, then touched her cheek. "Silvie? Silvie, wake up!" She merely groaned, stirred, and rolled over. "Silvie, talk to me. Wake up. Wake up!"

"She lives."

The woman spoke from behind. Her voice carried the weight of authority, gentle and calm. The two words flowed off her tongue, trailing back as if she could say more but preferred not to trouble him. In the dense fog he couldn't see the woman.

Johnis whirled around and jumped to his feet. It was her! He'd found her!

"Where are you?"

A bemused chuckle. The fog parted a little and two vibrant, glowing eyes sparkled at him. The left eye was a startling purple with a sliver of rich crimson. The right, a vibrant blue with the same crimson half-moon slice. Perfect almonds, shining like jewels in sunlight.

"Peace, Johnis. She sleeps. She will soon wake."

He lowered Silvie's dagger halfway. "You're . . . real."

"I am."

The woman had a sweet scent. Alluring, in the same way the smell of baking bread is alluring to a starving man. And her eyes—those huge, intoxicating eyes with thick black lashes.

"How . . . did you do that?"

"In time, my Chosen One." She shrugged the fog back the way she might a cloak and let it fall from her shoulders. It drifted to the ground. "Such is more easily shown than explained."

"I thought you were in trouble."

"So such appears . . ."

She was even more beautiful up close. Johnis lost himself in her. Her lips parted in a seductive smile. The woman was tall and exquisitely shaped, everything about her long and willowy. She wore a strapless white dress that fell to her ankles and made a feathery train behind her. A small chain circled her neck, silver with a blue stone pendant. Her feet were bare.

"Look upon me, son of Ramos . . ."

The woman's riveting eyes commanded his attention, and he was lost in them once more. She smiled and took a bite of the fruit he only now saw in her hand. It was pear-shaped, with purple translucent skin that seemed to glow.

His mind was drifting.

Elyon alive, she was breathtaking.

Fight, Johnis. Silvie's unconscious.

"What have you done to Silvie?"

The woman glided to him, stopping so close he could feel her warmth. She licked the wound on the face of the fruit.

"The female has not been harmed."

He stepped back, still holding Silvie's knife. "Why is she on the ground? And how do you know my name?"

Her eyes narrowed for a moment, displeased with his answer. "I am armed with fruit and drink alone, yet I pose a threat?"

She had a point.

"Did you see the hidden pool?" The woman asked softly. Her voice was even. Cool, like fresh water sliding down his throat and quenching his thirst.

"I saw you." Johnis maintained his stance, indecisive. "She hasn't awakened, either."

Something about this woman was heady, sent gooseflesh across his skin, and hypnotized him. He could drink her, he thought, and never thirst again.

The woman seemed amused.

"I do not speak of your red Forest Guard pool. And perhaps she sipped too long on my eluweiss."

He took a step back. "The mirage?"

More gentle laughter. "I merely made visible that which is invisible, Johnis. Your female wished for water."

"Eluweiss?"

She slid her fingers up the side of his neck and along his cheek, traced his lips with needlelike nails. All the world gave way, leaving only her eyes.

A purple haze fell around them.

"My water is soothing and sweet," the woman continued. "My food is rich and sustaining. My slumber . . ." She motioned to Silvie. "Complete."

"What did you give her? Who are you?"

Her free hand slid along his shoulder and arm—a tingly sensation—and gently slipped the weapon from his hand. The edge nicked his thumb.

"I am called Shaeda, a ruler among the Leedhan."

Johnis felt the cut start to bleed. Blood crashed through his veins, shoved through his body with the force of a sledgehammer.

Her eyes. Her strange, intoxicating eyes . . .

Her fingers slid up into his hair and fingered it. She circled until the train of her dress surrounded him.

"I've never heard of a Leedhan," he said.

Shaeda let her unfinished fruit fall to the ground. "I have journeyed from the far side of the River, my friend."

"What river?"

The Leedhan seemed amused. "Did I not show you, my pet? Beyond the desert, beyond a labyrinth of canyons, is a river that spans the world, my friend, and cleaves her in twain. On both sides of the river are the most glorious of springs. From the far side of the world I come, and therefore your eyes have never known me."

She recited a chant in a foreign tongue. Her presence clung to him like a garment. Engulfed him. He felt numb, dazed.

A silver goblet appeared in Shaeda's hand. She had summoned it from the air. "This is eluweiss. It is made from badaii juice, along with a few teas and herbs. I carry food and drink to satisfy your hunger and sustain your life."

Johnis could smell a pungent citrus stronger than any he'd ever known before. Something niggled at the back of his mind, a pinprick amid the haze and shadows, from an old legend Thomas and the older ones used to tell.

"Such your female has also tasted. She but sleeps."

"I can't trust the water."

"Such is not water. It is better than your water."

Still, the bitter thought would not relent—that he could trust no one.

"This is eluweiss, my pet." Shaeda sipped at the citrus-flavored drink and gave an understanding nod.

"Sustenance you seek, do you not?"

Johnis went wide-eyed. He was hearing her thoughts.

She seemed even more amused at his surprise.

"Look at me, my Johnis . . ."

How could he refuse her?

"Why refuse?"

Did she say that, or did he think it?

Looking into her eyes, smelling the drink, feeling her presence and the barely contained powers he'd seen only shadows of . . .

"Terrible legends fill your mind, do they not? Terrible things spoken by mortal man doomed to die." She took another sip and extended the goblet toward him. "Taste and see . . ."

He needed something to drink, he and Silvie both. If they didn't drink, they would die of dehydration. Johnis ran his tongue over his mouth. His mind was falling into a tunnel, surrounded by cloud.

Shaeda's eyes seemed to permeate his skin and go straight through into his soul. They beckoned him, asked him to trust.

The scent itself filled him.

She massaged his neck and caressed his flaking skin, soothing the pain. A single thought entered his mind, a small thing nibbling at him just beyond comprehension.

His mind's eye saw swarming bats, the Shataiki queen who had tried to kill them. He relived his mother's capture, relived the horrors of the other world, Billos, the hard chains of a Romanian prison. Darsal's stunning betrayal that nearly sabotaged the mission, destroyed an entire planet, and killed him and Silvie.

All of that for nothing.

All of that to find Scabs living in Middle.

Johnis furrowed his brow. The Leedhan offered him more than fruit and eluweiss.

Shaeda leaned close and smelled his neck, then his hair.

"Too much from you has been stolen."

A longing filled him. Weeping for his lover. No, Silvie was not dead. Shaeda's eyes swallowed him. Her lover. The Leedhan had a mate.

Shaeda shut down the memory. Another took its place.

A coppery tasted flooded his mouth, rich and dark. Memory of the cold shackles around his wrists and the horrific understanding that all was lost caved in on him. He'd come home to marry. To celebrate. To go home.

Sucrow was in Middle Forest.

He scowled.

"You are indeed chosen, Johnis. And your mission is not yet complete. That alone is why you and the female survived."

We share commonality, do we not?

Shaeda's eyes roved over him. Her smile faded. "Your mind is clouded, your body and soul weak from lack of sustenance. Taste

my healing drink. You are correct in believing I have more authority beyond the River. I have the power to heal, my friend, the power to exact justice and extend mercy, to provide rest for the soul."

A vein in his temple began to pound.

"I've never heard of the Leedhan," he rasped. But . . . still . . . she had food, and she had . . . what was it? . . . eluweiss . . .

"Why linger so long in doubt?" Shaeda's voice was low and soft. "Is life so difficult to choose, my friend?"

His throat was burning. She was right. This was foolish. Only a fool would be stranded in the desert, dying from thirst, and refuse water.

Shaeda extended the goblet. "Drink."

Johnis's hand accepted the eluweiss before he consciously thought to reach for it. The compulsion was too great. Shaeda?

He pressed the silver lip to his mouth and drank.

Or had she done it for him?

The smooth liquid was sweet and burned all the way down, filling his stomach. A sharp pain twisted through his gut and the rest of his body, all the way to fingers and toes, and sent a buzz through his head. Everything seemed sharper, clearer. His senses heightened.

Greedily he drank the rest, each swallow further intensifying everything around him: the haze, the sand grinding beneath his feet, the feel of his clothes, Shaeda's light touch.

His eyes narrowed, vision tinged with that purple haze. Heat coursed through him. Bubbles rippled along his bloodstream. The faces of his enemies now clearly shone in his mind's eye. Those who had destroyed Middle must die. All of them.

"Very good, my Johnis." Shaeda withdrew the goblet, and it disappeared. Her hand reached into the air and pulled down toward him. Now she held another badaii. She took a small bite from it, studied him.

"You please me, Johnis. Yet another gift shall I bestow, now that I see you trust me." She drew a small object from her hand. A ring. Small and silver. "This is most difficult. I fear your mother did not fare well."

His mother's ring.

A lump caught in his throat.

She cupped his hands and gently slid the ring on his finger. "Middle has been beset and overdrawn."

He was sick of running. Sick of being chased around in the desert with his life in his hands.

The days of being victim were over.

Johnis balled his fist as the internal river flooded and threatened to burst the dam that held his fragile sanity in check.

Shaeda's power continued to spill into him. Heady, never-ending, and potent. Where before his senses were only heightened, now he saw in a completely new spectrum.

The Leedhan's mind revealed to him what befell Middle. He saw it all, saw the carnage through her vivid, multicolored eyes . . .

Her siren song almost overwhelmed what she was saying.

Everything was a magnificent whirlwind, a cacophony of sensory pleasures.

"Much has occurred in five years, Johnis. The Forest Dwellers split; most became Horde and remained in Middle as you've seen it. Others became outlaws called albinos for their smooth skin. The Circle."

A split. Their forces split. Of course, there had been enough controversy when Johnis was last in Middle that this now made horrific sense. The council had been in upheaval, the leaders divided on how to address the matter of the Horde.

"Thomas became one of the outlaws," Shaeda said.

An invisible presence slid around Johnis's shoulders. Her spirit, the seat of her powers. Heady, bubbling to the surface. The dam was creaking. Small rivulets of water now broke through. The impending breach was near.

"In the end, Middle collapsed on itself," Shaeda said. "The outlaws raided the village and destroyed it."

Hate and bitterness clamped down and smashed through the dam walls. Something deep inside him fought for reason.

Johnis withdrew from her. "You could be lying."

"Regrettably, I am not."

Johnis glared at the silver ring and knotted his fists, heat rising in his chest. "Thomas would never do that."

From beneath the fog, Silvie moaned and sat up. "What's going . . . ?"

He helped Silvie up. "It's the Horde I despise," he said.

"Johnis, yield but a moment longer. Yield. Listen. There is more."

"Then tell me!"

"Patience." Shaeda fixed him with a gaze, and once more he could not move. He stood fidgeting. "Patience. It is not only for the books that you were chosen, Johnis of Ramos."

"What, then?" he growled, angry at his inability to tear himself away from this woman whom he suddenly desired more than anything.

Shaeda glided over the sand. "It is truth that restrains you, and such truth alone. Your eyes are open now, and you see clearly."

"Johnis . . . ?" Silvie trailed off.

Why was he so resistant?

He'd followed his heart.

She was here.

"In my half of the world, I possess all authority and power, my Chosen One." Shaeda placed her hand over his heart, palm spread wide. Her long fingers covered most of his torso.

No, no need to resist.

His heart would always lead him.

"Half the world is mine, Johnis. Consider this."

"I'm listening."

"Half the world is mine, and more power is at my disposal than the mere appearance of food and drink, fog and mist, pools and sleep. This much you have already witnessed."

Johnis clenched his jaw.

"Make alliance with me. Aid me in but one task—one simple task of monumental reach—and I will grant you my strength, my power, and my authority. You will inherit a vast and glorious land that your dreams could never fathom."

"Why would I want that?"

"We aren't interested in turning." Silvie had found her mouth and now spoke from directly behind Johnis. "Our minds will go."

"Why do you doubt, little female? My ways will prevent any such . . . deceptions." Shaeda returned her attention to Johnis. "Your mission will require you to forgo the bathing ritual a little longer. You also require clarity, vision, and single purpose."

She offered him the badaii in her hand. "I will give you all of these and share with you my powers."

Johnis withdrew. "Why?"

"Take my gift, Johnis. Together we can overthrow this Horde we so despise. Together we will rule this world. Will you hear me?"

He had already tasted the eluweiss. Surely it wouldn't matter if he ate the fruit from whence it came, this badaii. It couldn't have any different effect on him, could it? Johnis studied the purple fruit, reached out to take it.

Then again . . .

"You haven't answered the question."

Shaeda scrutinized him. "I have told you that I rule the far side of the River, correct?" He nodded. The Leedhan turned grave. "This Teeleh became jealous of us, because we are half-human, and he banished us to the other side of the River." Her lips pulled back, revealing needlelike rows of teeth. "Yet . . . Yet now, I, Shaeda, ruler of the entities, the Leedhan, have returned, and shall use this amulet to control these beasts and usurp that purebred to such completion as has never been done."

A moment passed. The Leedhan simmered, forcing a smile. "He calls us vampires, yet such is not so. And he will see the full might of an entity." Musical, dark laughter came from Shaeda's throat. "What say you, my pet? Shall we destroy this common foe?"

Shaeda still held the badaii.

Johnis plucked it from her hand.

"This isn't right," Silvie said. "We need to bathe."

Bathe.

Endure searing pain several times a day.

Why prolong the inevitable?

"You will not be required such," the Leedhan spoke to Silvie. "I force none. Yet, perhaps you will see for yourself the healing my fruit accomplishes."

Johnis stared at the badaii.

He was tired of the haze that had settled in. Tired of the transition phase. And hungry. At least as hungry as he had been thirsty.

Shaeda's eluweiss quenched his thirst. Now to quench his hunger.

He lifted the fruit to his mouth and bit. His eyes widened. It was like when he drank the eluweiss, but a thousand times more potent.

The haze vanished. Everything lay bare before him.

He chewed.

The flavor burst into his mouth and filled it. Rolled over his tongue and between his teeth.

Johnis swallowed. Power surged through his body, plunged into his veins.

He devoured the badaii. With each bite his purpose, Shaeda's vision for him, became a more certain reality.

Her power coiled around his mind and settled. Johnis's eyes widened.

A gentle laughter echoed inside of him. *"Enter, my Johnisss . . . The gift of knowledge I bestow . . . of knowledge and power."*

He knew the Leedhan's thoughts. Her power coursed into him. Dominated his mind. His muscles tensed.

All his thought converged on one task: conquer the Horde.

eighteen

Silvie stared in grotesque fascination at the striking beauty before her. She'd been separated from Johnis in the fog, and this woman had offered her something called eluweiss.

She had taken it. The last thing she remembered was falling into a deep sleep.

And now Johnis seemed spellbound by this same strange woman who floated in the desert.

The same woman from his visions.

The eyes—those incredible, dual-colored eyes—were stunning. No wonder he'd been so transfixed. She was gorgeous, this exotic goddess in gauzy, transparent clothing, with the delicate voice and glowing eyes.

Silvie forced her mind to refocus. The disease threatened

her. This woman threatened her. This creature was seducing Johnis.

Her Johnis.

"Hear me," the goddess commanded.

Johnis's expression had changed. The desperate look had fled. But his face was not that of the Johnis she knew.

"Yes." His voice was deep. He played with something on his little finger. He turned it over, and with every turn his brow furrowed deeper, mouth drawn into a thin line.

A ring. A familiar silver ring.

His mother's ring. The tart had Rosa's ring. "Johnis . . . ?"

Johnis remained transfixed. The look in his eyes was one Silvie had never seen. He'd never even afforded the Shataiki that kind of scorn before. That cold, vengeful hatred.

The woman withdrew a piece of yellow, rotten fruit, infested with maggots, and offered it to him.

Disgusting.

"Take this harach," the woman said. "Such is your means of enticing what shall be an army that cannot be thwarted and that will rid the Horde of all the albinos within days. An army you alone will command. But mind you, Johnis. This is merely the bait. Take such."

He scowled. "How is that bait?"

The woman smiled, amused at his ignorance. "What is detestable to some is tantalizing to others. Surely you remember the Shataiki."

"Pin yourself to a cactus," Silvie spat.

Johnis had heard the woman's voice in his head from over six hours away. And now she was before them. Changing him.

Johnis's menacing glare intensified. She'd seen that look before—from a throater right before a battle. This Johnis would count his bodies.

"I remember."

"Why don't you get away from my lover," Silvie warned. She brandished a knife.

But Johnis's now-visible woman only seemed amused. "The children of Tanis are indeed fascinating . . ." The woman gave a musical laugh. "I do not believe such necessary."

"No. But that doesn't mean . . ." Johnis trailed off.

"We wish to conquer Horde, do we not? The Dark Priest." A coy smile. "And what is this talon between their ribs? The thorn in their flesh?"

"What?" Johnis asked dumbly. He was struggling, Silvie could tell. The woman's power overwhelmed him. Consumed him.

"Him whom they despise more than anything else."

"Thomas."

"The Circle," she said. "If you were to solve this problem for the Horde, you would be greatest among all Horde."

"But he's not Horde!" Silvie said.

"No?"

Shaeda slid her arm around Johnis. Her hand stroked his

neck. "We Leedhan have our own power, this much you can see. Feel. Yet, there remains another."

"And what is that?" Silvie protested. "By Elyon, Johnis, why are you listening—"

Multicolored eyes drank her.

"Peace, little female."

"I possess knowledge of the acquisition of a final solution to all that haunts the Horde, Johnis. An eclipse that will force the diseased Scabs to eat out of your hand. Together we will destroy them at our whim."

Johnis shook his head, desperate to clear the fog.

Come on, Johnis, fight it!

But now Silvie understood.

No one resisted this Leedhan.

Johnis blinked, eyes wide with wonder. Clearly he was completely taken with her every word. It was *he* who was eating out of *her* hand.

"An eclipse . . ."

"A simple plan for your ears, precious. Would you like to hear it?"

He swallowed. "Yes."

"Consider this, my Chosen One. There is an amulet in the possession of a Shataiki queen named Derias. From him you must retrieve an amulet, an amulet by which you will be able to control the Shataiki. Of course, there is neither male nor female within Shataiki." Disdain shone on her face. Then she dismissed the slight derailment and continued. "This, this is our Eclipse. Remember, however, that there is an order to our mission. First you must gain the assistance of the priest."

The Dark Priest.

"Why the priest?"

"It will be a temporary alliance," Shaeda said. "He has the ceremony you require. There is no need to be sincere."

Johnis's jaw clenched, but after a moment he nodded. Silvie's hope sank.

"Allow me to continue," Shaeda said. "Go to the priest and acquire his assistance. You must then take the fruit and go to the Black Forest as I direct you. You first will need to retrieve the amulet from the Shataiki queen."

"How do we do that?"

Shaeda offered him rotten yellow fruit. "The harach offers protection. Retrieve the amulet and perform the ceremony. This will summon the Shataiki to you. Entice him with the harach I've given you. When he eats of it, he shall be yours for four days."

Johnis nodded. "So we use the Shataiki to destroy the Circle and return heroes to Middle. This is how we gain control of the Horde. Then we destroy the Horde."

"This is correct, my Johnis."

And then we find water, and Darsal, and Thomas, Silvie almost added. But that could wait. They could make their own plans once the wench left Johnis.

Shaeda kissed the birthmark behind his ear, caressed his cheek, and let him go. "You will accept, then."

He gave a single nod.

She appraised him, slow to approve, and gave him instructions on how to find the Black Forest.

"You will be unable to see such until the amulet is in your possession," Shaeda warned. "Do not be fooled. The canyon is filled to the brim, a boiling cauldron of Shataiki."

"One more question," Silvie interrupted. "Why us? The bats aren't going to just give it to us."

"The amulet is useless to all but the children of Tanis. I cannot wield it, nor can the queen. Only a chosen human can. Remember these things, children of Tanis: The harach fruit protects the bearer and weakens the will of him who takes such from the bearer's hand. In this manner, he who eats the fruit becomes subject to him who gives the fruit. However, the amulet binds the Shataiki guardian to him who takes such from him, granting power in days of four." To Johnis, "You have my heart and my mind, and you are mine. And you will follow your heart and conquer the Horde. There is your mission, and this . . ."

She pointed to the rotten fruit, the yellow harach that curled Silvie's toes even at ten paces.

"This is your path. To waver is to deny yourself my strength."

The mist thickened again. She offered a second fruit. "A gift." She smiled at Silvie. "For the female."

"I want nothing from you."

"Which is better, little female, to die needlessly or live for a cause? You despise the Horde, do you not?"

"You wish me to become Horde."

"You *are* Horde, little female." Shaeda extended the purple badaii. "This will only take away the pain of the transition and make you whole. Ease the anguish. Do with one bite what would take a week. Or do you wish to be less than your mate?"

Less than Johnis.

Silvie scoffed. This Leedhan could dream on.

"Look, has my fruit harmed your mate at all? No, and already his eyes are bright from the comfort of food. Did not my drink provide you rest?"

She did feel better; her throat no longer parched. Her body felt refreshed after the short slumber.

Shaeda still extended her arm, badaii in her palm.

"It's all right, Silvie," Johnis said. "It's just fruit."

She took it but didn't eat it. The skin was smooth and cool, transparent and almost glowing.

The woman slowly walked away from them, drifting in the fog. She glanced over her shoulder as if being called by someone, then fixed her brilliant eyes on Johnis. "East is to your left, Chosen One. Stay the course. Remember your mission. Do not fail me."

Shaeda gave a musical laugh, retreating into deepening fog and black night. "You will see me again, my handsome Chosen One."

Lightning split the sky, and the earth rumbled beneath their feet. A shot burst through the canyons.

All stilled.

Silvie continued to stare.

"I don't know that I want this."

Johnis turned to her with that wild-eyed, cocky look that usually wound up jeopardizing their lives. "Taste it. It's all right."

"I don't know. Didn't you see the way she reacted to Elyon's name?"

He flinched.

A long moment passed. Silvie could see him struggling with something. He ran his hands through his hair. Puffed out his cheeks. Paced.

Then he seemed to find control.

Purple flecked his eyes.

"Don't I look all right to you?" he asked.

"You look like a throater."

Pause. Johnis's mouth twitched.

Then, "If you don't eat it, I will."

Silvie sighed. "If I eat it, will you tell me what's going on?"

"There's no need to be sassy about it."

"Oh, I'm sassy now?" She raised a brow. "You haven't seen sassy yet, boy."

"Just eat it, Silvie. It'll clear your head."

"I don't know that mine's the one that needs clearing."

They stared each other down.

Shaeda's multicolored eyes flooded Silvie's mind. She could see the Leedhan's face. Feel her touch.

There would be no escape.

They belonged to Shaeda now.

"Can you still hear her thoughts?"

Hesitation. Finally he nodded. "Middle," he breathed. Sweat beaded. "We have to go to Middle. But . . . eat the fruit. Please."

She drew a breath. "All hail the Leedhan."

Then took a small bite.

The nectar flooded her mouth, sweet and intoxicating. She swallowed hard and felt warmth flood her belly then spread out toward her arms and fingers.

Then it rose and gulped down her mind.

Even as it swept through her she realized that something fundamental had just changed. As the seducer had said, she'd just become wholly Horde.

Reasonable. Encouraging even.

No, something's still wrong . . . Do I care?

No more confusion. No more pain.

Shaeda was right. Silvie and Johnis were equal again.

No, she didn't care.

She took another big bite and handed the badaii to Johnis.

He scarfed down the rest and studied the yellow, rotting harach in his hand. "It is by fruit," Johnis murmured, as if repeating something he was hearing. "By fruit do temptations come, by fruit do they fall. Him who takes such as offered subjects himself to the giver, one and all . . ."

A chill swept through Silvie. Johnis studied her, barely aware of what he'd said. She cleared her throat. "So, now we find the priest?"

He hesitated. Seemed conflicted. "Yes. Yes, we find the priest. And use him . . ." Johnis trailed off as if listening to someone else. "Use him to help us bait the Shataiki. The harach weakens the Shataiki amulet guardian's will, and that allows us to use the amulet to bind their will to ours." His eyes narrowed.

Scorn. Nothing but pure scorn.

Silvie's eyes narrowed. "It doesn't strike you odd that you would actually consider helping the Horde go after Thomas and this Circle of his?"

Johnis thought about it for a moment. More listening. Then, "Well, yes. But Thomas could join the Horde. He doesn't have to hide out in the desert. Right?"

"Talk like that would have sent you into a fit a few days ago. That doesn't bother you?"

Hesitation. Johnis was hiding something.

"Well, yes. I suppose it should. I don't hear you screaming in outrage. You?"

They were discussing the whole matter with hardly an emotion.

Worse, going after Thomas was no longer sounding so horrible.

No, they were after the Horde, not Thomas.

"It's a means to an end," she said, ignoring the slight chill sweeping over her skin. "That doesn't mean I like it, mind you."

"No, me neither."

"But if it's the only way to overthrow the Horde . . ."

"Exactly," Johnis said. "And maybe we can find a way to save Thomas and the others. But I do think we have the final solution to the problem of this Circle. And I think Sucrow and Qurong will hand us the keys to their kingdom for it."

Something wasn't right here. But Silvie was having a hard time remembering what.

She looked at his flaking skin. "I don't trust Shaeda."

"Then trust me. Please, Silvie, do you truly think me a fool?" He smiled. "We're going to follow along, but that doesn't mean we have to do it precisely Shaeda's way."

He winced.

She frowned and thought about it.

Leedhan powers.

Shaeda's powers.

But maybe Johnis wasn't as taken with the lusty-eyed Leedhan as she'd thought.

Maybe he was using his head after all.

"Well . . . The plan could work. I just don't know that I—"

"What's the harm, Silvie? We're using a ruse to destroy the Horde. Besides, I'm not going to turn it over to her. By the time we return to Middle, we should have a plan in mind. What do you say?"

Silvie hesitated.

"I can't do this without you. I can't." Johnis extended his fist. There was more to this than he was saying. Johnis, pleading?

No. The jealousy was getting to Silvie's head. Or the disease. Or both.

"Are you with me?" she asked. Searched his face. His skin was so pale . . . his eyes . . .

His eyes were round and wide, face lit with excitement and anxiety. "My heart is with you."

"Then follow it."

Another minute passed. *Follow your heart.* The words echoed. *Follow your heart.* Such words had been their mantra for a long time now. Thus far it had kept them alive.

Silvie placed her hand on Johnis's. "For Middle."

nineteen

Johnis's senses were on overload. Before the fruit Shaeda had merely sharpened them a little. But now, now he could likely count the grains of sand if he chose. Everything was purplish-red.

Shaeda's eyes . . . her intoxicating eyes. He could see through them as before, still hear her siren song in his head. And more. The fruit . . . changed everything.

And his feet seemed to have a mind of their own.

Shaeda's mind.

As she had drawn him into the desert, now she goaded him toward Middle City. Toward Sucrow, Teeleh's priest.

"You are near Natalga Gap," her inner voice instructed. *"You are not far, my pet . . ."*

Johnis tried to ignore Shaeda's voice. Silvie still couldn't hear it, and it aggravated her to know Johnis and the Leedhan shared secrets.

But how much did the Leedhan know? Did she know his plans to use her power for his own devices? Could she read *his* thoughts or only implant her own?

A gentle, musical laugh. Invisible talons tickled his neck. His mind's eye saw only the alluring eyes, the seductive smile . . .

"Can you hear me?" he asked. Silvie glanced at him. It was strange, but important. He had to know how this worked. What to expect.

"I hear much, my Johnis."

The slithering presence seeped into his mind. Johnis saw a thousand Leedhan, male and female, on the far side of the River. He saw them engaged in fierce battle with a throng of Shataiki. Felt someone strike him down. Felt his limbs torn and hot blood seep from the wound. Knew—

The vision stopped abruptly. A low growl of disapproval.

Shaeda?

"What happened?" he asked. "Tell me. At least explain it."

The talons dug into his spine and tore. Johnis doubled over, knees buckling. He saw nothing but multicolored eyes. Smelled the sweet scent of Leedhan. Heard the siren song.

"Johnis?" Silvie grabbed his arm, but he pushed her away. She stared for a minute, then backed off. She smelled of anger and fear.

Another vision. Johnis saw an enormous male Shataiki, a queen's rank. The Shataiki was Derias, Shataiki guardian of the amulet.

A coppery taste flooded his mouth. He hated Derias.

No, Shaeda hated Derias.

Same difference.

"Do you see now, my Johnis?"

Yes. I see why you hate the Shataiki. But what does this have to do with conquering the Horde?

"Johnis." Silvie's voice shut off the image. He shook his head. He was on his knees, palms flat on the ground.

"Shaeda," he whispered. "Shaeda, come back. Explain the rest. Tell me."

But Shaeda was quiet.

Why did Silvie always seem to silence Shaeda?

Silvie said his name again. Shaeda's will was so strong. But he couldn't ignore Silvie.

"I saw . . . I saw into Shaeda's mind. Her memories . . . I saw . . . She hates Shataiki, Silvie. Hates them. And she wants to control them. She's angry, very angry."

"You can read her mind?"

"Not all the time, I don't think." Johnis shook his head. "Sometimes."

"Rely on me, my Johnis. You must learn to trust in my power."

Shaeda's power.

Johnis licked his lips. He'd had a taste of it. His mind fantasized what the full measure of her might could do. Heady, really.

She chuckled. *"Trust me, my Johnis. You will see, in time . . ."*

"See what?" he asked.

"I didn't say . . ." Understanding came into Silvie's eyes. "Are you two going to continue these private conversations?"

He shook his head. Shaeda prodded him along. "We have to get to the priest."

MARAK LED DARSAL THROUGH THE STREETS, TURNED down an alleyway, and came upon a single-story house that was larger than the ones around it but mostly plain to look at.

"This is home. Per our arrangement." He hesitated, almost unwilling to say whatever it was he intended to next. "There's a spare room with a mat you can sleep on."

"A mat." She crossed her arms as best she could with the chains. "Am I your pet dog now?"

Love him, Darsal.

Right now she wasn't sure how, much less why. He was a brute. Uncouth and cold to the touch. And he smelled.

"Just tend the horse." He reached for her neck.

Darsal struck him in the chest on instinct.

Marak took a step back and absorbed the blow. His expression was both frustrated and surprised. "You want to wear the tether all night?"

"You went for my neck. What was I supposed to do?" Her instinct, her head, said to snatch out one of his knives and run him through. Her heart said that he hadn't meant anything and that she'd overreacted. And a third part of her said she hadn't overreacted but she could still get away without killing him.

Maybe Elyon himself had gone loony.

She could almost hear him laughing at that one.

Marak gave an exasperated sigh. "Just hold still." He removed her tether and shoved the lead to his horse in her hand. "Come in the kitchen when you're done."

"You want me to tend the horse?" From Forest Guard to Shataiki killer to traitor to mucking horse stalls. Although it was a step up from Alucard. As if that took much.

Marak stopped and turned around. His gaze lingered longer than necessary, studying her with an expression she couldn't read.

"You've made your agreement."

"To serve you, not the horse."

"My experience is that albinos rarely break their word." His voice was hard, edgy. Tense. "Don't disappoint me." With that, he went into the house.

Darsal started to protest, but he was already inside. She scowled. Maybe this was a bad idea. The horse reeked. Marak reeked.

He'd left her alone.

She could escape now, easily, without ever touching him.

But . . . but her fool's errand, her mission . . .

Elyon, what do you mean? How do I love a mongrel? He's rotten through, as good as dead already.

But the resounding, soft voice continued. *"So were you."*

There was no winning that one.

"For you, then," she grumbled. "For Johnis. Wherever the lunatic and his lunatic girlfriend are."

She went around back and unsaddled the Scab warhorse, rubbed him down—a disgusting, smelly task. She fed and watered the animal then entered into the living room from the back door, bracing herself for a fresh dose of spoiling Horde stench.

The inside was clean and smelled of dinner. Marak had drawn the curtains and lit a few candles and a standing torch.

Darsal rounded the corner into the living room and didn't see him. A couple of chairs, a low table, and a couch. Five candlestands and the torch. To her left was a small, round kitchen table big enough for two, maybe three people.

To her right was a narrow hallway.

What was in the rest of the great Horde general's house? No harm in looking. Know thy enemy, right?

Love thy enemy.

She remembered the line from somewhere but couldn't place it. The other Earth, somewhere. Not Alucard.

Darsal entered the hall and found three doors on the left, one on the right. The hall was a dead end.

The first room was a study. Qurong's general liked to read. The room was full of books and scrolls. A small writing desk lay half-buried under a mound of paper, and several candles had gone to a waxy grave.

Darsal looked in the second room. Bathroom. Nothing special.

The third was a storage room. She approached the fourth with some care. It was farthest from the door and on the far right end of the hall.

She turned the handle slowly.

Yes, this was the great general's bedroom.

Darsal remained in the doorway, taking it in. A small bay window, curtains drawn. A single candle on a stand right beside his bed. Two trunks: one red, one brown.

A worn journal lay on the bed, open.

Thinking maybe it was battle plans, Darsal ducked inside.

If she made it to Thomas, to the others, she could . . .

Her hand touched the leather.

The cover had an inscription in neat, flowery handwriting. A woman's. Curious. She flipped it open. Definitely not battle plans. She started to read.

"Dear Marak, we've been in hiding two months now. Forgive the long secrecy, but you understand how it is. We parted ways so angry, so hurt . . . Jordan's been good to me, but I fear too much is left unsaid. So listen to me, love . . ."

A hand grabbed her by the wrist and spun her around.

Her head slammed on wood paneling.

Darsal wrapped her hands around Marak's wrist and squeezed until he released her. He swore. She went into a defensive posture.

The general shoved past her and slammed the journal shut. Picked it up and studied it for a long time. Then set it on a bookcase.

Darsal was between him and the door, but experience fighting with and against Silvie taught her well the meaning of knives in thigh sheathes.

Do not run.

"What's in the journal?"

Marak's expression was unreadable. He looked surprised and enraged. Barely restrained fury. A caged, half-starved lion.

"Does this look like the kitchen to you?"

"I was looking around. For that you grab me by the wrist?"

"Did I *tell* you to look around?"

"I repeat the question. I trained under Thomas Hunter, supreme commander of the Forest Guard. I'm hardly some simpering wench you can throw around at will."

Marak studied her a minute, then relented. "Learn your place, albino." He stalked down the hall into the kitchen.

Thoughts of the journal made her hesitate.

If she could get to it . . .

"Go clean up," he growled from the other room.

Darsal opened her mouth to protest.

No.

His reaction to the journal was potent.

More mysteries.

Shake it off, Darsal. It was nothing. He's a brute. A brute who hates all things Elyon, including you.

She retreated to the bathroom and found the clean clothes and jar of morst. For a long minute she stared at the basin of murky water with which she would have to bathe. Finally she wet a cloth and washed herself. Darsal washed her hair, too, as best she could. After she was clean and toweled off, she examined her cuts and bruises, fingered Jordan's pendant at her throat.

The one Marak kept staring at.

Marak with his flaking skin covered in disgusting white powder that barely muted the noxious fumes. Marak, the Horde general out to eliminate the entire Circle because of their skin.

The beast who allowed those things to happen to Rona and Jordan and Xedan.

Her hand brushed the jar of morst as she reached for her clothes.

She paused. Studied it. On impulse she opened the lid and smelled. A floral scent. Water dripped from her dark hair into the jar.

Darsal brushed the wet lock back over her shoulder and put the morst down.

Wrung out her hair better.

How miserable, to smell and look so grotesque that you would cover your entire body in a white powder out of embarrassment. The only thing worse than Scab skin was Shataiki flesh.

Darsal mulled it over.

Curious, that partial journal entry.

Disgusting, the mere suggestion of loving a Scab.

This mission is stillborn.

As she used the comb, her eyes fell once more to the jar.

Her skin was as mortifying to the Scabs as theirs to her. Yet she had chosen to love them as penance to Elyon.

She pressed her lips together.

Love them.

But first they had to be able to stand the smell of each other.

She smelled at least as bad to Marak as he did to her.

"That could work," she whispered. She braided her hair in Horde fashion, then opened the jar of morst, which really did smell nice. Quickly, she rubbed the white powder over her body, over her hands and arms and as far under the shackles as she could.

Ten minutes later she came into the kitchen.

Two bowls of stew waited at the table. Marak had flung himself into one of the chairs and was eating his meal in a brooding silence.

Darsal waited in the threshold, watching him eat. *Elyon, how do you win a Scab that won't even look at you?*

Just looking at the white skin made her itch and feel stiff.

Stop it. You're sympathizing with a monster.

Then she narrowed her eyes. For one, the rotten-meat smell was heavily muted and she could stand it, even in the minute or so they'd been in close proximity. Two, aside from the places on his arms where their skin had made contact when he grabbed her, fresh morst had been applied in generous amounts.

General Marak had taken great care that no cracks and no obvious flakes showed.

Why?

"Get out of my blind spot," Marak said without looking up or turning his head.

Darsal's eyes narrowed. "I like this spot."

Marak jabbed a finger at the chair in front of him. She started to argue again, but that tiny little voice in the back of her mind kept reminding her of her mission.

Fighting Marak every step of the way would never work. Forcing herself to obey, she took her seat.

Marak's eyes were dull, clouded, concealing some skeleton rotting in his heart. Darsal returned the steady gaze. The longer she looked the more she saw—and the more questions she had.

What exactly *had* caused him to come into the dungeons? To stay his hand? And then there was that journal . . .

What lay beyond the skin of this general?

"Are you a spy?" Marak continued to study her.

"No." So now the interrogation would begin. Now he would force her to lay bare her sins. She braced herself. "I'm sick of spilling blood."

"I spill albino blood."

She didn't flinch. He was watching for her reaction, and she didn't want to witness his satisfaction as he gloried over his exploits, reveled in the slaughter of Middle, of innocent men, women, and children. She should burst across the table and spear him through with his own knife.

But the memories served as pointed reminders. She thought of Johnis and Silvie, who had stayed true to her even when shackled to the wall awaiting their doom. Just like Jordan had.

Was that what the books were about?

Her hand went to the necklace. "I've done worse."

That answer surprised him. She looked away.

Silence.

"You're wearing morst. Why?"

That surprised *her.* "I . . . thought it might help."

"It helps."

"You think I lie."

"I don't trust you. Eat. We've a long day ahead. Tomorrow I'll have a brood of albinos to deal with and a meeting with Sucrow. Unfortunately." Marak stood.

He was becoming more and more curious. So the general hated the priest as well. But then, Sucrow was easy to hate.

"To discuss killing the Circle."

The general's eyes went cold. "To discuss our mission. Desecration."

"Fitting title. Did you name it?"

Silence.

Darsal couldn't withhold the question anymore. She lowered her spoon and twisted sideways in her chair. "Why didn't you kill me in the dungeon?"

Marak's expression turned dark. He cracked his knuckles. One hand pressed flat on the table, he leaned down to her.

"I'm beginning to rethink that decision."

"Does it have something to do with Jordan?"

He instinctively raised his fist, then lowered it and swung away from her, red faced.

"What makes you think that had anything to do with him?"

The mighty general had an underbelly. Jordan.

What did she care about a Scab's feelings?

But . . . she couldn't hide the overwhelming impulse to keep pushing.

Elyon help them both.

"You seem upset by his death."

Marak stalked away from her. "Stop it, albino."

Now she *had* to find the source of his wound. It was non-negotiable. And the evidence all pointed to one man: Jordan of Southern. She stood.

"You know his name. It's his necklace I'm wearing. He gave it to me."

His fist smashed against the wall. Understanding came.

One clean-skinned and warm. One disease-riddled and cold.

Darsal lowered her voice, seeking softness she didn't possess. "He was your brother, wasn't he? And you executed him."

Marak pivoted on one heel, his face stopping inches from hers.

Darsal froze.

"Never, *ever* speak like this to me again." His hot, acidic breath basted her skin. Darsal choked on the smell and fought back a cough.

Marak stormed out. Darsal could only stand there.

He didn't come back. She pushed aside her bowl, put her head in her hands, and closed her eyes.

twenty

Silvie marched across the final stretch of desert to the southern edge of Middle with the sun flickering at her back and the bitter taste of sand in her mouth. Johnis gained speed with every step.

They'd both been different since Shaeda. But their alternative plans were forming. Thank Elyon, Johnis was thinking.

Unfortunately it required a temporary alliance with Teeleh's priest.

Shaeda could read his mind. He could sometimes see into hers. How much was the Leedhan controlling him? Was she guiding or forcing?

Silvie grabbed his shoulder. "Listen to me!"

He whirled. His eyes were completely void of emotion.

Cold. Hard. Calculating. He was on a mission. The clarity of what he wanted to do completely blinded him to everything else.

Silvie's eyes widened. She backed up, horrified. "You can't do it this way."

He wanted to go tearing through Middle like a wild animal, rousing Marak of Southern out of bed and demanding to see him, as if Qurong's general was little more than a servant to be summoned at will.

"You'll never get Marak to listen to you if you don't do this right the first time," she argued as they headed north along the eastern edge of Middle Forest. "And if you can't get in to see him, this quest of yours will be the death of both of us."

"What do you suggest?"

"Clear your head."

After arguing the matter for a few minutes, Johnis complied. They would not attack General Marak in his bed. Instead they would demand an audience like civilized people and hope for the best.

Following this decision, Johnis appeared somewhat conflicted. The more she got him thinking—forcing him to do something not directly obedient to Shaeda's instructions—the less he was able to reason.

What *had* they gotten themselves into?

Shaeda's directions guided them to the edge of the canyons and set their course back toward Middle. Shaeda had proven trustworthy on this matter, Silvie finally conceded.

"But this alliance with the priest is temporary," she reminded. "This is all temporary. It's Horde we're after."

"Right. Once we have what we need from Sucrow, we'll kill him and use Shaeda's power to take out the Horde. We don't need her forever. And I don't have to give her the amulet."

He hesitated. The emotions shifted on his face. He muttered under his breath. Johnis finally looked up at her.

"Sometimes she seems to be in my head, sometimes she doesn't," he explained. "I'm not sure we should talk about this until I know how often she's listening."

"We may not have that luxury."

He fell quiet.

Silvie understood.

She would have to do the bulk of the planning until Johnis found a way to stave off the Leedhan.

Neither spoke for a while.

The desert gave way to forest, and they found a cool stream of muddied water to drink their fill.

"What about Thomas?"

He paused. "We do what we have to in order to complete the mission. Our mission is to defeat the Horde."

"By defeating the albinos. And who will we be left with?"

He answered after a pause. "Each other."

Thank the stars he hadn't said Shaeda.

Strange how quickly her loyalties had changed.

Before leaving this place a few years ago, she would have died for Thomas and the Guard.

Now she wasn't sure who she would die for.

Besides Johnis.

Who now looked completely Horde. Generous flakes of white skin dripped from his limbs, face, and neck. His hair had turned ashen and his eyes a smoky color. He was withdrawn, almost as if drugged. Her heart should be twisted by the sight.

But she was no different. Of course their skins flaked. Logical. Even compelling.

Silvie realized her mind was drifting a little. She refocused. She had to help Johnis.

And Johnis needed his head clear to fight Shaeda.

"You're certain this plan to find this charm in the Black Forest will give you the power you need to control the Shataiki?"

The effects were immediate. Like magic his expression cleared. His eyes focused on her. He finished drinking and stood.

"I know it will." Johnis cast a wicked grin.

A cold chill curled around Silvie's spine. Letting Johnis focus on his mission was the only way to keep him out of the abyss threatening to consume him.

"What aren't you telling me?"

Johnis marched past her into the woods. Silvie followed. After another half hour they approached the road leading back to the city.

"I know how to do it. Shaeda let me in again."

Silvie paused. "What?"

"Convince Sucrow to help us."

"RISE AND SHINE, GENERAL."

Marak woke to the raw smell of an albino. He jumped and reached for his knife, then forced himself to relax.

Darsal stood in the doorway, her arms crossed. Who knew how long she'd been there. Pale sunlight streamed down on her face. Dawn.

"My clothes are in the trunk," he growled.

"A grown man can't dress himself?"

"I really should just cut out your tongue."

"You couldn't stand the smell long enough."

"Would you just hand me my tunic?" Marak pointed at the trunk she was standing next to. She looked coy.

"You could ask me nicely."

He bit back the urge to swear at her. "Fine. Would you hand me my shirt *please*, albino?"

"My name is Darsal of the Far Northern Forest." She flung it at him.

"Fine. Darsal of the Far Northern Forest, thank you."

She turned her back and went quiet while he dressed.

After their confrontation the night before, he'd stormed outside and taken a long walk around the lake, bathed in it beneath the moon.

Darsal couldn't possibly know anything.

Most of those secrets had died yesterday. After Jordan and the others had helped her escape, Sucrow had ordered their executions, and Marak had no choice.

At least the priest couldn't torture them any longer. Couldn't use Rona against him.

Marak had hoped beyond logic that he would be able to come up with an excuse to free them, even if it meant making them all look like traitors to their own kind.

Darsal's escape had ruined all of that. And then she had come back.

The bloody little albino had sentenced to death three people he'd tried to save and then rendered their sacrifice worthless. He'd come to retrieve their pendants, and there she was.

Marak put on his shirt.

He should have killed her just for having Jordan's Circle pendant.

The commanders had asked why she was still alive. Cassak hadn't. Maybe Marak should ask him.

She'd never touched the stew. It had been cold. He had put it away and could only lean against the counter until Darsal had come back to ask him where he wanted her to sleep. He had tossed an old cloak at her and had told her to sleep on the floor.

Marak put on his boots. One scuffed the wood.

"Sleep well?" Darsal turned back around. Her voice was steady, a very controlled effort. He didn't answer. Of course, that didn't prevent her from speaking.

"About your brother. I didn't intend to overstep last night," she said. "Forgive me."

His stomach lurched.

Jordan had looked up at him from the floor, his arms bound behind his back, face bloody from Warryn's beating, and had used that same word.

I forgive you.

The knot shifted from Marak's gut into his heart and up into his throat.

He squeezed his fist. "I didn't say you could speak."

Darsal pressed her lips together, then lowered her head. She removed the necklace and let it dangle from her hand. Extended it toward him.

"This is what you wanted from the cell, isn't it? It's yours by rights. He gave it to me, for when I found the Guard."

He looked at her, surprised.

Someone knocked at the front door. "General, I've a message for you from the priest."

Marak shoved past her and barreled through the house to the front door. "What in the name of Teeleh do you want?" he snarled.

"My lord does not think he's been advised of everything regarding this Desecration of yours. He also wishes to know who is on the western side of the forest." Sucrow's servant glowered with beady eyes at the slave.

Marak crossed his arms. "And for this he's decided to send you to fetch me at dawn?"

"I . . . he says you may come at your leisure, General."

"How thoughtful of him. Tell him not to waste my time." He swung the door.

"General—"

The door shut. Sucrow's servant knocked again. "General, the priest was quite insistent that—"

Marak whipped the door open, into the wall, and grabbed the worthless youth by the tunic, right off the ground. "I will meet with Sucrow when I desire to meet with Sucrow and not a moment before!"

He flung him down the steps. "Get out of my sight!"

The servant scrambled to his feet and scurried away.

Marak slammed the door so hard it rattled the walls. Darsal retreated into the kitchen. He stormed back to the bedroom and strapped on his weapons. Throat constricted, chest heaving. Then went into the kitchen to the slave.

Darsal stood at a distance, her face devoid of emotion.

He snarled and sat down, unwilling to deal with the albino in his house—the one he'd spared only because for a fleeting second, with Jordan's medallion dangling around her neck, she looked like Rona.

"I haven't got all day!"

"There's no cause to yell," she snapped, putting the refused necklace back on. "I didn't do it, you big idiot!" Darsal went to the cabinet and pulled out bread, then rummaged for the butter.

Teeleh's breath, she really does look like her. Marak watched her for several seconds.

"It's in the bottom. I don't use it much."

Darsal retrieved butter and cheese and set both out on the

sideboard with the loaf of bread. The idea grew as he watched her, demanding he express the comparison. Marak considered whether or not he should say something. She hadn't deserved his bellowing, and she was here of her own volition. Why not?

He would explode if he didn't make the connection.

"You remind me of someone."

She glanced up at him with wide brown eyes, then returned to his breakfast, not slowing down. "Really? Who?"

Marak watched her arrange cheese on a plate. "Rona. My sister-in-law."

Darsal started with the bread and butter. "Your brother's wife."

"We were engaged."

She finished and got him something to drink. "And once she became albino, you couldn't get married."

Marak looked away, avoiding her. Why was he saying all of this, to an albino nonetheless?

Still, he'd started, and now it was out in the open.

Darsal brought his breakfast, then retreated to the other side of the table, well within sight. She'd remembered to stay out of his blind spot.

"What happened?"

He stared past. "They were forced to flee. Jordan promised to take care of her. Six months later a note saying they were married arrived. They both signed it. Rona sent her journal along. It was good-bye."

Silence.

"I'm sorry."

Marak shook his head and started on his meal. "Thank you for breakfast."

"General, I . . ."

"We're leaving in twenty minutes. You can go until then."

twenty-one

Shaeda said the fruit would complete the process," Johnis argued.

"It's still strange to walk into a Horde city without wanting to vomit from the smell." Silvie pressed her lips into a thin line. "Not that I miss it. Nor do I miss the Dark Priest."

She meant Sucrow.

I don't want to see the priest!

"You must, my Johnisss . . ."

He stopped in his tracks. "Why?"

She didn't answer.

"Tell me!"

"Johnis." Silvie touched his shoulder. He held up his hand.

His body, his mind, his soul, ached. Shaeda's spirit was so heavy, so potent. He felt crushed under her weight. But something wasn't right. He could sense it, and Shaeda knew he sensed it.

Why must I kill Thomas to destroy the Horde?

"Conquer, my pet, not destroy."

He chewed his lip. Put his hands on his knees. Struggled for breath.

The dark presence cinched tight.

"Resist me not, my Johnisss . . ."

Let me go!

"You have sworn your allegiance . . ."

"Johnis." Silvie interrupted the inner fight.

"I'm listening, I'm—"

Shaeda wrung his will with an iron fist.

All right! My allegiance is yours.

The noose slipped. His head cleared. "Talk to me, Silvie. It helps. You're the only one who makes her let go. I don't know why."

Silvie's eyes narrowed.

Johnis continued. "Unfortunately the mission comes before our preferences. It won't be for any longer than it takes to get rid of him. This way." They neared the gate.

"Let's get it over with," Silvie grumbled.

Johnis gave a swift nod and approached the guard speaking to an officer. Silvie hurried after him. As they neared, he could make out the captain's insignia.

Shaeda filled his mind, whispering words to him. Words to speak to this guard and to the captain. They would hear, they would give him entrance.

"Trust me, my Johnis. Trust me."

"Johnis," she whispered. "They won't take us seriously."

He felt Leedhan might surge into him. Smiled.

"Trust me."

The pair turned when they saw Johnis and Silvie. The guard turned to assume his duty. "Names and business," he said.

"Josef and Arya of Southern," Johnis said. His mouth seemed to work on its own. He spoke with her voice.

Shaeda's eyes were on him. He struggled, his will melding with hers. And he knew what to do.

"We've been helping hunt albinos, if you must know. Tell me something: if a fellow had information for a man of authority in this town, to whom would he go?"

"What kind of idiot asks a question like that?" the guard mocked. "The priest."

The captain's eyes narrowed. "Really. And you, a lowly guard, know this."

"No offense to the general, Cap'n," replied the guard. "But some say—"

"I'm not interested." The captain rerolled the scroll in his hand. "Though I am interested in a man who asks a fool question like that."

"But you are," Shaeda chuckled.

Her eyes filled his mind. Everything turned reddish purple.

Shaeda's mind whispered. She knew this one . . . this captain named Cassak . . .

Johnis turned. "I meant no offense, Captain. I'm from out of town, and Middle was close. We need fresh supplies. And I do have information that might interest whoever's in command here."

"The albinos are in the desert. Lost your sense of direction?"

"That's part of my information."

The captain tucked away the scroll and started off. To the guard, he said, "Pass the word. Desecration goes down as soon as final orders come in." To Johnis and Silvie, "Get gone. I've got a job to do."

"I can deliver the message for you," Johnis called out. "Save you time." The captain kept going. Johnis caught up. "Don't you have better things to do than play messenger boy?"

"You aren't authorized to carry it," the captain replied. They were coming up the main road into town now: lake to their left, palace to their right. And across the lake, the Thrall. The captain broke off and headed for Qurong's expansive home.

And they now stood in the streets.

Shaeda coaxed him. A girl, he needed a girl . . . she knew where to find the general, who could take them to the priest . . .

Silvie scuffed up dust. "I told you he wouldn't listen."

"I'm not done yet," he said. Johnis scanned the town. They now stood in the middle of the road with people bustling everywhere. "There."

There she was. A child. A small girl. Johnis hurried toward her and crouched. "Hello."

She withdrew and stuck her finger in her mouth. Johnis went down on one knee.

"Do you know who the general is?" Johnis asked.

The girl looked up with wide gray eyes and brushed hair out of her face. She nodded.

Johnis smiled. "Excellent. So you know what he looks like?" Affirmative. "Do you know where I can find him?"

Hesitation. The kid was a beggar. She wanted something. And she was eyeing his mother's ring.

She couldn't have it.

Shaeda's talons drove into him. Screaming pain flashed through his body.

Not my ring, he protested. *Not my . . .*

Silvie dug a fruit out of their sack. "Will you take this and show us the general?"

But the girl was uninterested. Unlike a previous Scab girl they'd once encountered.

"What do you want, pup?"

The child opened her palm. "For my mommy."

"Well, the ring belongs to his mommy. He can't give it to you. You wouldn't take anything from his mommy, would you?"

The little girl thought about that. "I suppose not. But I want something for my mommy."

Silvie had no patience for this. "Listen, girl . . ."

Neither did Shaeda.

"Did your mommy tell you about the albinos?" Johnis asked, interrupting Silvie. The girl's eyes widened. "They do bad things, don't they?"

She nodded.

"Well, wouldn't you agree the best thing we could do for you and your mommy would be to make the bad albinos go away?"

"Mommy likes pretty things."

Johnis sighed. "Let me see the sack, Arya."

She offered it to him. "What?"

"In my other pocket." He fished in the bag and found the pants from the other world. His hand brushed against the Book of History.

Johnis paused.

"Another time, my Johnisss . . ."

Yes, they were in a hurry, weren't they?

No time to ponder.

He dug out a coin with a man's face on one side and a big star on the back.

"This is silver, and it's worth more than the ring. You can get your mommy something pretty with this, can't you?"

The girl's expression turned greedy. She reached for the coin, but Johnis pulled it back. "No, no. Show us the general, and then you can have the coin. Promise."

Her face scrunched up. But she nodded. Johnis took her by the hand, and the little beggar led them through the streets.

It didn't take long.

"There." The girl pointed.

The general was well out of earshot and getting smaller, barreling down the road toward the thrall with a woman hurrying behind him. The woman wore a plain brown tunic and pants, sandals on her feet. A veil covered her head. Her master wore tans and browns and a dark blue cloak with the hood flung back, sword strapped on, knives in place, just as before. Long, white dreadlocks bounced along his shoulders. He marched proudly through the streets of Middle.

The girl grabbed the coin from Johnis and fled. Silvie and Johnis didn't bother protesting the little beggar.

He had the sudden urge to run.

Fast.

Breathtakingly fast.

Johnis grabbed Silvie by the hand. "Come on."

DARSAL'S VEIL BOUNCED AS SHE HELD IT AGAINST HER throat to keep it from flying off. She had to run to keep up with Marak. His boots pounded up the road. Her sandals could only slap.

And now she'd found beneath the Scab exterior even more layers, as with an onion. Like the pool, far deeper than she'd first imagined.

The journal belonged to a dead lover.

They weren't battle plans. They were good-bye.

Touching those pages was a violation of his inner sanctum. She might as well have defiled water with human blood. But at least after Billos she could imagine the sentiment.

The general rounded a corner, and she almost lost him, fumbling with the leg chain. She was fast, but his legs were much longer, and he was furious at Sucrow for summoning him like a commoner.

Marak's rage at the servant had been almost more than she could take. It reminded her too much of her uncle in one of his drunken states. Or had her uncle been sober?

At least now she understood. Somewhat.

She clutched the necklace he still hadn't taken. Today she would help a Scab general kill albinos. Elyon help them both.

To love a Scab who would slaughter his own lover, his own brother, before allowing an albino to live . . .

"General!" A voice bellowed from behind.

She whirled, eyes wide. Stunned at the familiarity. A man and a woman raced toward them. Two Scabs. Darsal stared.

"General Marak!" Johnis's voice called out again.

Darsal could barely breathe. Johnis and Silvie were alive. Alive but dead.

They were Scabs.

And running. Fast.

"Go tell Sucrow I'm coming," Marak said.

She couldn't move.

They were Scabs looking for Marak. She was an albino slaving for Marak. Disguise or reality?

Johnis looked strange. Blue veins stuck out beneath pale skin. And his eyes . . .

"Darsal." The general's voice snapped her out of her stupor.

She blinked. Johnis and Silvie were almost to her.

"I'm going."

She gave him a half bow then hurried over the bridge and headed up the white steps into the thrall.

JOHNIS THRUST HIS SHOULDERS BACK AND STAYED ON TASK. Again, Shaeda coaxed him. He was beginning to enjoy these bursts of power and insight.

"General Marak, we meet at last."

The general crossed his arms, face hardening. "Who are you?"

Shaeda's inner voice whispered the words he would say. She willed him to bow.

He obeyed. Hated it. Loved the increased gift of persuasion.

The allure of men . . .

The siren song . . .

"My name is Josef. This is Arya. We have a proposition for you, a valuable piece of knowledge that will enable you to destroy the albinos for good."

Marak quirked a brow and snapped his finger at a scout approaching from the west, who hurried forward and presented him a scroll. The general scowled at it.

"From Cassak," the scout explained.

How had he known—or even Shaeda known—the captain he'd addressed earlier was named Cassak?

"Your attention, my pet . . ."

Right. The mission. Questions later.

The general grunted. Nodded. "You can go." The scout hurried off, and Marak resumed his march toward the temple.

"I've already taken my plans before Qurong and had them approved. They're proving quite sufficient."

The general was getting away.

"Release him not, my pet. Tell him."

"I know a weapon that can kill the entire Circle in three days."

Marak allowed Johnis and Silvie to catch up. He broke the seal on the scroll and proceeded to read it.

"Think about it," Johnis continued, consigning himself to Shaeda's rule. If for no other reason than so he could think.

Temporary, he reminded himself. Temporary.

"Three days, General. Three days and the albinos will be dead. All of them."

Marak rolled up the letter and resumed his march.

"We use this." Johnis whipped out the rotten yellow fruit. Maggots fell out of the disgusting thing onto the bridge.

The general stepped on one, squishing it beneath his boot. He sped up. "You're wasting my time."

"It's bait."

"Get out of my way, boy."

"The bait is for the Shataiki. Who better to rout out albinos?" Johnis grabbed the general's arm.

Marak flung him away. Johnis struck the ground hard. "The Shataiki are a myth, you fool." He stepped off the bridge onto the sprawling white steps of the thrall, where worshippers stooped to bathe in the muddy waters below.

Johnis ignored the pain in his arm and shoulder and hurried after Marak. How in the name of Elyon was he supposed to do this? "General, I've seen them."

"You were dreaming."

"General, the Circle is protected by an invisible covering that also blinds us to the Shataiki. By doing this you remove the veil."

Agitated silence.

Johnis continued. "You kill the Circle without the priest. He's holding out on you."

One of Marak's hands was on his sword. "How did you come across that information?"

"In fact, I believe the priest has had your solution all along."

The general scowled.

"His book of incantations," Johnis explained. "He will know the road, but I possess the horse, so to speak. The priest will be necessary for this to work. What have you to lose, General? If I'm wrong, the priest will know immediately, and you lose nothing. If I'm right, then it is to your benefit."

Marak mulled it over. Johnis could see on his face that the man despised Sucrow just as much as he did.

Good.

Of course, the priest was easy to hate. It could work to his advantage.

"Five minutes."

twenty-two

Priest!" Marak slammed the thrall's double doors against the walls and bellowed into the hall. The few servants and acolytes around scurried out of his way. He roared through the atrium and between two shrines of the winged serpent, boots pounding against the floor.

"He's—he's in his study, General," a temple guard offered. The man bowed and scurried out of Marak's way. Smart man.

Marak swung open another door and knocked one of the serpent-idols off its stand. The silver god clattered on the floor as the door crashed against the wall.

Sucrow looked up from his study, pen in hand, and drilled him with a malicious scowl. "You dare show such irreverence. Announce yourself like a civilized man."

"I announced my entry from the front door, Priest. It's no

fault of mine if you're deaf." Marak stomped across the room and slapped both palms on the desk, leaning over the wood into Sucrow's hawkish face.

Sucrow stood and came around the desk. "Don't send me albino slaves, Marak. The smell is atrocious. I had the guards take her to a holding room. In fact, I don't want her to exist. Who are these?"

"They wish to make a presentation. Apparently they think they can do in three days what we've been trying to do for years."

Listen to yourself, he almost heard Jordan say. *You talk like you're pulling weeds. I'm not a weed, Marak.*

Qurong wants dead albinos, I give him dead albinos, his mind argued back.

The invisible knife twisted inside his stomach. He remembered that argument. One of many.

And when Qurong asks for my dead body, brother? When Sucrow takes Rona for his reprobate rituals? Then what? For Elyon's sake, Marak, you were going to marry the girl! Don't tell me you don't love her still!

Marak stilled. He turned his back. *I can't love the dead.*

We're not dead.

Sucrow dismissed the young couple. "They can wait. I have another matter to discuss with you."

Ignoring Josef's angry expression, Marak motioned for them to remain in the hall. The door shut on the pair of nutcases, then Marak was alone with Sucrow.

The priest opened a cask of wine.

"Why did you decide to keep an albino for a pet?"

Marak shrugged. "I just haven't decided how to kill her yet. She's the one responsible for the death of Jordan of Southern."

A sly grin spread across Sucrow's face. "You are cruel."

Funny, Rona had told him the same thing.

"She hasn't tried to convert you, has she? The albinos can be persistent."

"She'll keep her mouth shut, or I'll cut out her tongue."

"Just like your brother," Sucrow cackled. "And now he's dead."

"Get on with this. I have duties that don't concern you."

Sucrow fingered his necklace and folded his hands. Chuckled. "Very well, General. Let's get down to business. My report to the supreme commander included your compliance to the new laws regarding the albinos. As expected, the execution of your albino relatives has reassured us both where your loyalties lie."

Marak growled. He'd given the order. His captain carried it out. As promised, he'd watched their executions.

Cassak sent him home. Then he found Darsal in the dungeons.

Sucrow sneered, enjoying his newfound power too much. "I will be placing my serpent warriors over each of your commanders. They will report to my men, just as you will report to me."

"My men report to me."

"You'll have to take the matter up with Qurong, General." The priest still looked amused. "But don't think that will aid you. I have my own means of persuasion."

Rumor had it Sucrow used spells to control the throaters. If you believed in that kind of thing. Regardless, the man obviously had some sort of control over them. They were all unquestionably loyal to their high priest.

Once again, Marak wondered how this man had gained so much power and favor with Qurong. Thus far, Marak had resisted the priest's influence. On that point alone he agreed with the rebel Eram.

The priest needed to go. No religious man should have equal or greater power than a governing ruler. Exactly who ruled whom, the priest or the supreme commander?

Sucrow poured two glasses and gave one to Marak.

He pushed it away. "Qurong wants me to let you at the helm of my project. He did not order me to drink with a superstitious old man who worships a snake with wings, Priest."

Sucrow threw him a cold stare. "Blasphemer or not, you will show respect for the Great One while inside my temple."

"Your temple or his?"

"You know what I mean."

"Then say what you mean."

After a few moments, the priest conceded. "Killing kin. Something your grandfather never would consent to."

Marak ground his teeth.

The priest chuckled. "Still reeling over their deaths, Marak? They were diseased. Far better to die quickly than slowly, don't you think?"

Marak fought the urge to turn this priest into a mound of clay on the ground. But the old sorcerer had far more to his advantage than met the eye.

"I think a wise man knows when to mind his tongue. He never said I couldn't kill you."

Sucrow's amusement only increased. The viper needed to die, slowly and painfully, the most excruciating death available.

"Marak, Marak, such a temper."

"Don't tempt me, Priest. You've seen what I'm capable of." Marak turned. He hadn't touched the wine and had no intention of doing so. Sucrow likely meant to get him drunk and wave some spell over him.

"General . . ."

Marak paused but didn't turn around, hand still on the door.

"As you've said. You're capable of anything, correct?"

"Say what you mean, Priest. This is why religious idiots have no business leading an army. You'd kill us all with your yammering."

More cackling. "Very well. Since you're so adept at killing albinos, take care of the one you've been dragging around."

Darsal.

"I do things my own way, Priest. She'll die when she dies."

"I want her dead, General. You can kill your own brother, surely you can take care of a nameless wench." Pause. "Or you could give her to me. She'd make a lovely replacement for the other wench."

Rona.

"Fine," he growled. "I'll kill her."

Sucrow chuckled. "Pity. She might enjoy Teeleh's caresses as much as the other one did."

"Leave it, Sucrow. I said I'd kill her." He tried to leave.

"Ah, General?"

"What now, Priest?" he snarled.

"Are you curious what the youth might say?"

"Send your servant with a report. I'm taking the wench now."

He shut the door. The young man and woman were still waiting in the hall. "Enter." Without waiting for a response, he stormed off.

Sucrow was trying to usurp the military arm.

Qurong was breathing down his neck to finish off the albinos.

Eram threatened rebellion.

He'd killed his own his brother and sister-in-law.

Then taken in a pet albino.

Lunacy.

Darsal had to die.

Then Sucrow would get off him and he could see to getting his command back.

SUCROW HAD LOCKED DARSAL IN WHAT LOOKED LIKE A small ritual room and posted a guard outside. A room with Teeleh's winged serpent image leering at her and an altar and a silver bowl of unlit incense. She'd had neither the time nor stamina to resist being placed there.

Not that it would have mattered.

Marak might kill her.

Sucrow *would* kill her.

And that was counter to Elyon's mission for her.

She couldn't do penance if she was dead.

Once the door shut she started to pace. Johnis and Silvie were alive. Alive and Scab. Alive and coming to deal with Sucrow.

What to do, what to do?

Darsal sat, one knee up, as far from the feet of the idol as she could get. No way would she take a kneeling posture before the image.

"Elyon . . . ?"

She tried to wrap her head around this idea that Johnis and Silvie had not found water, had not gone on as they should have to bathe and find Thomas.

This was not what was supposed to happen.

"Elyon, why?"

Everything in her screamed to break out of the temple, rush out, and find her friends. Shake them, reason with them. She could try it. Overpower the guard, steal his weapon. Grab Johnis and slam him against the wall, fling him into a red lake and drown him.

But no—even if she could get out of the room, she'd never get beyond the first corridor before someone ran her through.

She couldn't help Johnis and Silvie. They were in agony. The Scab general was to blame.

How could she choose Marak over Johnis and Silvie? Hopeless.

Return to the Horde and love them for me. For Johnis.

"Do you want me to help Johnis or stay with Marak?"

The seconds turned to minutes. Darsal laid her forehead on the cool floor.

Arguing outside. Marak burst through the door. Darsal stood. Her leg chain clattered on the cold stone floor.

"Come," he snapped. "We're leaving."

She squeezed between him and the door, under his arm, barely brushing his clothes. Marak poked at her with the butt of his knife.

"What's—"

"Silence!" he ordered.

She obeyed.

"WHO ARE YOU?" SUCROW DEMANDED. THE SNAKE WAS just as disgusting and slimy as his predecessor.

"My name is Josef of Southern. This is Arya, my betrothed."

They had both agreed to change their identities. Josef after a story Darsal's niece once told them. Arya after Silvie's mother.

Of course, Silvie couldn't be sure if the suggestion was Johnis's or Shaeda's.

She wasn't sure what she knew anymore. Johnis wasn't himself.

Johnis approached the desk and leaned forward. "I've a solution to the albino problem. We can be rid of them all in three days' time."

Sucrow squinted at him. He had the look of a man curious but trying to appear indifferent. With one hand he pushed Johnis back.

Silvie kept a hawk's eye on the cretin's fingers. Though the more rational part of her told her Shaeda, if she was really controlling him to any degree, would not allow him to be injured for long.

As long as he obeyed.

"And what might that be?"

Silvie tried to keep their greater purpose in mind: conquer the Horde. With them Sucrow would die too.

Shaeda's will was infinitely potent.

Soon enough. Soon enough. Johnis's plan included breaking free of the accursed Leedhan's stranglehold and keeping her powers for himself. Then they could kill the Horde instead of just conquering them.

Silvie toyed with her knife, imagining slitting the woman's throat.

Under normal circumstances she would already have planted one in the Dark Priest's brain and another in his torso.

Soon.

Very soon.

Her hand was getting itchy for a throw. The blade would have to go right past Johnis's ear, likely touching it, to reach the priest's skull. She'd made that throw before. Her love was in no danger if she made a second attempt.

"An ancient power," Johnis answered, "beyond the likes this world has ever seen."

The priest picked up his pen and started rummaging in his desk, apparently bored with Johnis's assertions.

Illusion, of course.

If anyone knew the old tales, Sucrow did. That was why Johnis had been confident selling the point to Marak. Sucrow would know.

"I've been given the means and locations required to retrieve it."

"Is that so, boy?" The priest's coyness made her blade-finger twitchy.

Johnis's cutting glare hardened. "It is."

"And how do you propose to get this . . . weapon?" Sucrow sneered.

"With this." Johnis withdrew the maggoty, rancid yellow grapefruit-thing and held it right under Sucrow's nose.

The priest's eyes widened. Only for a second, but enough for Silvie to notice. Johnis was right.

Which meant Shaeda was right too.

Her stomach turned.

But why was Sucrow pretending he didn't believe? Or maybe Johnis really had surprised him with a fruit that no one had seen before. Comforting, that thought.

"We use this as bait, then go to the Black Forest into a Shataiki lair and recover a certain charm," Johnis said. "With that, and your summoning ceremony, we can gain control of the entire horde of Shataiki for four days. Nothing can stop them once they've flown. It will be perfect. You will see."

Sucrow slapped the fruit away. It rolled across the ground, a single maggot landing on the desk, several more falling out when the fruit struck. Silvie almost gagged.

"And what makes you think these Shataiki are more than legend, boy?"

Johnis leaned close. Very close. "I think we both know that's a fool's question."

They stared each other down for several minutes before Johnis straightened. Sucrow chortled and went back to his work.

"You're the fool, boy, to come waltzing in here with rotten fruit and a child's notion of controlling Shataiki."

Johnis retrieved his fruit and slapped the desk. "I alone have the location of the Black Forest, and I alone have the bait. You'll never find the place without me."

Sucrow picked up a maggot from the desk, inspected it. Then squished it between his fingers. "You have nothing but empty words. Now go."

"Sucrow, you must listen—"

"Guards! Escort these children back outside and inform them that if they're caught trespassing again, they'll be executed."

Four muscular temple guards entered, two through the side door that likely led to the library, and two from the front. They grabbed Silvie by the wrists and began dragging her out.

The other two had Johnis. He kept protesting, but no one would listen.

Silvie cursed the priest as they were taken down the halls. Out on the patio, toward the steps.

"Let me alone," Johnis growled. Silvie snapped her head around. The voice wasn't Johnis's. It was lower, more sinister. His eyes had a cast to them she couldn't describe.

The guards were stunned too.

Johnis jerked free. Lowered into a crouch. Readied for a fight. The guard holding Silvie had let go.

Shaeda.

She didn't like her little pet threatened.

A chill wound around Silvie's spine.

Johnis lunged.

Silvie grabbed his arm. "Don't. They'll kill us."

Johnis ground his teeth, fists balled, muscles in his arms tightening. His eyes were dull, narrowed to slits, and very dark against his flaking, mosaic skin. He broke free of her and snarled.

"Follow us and it'll be the last thing you do," he warned the guards. Johnis grabbed Silvie's arms and marched off. Left Sucrow's men standing there gawking.

"What was that?" she asked when they were away.

He didn't answer.

"Johnis."

He was wrestling Shaeda again.

Finally his head cleared. Clarity came into his eyes.

Johnis's mistress had spoken.

He looked at her. "We'll have to find another way to convince Sucrow. The fruit he'll blow off as coincidental. We need more."

He grabbed her by the hand and hurried into the trees.

Silvie yelped. "Where are we going?"

"To get the amulet. We need to get supplies and some horses. I'll explain on the way."

SUCROW WAITED UNTIL THE TWO YOUTHS WERE OUT OF HIS sight and the door shut before reaching into his desk.

The boy had said far more than he likely comprehended. And he knew what the boy wanted, what he needed.

Josef had the means, but he would require a particular ritual to bring his plan to fruition. A ritual only a priest of Teeleh would know.

He retrieved parchment and pen and a small, leather-bound book tied with gold twine that contained a series of legends and incantations. His guest had made him suspicious of an old tale that few remembered.

Sucrow flipped through the book to a dog-eared page and read it again. His frown deepened.

That fruit the boy carried wasn't supposed to exist.

It was a harach, supposedly from a purple-leafed tree that simply did not grow anywhere in the world. Only a precious few even knew the tale. Rumors, scarcely whispered stories from a tight-lipped, waning number of priests who devoted themselves to ancient practices and to the winged serpent.

Leedhan magic. The entities.

Vampire lore.

The *amulet* wasn't supposed to exist.

"But if it did," he mused, "if it did, it really could mean the end of the world as we know it. This truly can become a world without albinos."

But what else would it mean?

With trembling fingers he scanned the pages, looking for the location of ancient things. A simple ritual would gain him access.

Teeleh would not be pleased if these abominations gained control of his following. If this amulet of Josef's really was the same, he could control the world. Surely Teeleh would prefer his own trusted priest to hold that Shataiki's bane. Not some fool who would enslave him.

This meant he didn't need said fool running around unsupervised. Josef and his lover needed to be under Sucrow's control.

"Yes," he muttered. "That would do it." He needed to send Warryn to catch up to the couple he'd too quickly dismissed and have them go after the amulet together.

Upon their return he would deal with them and take the Leedhan magic for himself. And then the girl would make a nice addition to his rituals. She was extra baggage, anyway. The boy would be more compliant locked in a dungeon.

Or dead.

Sucrow called to his apprentice in the library next door. "Come. I have a message for Warryn. A special assignment." Sucrow wrote on a parchment, rolled it up, then sealed it.

The skinny youth bowed upon his approach. "Furthermore," Sucrow instructed, "I want to know where the lair is."

"It is done." The servant's hand closed on the scroll.

Sucrow grabbed his wrist and gripped it with his long, sharp nails until the youth's flesh tore and began to bleed. "Do not let them leave the city."

twenty-three

Where are we going, General?" Darsal asked, fighting the butt of his knife against her spine.

"Keep moving." Marak ignored her questions, marched her to the north end of the lake. Ignored the diseased flesh and the Circle pendant that made her look so much like the woman he'd almost married.

"Where are we going, Marak?" Rona's voice echoed. He remembered taking her here. She'd brought a meal from the market, and her long braid bounced as she ran to greet him. Loose tendrils had fallen around her eyes and cheeks, and she'd flung her arms wide. He'd caught her up in his arms . . .

Darsal broke free and faced him. "What's going on, General?"

Jordan's pendant still hung around her neck. She'd tried twice to return it, but he'd been so frustrated with her he'd never taken it.

His uneasiness grew.

"You don't have to do it, Marak," he heard Jordan protest in his head. *"You don't have to give in to Sucrow. And you don't have to stay Qurong's general. You can leave. You can come live with us. No one's going to force you to drown. Come live with us."*

Jordan was an idealistic fool. No one just walked away from Qurong. And Sucrow was right. He'd had no business making promises to albinos. They were dead. And it was Marak's job to keep them dead.

But his little brother's face wouldn't leave his mind.

"Stop asking me questions and march." Marak gave her a push. Not hard, just enough to make her move.

No one was in sight. There was a thick grove of trees off the beaten path, on the north end of the lake, that would afford them some privacy. He didn't want company. He just wanted to kill the diseased albino and be rid of at least one problem.

"Tell me what's going on," she demanded.

Curse the wench. She was going to be difficult, wasn't she? The gnawing in his stomach grew. "Go, albino."

Her arms crossed.

Teeleh's breath, she was Rona again.

Enough of this lunacy.

"Fine. Here's as good as any." He drew his sword. "Get on your knees."

Darsal's wide brown eyes drank him in again. She stepped back, but didn't scream. "Why should I?"

Teeleh, Elyon, anyone help him.

"I said kneel." His heart started to pound against his chest. She wasn't screaming; she didn't try to run. She had Rona's backbone. Marak's skin crawled.

She didn't kneel. Marak pushed her to her knees. "Hands on the ground." He held her by the collar as she put her palms on the grass. The pendant dangled.

Marak stepped to the side. The minute he let go, she sprang up. He grabbed her arm. Darsal fought loose and punched him, sent him backward. He righted himself and tackled her.

Teeleh's breath, she was strong.

Darsal kicked free. They grappled for several minutes.

Finally he snatched her leg chain and yanked her feet out from under her. Marak pinned her facedown and tied her wrists. He hated himself for it, but what was he supposed to do?

"Don't be difficult," he snapped. "It has to be done."

Darsal quit struggling. She turned her face to the side. Jordan's pendant stuck to her skin. "Says who? You're a general, for Elyon's sake!"

He stood. "I'm under orders, albino. That's all you need to know."

"My name is Darsal."

He placed his sword at her neck. Raised it.

"Marak, I love you," he heard Rona plead. *"Why are you doing this? Don't throw me off, please!"*

"Marak . . ."

He tensed.

"Jordan and I aren't sick. You are."

"I'm not the one whose skin's been eaten right off—"

Jordan grabbed his hand, turned the inside of his arm outward, and rubbed hard at his skin. The morst smeared, and his flesh cracked and flaked onto his fingers and palms. "Then what is this, Marak?"

He jerked away. "It was fine until you did that!"

"Until I revealed the truth!"

"For the love of Elyon, Marak . . ."

"Silence!"

He couldn't do this if she kept saying his name, if she kept making him think of his brother and Rona. There was no option.

Qurong ordered him to submit to Sucrow. Sucrow ordered him to kill this albino.

Darsal worked her way to her knees. She went to one knee, then into a crouch. Now standing at attention with her hands behind her back, she waited.

The wench looked him right in the eye, pendant suspended from her throat.

Jordan's defiance and Rona's gaze stared at him. Waited for the blow.

A buzzing flitted like a dozen hummingbird wings in his head.

Looking at this woman, he could see only Rona, only the woman he'd loved and cast aside because she'd become albino. The woman his brother married because he refused.

He had to.

Marak brought up his sword. Moved to strike. The seconds felt like forever.

He lowered the blade. Then raised it again.

Slung it into the dirt along with a scream that tore at his throat and lungs.

Quiet. For better or worse, Marak could not kill her.

He clenched his teeth and swore. Slid his blade back into his scabbard, his stomach twisted in knots.

She was Rona. And now he had to deal with her. Deal with this albino and all the trouble that came with her.

His hand touched her shoulder. They both jerked away. Darsal stared up at him, eyes and mouth wide. Marak could only stand there.

Finally he cleared his throat. "Let me untie your hands."

"ARE YOU ALL RIGHT?" SILVIE SOUNDED LIKE SHE WAS TALKing underwater.

"She's wearing me out. I'm exhausted."

The dark presence seemed to wrap around his mind, sinking invisible claws into his brain. He could almost taste something coppery and salty on his tongue and lips. The siren song in his head grew louder. Louder.

"I am with you, my Johnisss . . . I and all my power, if you will but yield entirely . . ."

What did that mean?

"What do you mean?"

"I mean . . . I mean it's like . . ."

Johnis fell quiet. Admitting he wasn't entirely acting of his own will wasn't really something he wanted Silvie to know. But she seemed to already notice anyway. She wasn't stupid.

The siren song heightened. With it came the impulse to destroy everything in his path. To conquer.

"Johnis." Silvie's hand snatched at his arm.

Shaeda wanted him to give her total control. Yearned to share power with him. The pull intensified with every step. Drove him back into the southern desert. Drove him on like a wayward steer.

The guard had been but a taste. Like the badaii.

Like seeing Shaeda face-to-face.

Her mesmerizing gaze flooded him. He could feel her cool skin, hands sliding over his arms. Smell her perfume as she whispered in his ear.

Her thoughts came flooding in. She showed him the desert, a place called the Teardrop Canyon, showed him an eclipse of Shataiki at his command . . .

Showed him Middle as he ruled the enslaved Horde. The Horde he would destroy.

He struggled to clear his head. What had he been telling Silvie . . . ?

"I mean it's as though I only know what I'm doing when it's directly related to Shaeda's instructions."

Silvie mulled that over. "So you're her prisoner."

How dare she insinuate he was some kind of slave. Sassy wench.

"I belong to no one, Silvie."

"Continue speaking such sweet deceptions to yourself, my pet . . ."

"Well, what are you going to do?"

The noose tightened. Shaeda's ominous pronouncement echoed in his head. Yes, she'd given him power. But . . . what kind of power? And . . .

"You are mine . . ."

Johnis growled. "Figure out a way to keep her from reading my mind. She's strong, Silvie. So much power . . . what she's offering me . . . it's beyond comprehension. What she's shown me is but a fraction of what she's capable of, I feel it."

And to access the depths of that power meant he had to die to himself.

Become utterly and irrevocably one with the Leedhan monarch.

Secretly, though the understanding unnerved him somewhat, he liked the rush that came with her power whenever her spirit came upon him.

Shaeda was indeed with them. Better with them than against.

"Now you begin to comprehend, my pet."

He heard a rustling in the trees behind them.

Silvie jumped up and whirled, blade drawn. Johnis was right behind her with his sword.

A man rode out of the trees, dropped off his mount, and came forward, palms extended. He was tall and broad and wore black and purple like the priest. Thick dreadlocks fell almost to his waist. Dull, gray-white eyes scrutinized them.

A throater.

Behind him well over a dozen men on horseback split in half and surrounded them. Two extra mounts were with them. Saddled.

Almost two dozen throaters, all spellbound and loyal to the Dark Priest alone. They dressed alike, with gold and silver jewelry and armbands fashioned into silver winged serpents. Curved, wicked blades gleamed at their sides.

"My name is Warryn," the first, the leader, said. A jagged smile overtook his face. The kind few would ever trust. "I come on behalf of our illustrious priest."

"The priest had his chance," Silvie snapped.

Warryn raised a brow. "He's reconsidered your offer."

Johnis felt his mind sharpen and reorient itself. Shaeda's vise grip held fast. She shared his hate for the Dark Priest, this one who served the lord of the Shataiki.

He would rather deal with Marak. But now the priest had come to him.

"Accept his offer, my pet."

A heady, powerful sensation washed over him. His interest overshadowed his disgust.

"And what might that offer be?"

"Our lord wishes to commission you on this errand." Warryn came forward, hands behind his back.

"Do I look like a servant or a dog to be summoned and dismissed at will?" Johnis asked.

Yes, he was interested.

No, he would not accept too readily.

Shaeda's invisible grip strangled his will.

The chief serpent warrior looked irritated. "He has sent me to go with you to retrieve the amulet. If we return with it, he will mount a full-scale expedition to escort you to the lair, and he himself will lead it."

"And what makes—" Silvie started.

"Arya." Johnis held up a hand. Silvie's new name still sounded strange on his tongue. He didn't like hushing her in front of the priest's men, but they couldn't irritate Warryn too much.

He stepped forward, sheathed his sword. "Why does your priest change his mind?"

They needed the priest. Who would no doubt double-cross them. He'd come up with a way to circumvent that. The Dark Priest did not share power. And Johnis needed to think. The claws in his mind dug in, punishing his hesitation, driving him to obey.

"Ally yourself with the priest . . ."

Johnis stiffened. No. He couldn't do that. Could he?

She was so strong . . .

Could he defy her? Should he defy her?

Not yet. *Patience, Johnis . . .*

"Upon your exit—" Warryn said.

"You mean our being thrown down the temple steps like garbage," Silvie snapped. She sheathed her last knife.

Was she listening? Did she know he planned to betray her?

Could she stop him if he tried?

That was foolish. Shaeda could kill at will.

Focus, my Johnisss . . .

He sucked a breath. She'd heard that.

"A mistake our lord intends to remedy," Warryn replied.

"I won't tolerate anymore such 'mistakes,'" Silvie fired back.

She really needed to learn to let him do the talking.

Warryn gave a sharp nod. "We have supplies and horses. We can set out as soon as you are willing."

"Give us a moment." Johnis motioned to Silvie.

The throater nodded. "Of course."

Johnis and Silvie went aside. Her skeptical look showed what she was thinking. "What do you think?"

"You know what I think," she whispered back, too quiet for the throaters to hear. "I won't go surrounded by the priest's Scabs. Thomas would never stand for this."

"Thomas isn't here," Johnis snapped. Shaeda's sight tinged his vision reddish-purple. Had he said that or she?

Silvie stared at him. Johnis's face heated up.

Thomas wasn't dead. And he wasn't betraying him.

He just had to keep remembering that. He would leave them a way of escape. Just like last time.

Somehow.

Somehow this would all work out, and maybe he could get control of the Horde without killing the entire Forest Guard.

Maybe. The details would work themselves out.

"Fine. We'll go, but only because I don't see another way."

Compulsion forced his hand.

Johnis nodded and turned back to Warryn. "Very well. We accept. But for the duration of the journey you are under my command and not the priest's. Understood?"

Warryn scowled.

"Understood?"

After a few minutes of arguing, the throater consented, however reluctant. Johnis and Silvie mounted the offered horses and rode to the head of the group.

"Where exactly are we going again?" Warryn asked.

Johnis pursed his lips. "South." Despite the throater's protests, he refused to say more. The minute he told them, they wouldn't require him any longer. Johnis settled on that as they headed for Natalga Gap.

"You know where we're going?" Silvie asked.

Immediately his mind focused. Shaeda's mind overpowered him, poured her thoughts into him. He was a human dam. This entity was the river. Information burst out. The onslaught overwhelmed him.

"I can . . . She showed me . . . just now . . . Silvie, it's amazing."

Silvie raised a brow.

He checked to make sure Warryn and the others couldn't

hear him. "The canyon will be on our west. It's shaped like a teardrop."

"How steep is it?"

"Steep. We will be able to see a muddy road that goes underground. There's a tunnel leading into an underground lake. We find a cavern."

Everything went reddish-purple. He could feel himself changing. Feel Shaeda slip in. Slowly their thoughts grew together. Her siren song grew louder. Her gaze pulled him toward her, toward the canyon.

"You will need me, my Johniss . . ."

His mind's eye saw the lair, the Black Forest with its black lake gouged out of the desert with the hands of the dead. A lair housing Derias, the Shataiki queen. Her enemy. The enemy.

Shaeda despised this one.

He had something she wanted.

Desperately.

"Johnis." Silvie snapped to get his attention. He had yet to figure out why she alone broke Shaeda's vise.

She was staring at him. "I don't want to do this."

Shaeda's pull grew taut.

Johnis tightened his jaw and wouldn't look at Silvie, who really needed to learn her place and be more respectful. Ask fewer questions.

"It's all about the mission, Silvie. Our Eclipse."

twenty-four

"Sucrow ordered you to kill me."

Darsal hadn't really quit reeling. Johnis and Silvie were Scabs. The general she was supposed to love and serve was under orders to execute her. Had tried to execute her. And once more, only his little brother's pendant around her neck had saved her.

That and her resemblance to his dead lover.

"Shut up. Let me think." Marak paced in the secluded clearing they'd retreated to. Darsal watched, ready to fight him off if he got the idea in his head to try to kill her again.

Unfortunately for him, her death was counterproductive to her mission.

His hand played at his hilt.

"Tell me what you're thinking," she demanded.

Marak's boots trampled damp grass and flowers. Black mud from a streambed blackened the worn leather. His hands kept moving.

Big, calloused hands, like Billos's.

Big, muscled Billos, who had fought with and loved her with all his heart and soul and saved her twice over.

He hadn't just tried to kill her. He'd touched her.

Worse, that little touch sent something through her she hadn't felt since Billos.

The last few minutes left her completely out of her element. Billos had never tried to kill her. Why Billos? Why now?

She shook it off. "Let me help you."

Marak stilled, but did not, could not, would not look at her.

"Tell me."

"Rona, would you *please* be quiet! You—"

They both stopped.

Elyon's voice whispered in her ears.

Marak had killed on a principle he was no longer convinced he held.

Return to the Horde and love them for me. For Johnis.

The silence was finally more than she could take. She wasn't sure what Elyon wanted. But something had to happen.

Elyon had forgiven her.

Johnis had forgiven her.

And now . . . now she had to forgive a Scab.

Darsal struggled to her feet, untangled her leg chain, and

shuffled behind Marak. Her palms started to sweat and felt clammy.

His smell didn't bother her like it had before. Time would increase that acclimation. But she didn't have that kind of time.

She hesitated.

The very idea of touching a Scab repulsed her.

This mighty Horde general had shown her his underbelly. His brother's death had wounded him deeply. He had loved and lost.

And now he'd defied Sucrow and Qurong all in one moment.

Elyon . . .

A bird warbled from overhead. Darsal glanced up, recognizing the song. She smiled shyly at the snowy white bird with its red plume and red-tipped wings and tail. A swisher no bigger than both Darsal's hands cupped together. The little creature called out again then darted above the trees and vanished.

Love him.

Darsal approached him from behind. She put her hand on his back.

JORDAN'S VOICE TAUNTED MARAK. HE COULD SEE HIS LITTLE brother's accusing finger and red face in his mind's eye, demanding answers Marak couldn't provide.

And Rona, huddled on the floor, catatonic after whatever cruel ritual the throaters had subjected her to at Sucrow's command.

A pair of hands touched him. Marak's insides jolted. Who was . . . ?

Slender brown arms slid down his torso and locked smooth, brown fingers.

Rona?

No. Darsal. The slave.

The one who was supposed to be dead right now.

Teeleh's breath, he'd called her Rona. And now she was touching him.

For a second he was too stunned to respond. Nothing in him wanted to touch her. Nothing. He couldn't even rationalize what he'd just done.

He couldn't keep her.

He couldn't kill her.

Everything in him told him to turn on her, to throw her off and finish her. It would certainly rid him of one of his many complicating factors.

Blood pounded in his ears.

Darsal put her head against him, hugging him from behind. But why was she . . . ? What was she trying to do?

Then, against his will, he reached up and rubbed her arms. Held her fingers to his chest. Seconds passed.

Good grief, what was he *thinking*?

Marak broke free of her. "This is lunacy."

He should never have allowed himself the connection between Rona and Darsal. Both were albinos doomed to die. He should not have spared Darsal's life the first time. That was it—that was the reason he could not execute her now. He'd allowed himself to sympathize with the enemy.

She stepped back. "You called me Rona. Before."

"Also lunacy. You should be dead."

"But I'm not." Darsal let her arms drop to her sides.

"Don't ever do that again."

"Don't try to take my head off again."

His jaw clenched. "I'm not going to—" Marak cut himself off and turned away from her. Rona was right.

Overnight he'd become a monster.

"I don't know the way out of this one, Darsal. One or both of us has to die."

"There's a way."

"What way?" He knew without asking. His fist tightened. "I am not diseased."

"Then explain how any of this makes sense."

"You're ill."

"One of us is. But it isn't the albinos trying to eliminate the Horde."

He turned to confront her and froze.

Sucrow's servant stood gawking at them, face a mask of horror and disgust. Darsal turned to look and grew still.

Marak bore down on the servant and grabbed him by the throat. "What do you want this time, fool?"

The apprentice was still gaping. "What did you see?" Marak snarled.

"I—nothing, General." The wretch cowered.

Marak dug the edge of his blade into the man's flesh. "Liar."

The fool gulped. "Sir . . ."

"You wouldn't lie to me, would you?" Marak sneered. "I will kill you if you don't answer." He dug in. Blood oozed from the cut.

"Wait, General, wait! Cassak sent me."

Darsal scowled.

Their captive flinched away. "You can't kill me, General."

Marak gave a dark chuckle. Cassak had his own means of getting things done. He wasn't above using one of Sucrow's useless servants if that was the swiftest means available. "I can kill anyone, fool. I killed my own brother. Now tell me the truth, pup."

Hesitation.

"The priest cannot save you from me."

"N-no, sir."

"Now, you weak-willed, half-brained excuse for a piece of meat, what did you see?"

His eyes widened. "I saw . . . you and the albino . . ."

Beat.

"And in the event you breathe a word to a soul, living or dead, what do you think is going to happen?" Marak cut a little deeper.

"You're going to kill me."

"Very good. Say it again, to make sure we don't have any misunderstanding."

"Under penalty of death will I repeat anything I saw today."

"Good boy." Marak let go. "What's the message?"

The little weasel glanced around, looking for a way out and seeing none. Cassak must have been desperate to tax his general with this fool.

"Sucrow is sending warriors into the desert with the boy and girl to find the amulet and bring it back."

Marak frowned. Imbeciles, all of them. "Fine. But tell him not to provoke Eram or I'll make sure the whole mess comes down on his head. He is not to engage or frustrate them."

The apprentice hesitated.

Marak growled. "Do you understand me?"

"I—yes, General."

"You may go."

The idiot bowed.

"And what did you see today?"

Pause. "Nothing, General."

"Keep it that way." The servant bowed and fled.

Marak grabbed his cloak and pulled it over his shoulders. He let out an exasperated sigh and squeezed his fist.

Darsal stood waiting, head bowed. Jordan's pendant gleamed in the sunlight.

For an awkward minute they just stood there.

He broke off first. "Come on."

"Where are we going now?" Darsal's eyes narrowed. He deserved that.

"To find my captain who had the audacity to send me one of Sucrow's ingrates." Marak frowned. The frustration was starting to mount again. "I don't want that priest starting another war."

"War and slaughter aren't the same thing," Darsal said. Then she spoke again, the bite leaving her voice. "I should know."

"I'm still under orders . . ." He didn't finish that.

Grumbling at himself, Marak went back through the trees toward the lake. It didn't take long to find his captain and friend along the shore, sweeping for them.

Cassak saw them and turned. Surprise took over his face at Darsal. He tried to mute it but was too late.

"I see my beggar found you," Cassak said.

Marak grumbled. "What did you send that idiot for if you knew I was here?"

"He was backup, in case I didn't find you. You scared him pretty good." The captain surveyed his general and the albino slave.

"I really do have to ask why she's alive, Marak."

"She's the reason they're dead," he snapped. "She'll die when she's paid for it."

Cassak was openly taken aback. It took him a minute to recover from Marak's announcement.

"A little cold, but you're the general. You got my message, then."

"Sucrow agreed to send throaters into the desert with those idiots." Curious. Marak didn't see any point. Although, if the priest thought there was some merit to all this nonsense . . .

"Right." Cassak kept glancing between Marak and Darsal. What was going through the captain's mind? Did he suspect anything?

"You really should have just come yourself," Marak grumbled.

"It was more fun watching you toy with him. What did you say?"

A chill worked its way down Marak's spine. Cassak was a good man. Loyal to the bone. But Marak had taught him well. He would go to Qurong. Besides, it wouldn't happen again.

At least Cassak hadn't heard.

"Told him if he bothered me again I'd slit his throat." Marak shrugged. "He's one of Sucrow's, Cassak. I wasn't in the mood."

"He was available. Sorry."

Marak tapped his chin, eager to be off the subject. "How many men is Sucrow sending?"

"Twenty, twenty-five. My source is bad at math."

"I don't want the idiots giving Eram the wrong idea. And if this thing is legitimate, I don't want Sucrow getting credit for it."

Cassak beamed. "I'm up for a ride."

"Good." Marak clapped his friend's shoulder. "Take twenty-five men and follow them. Don't be seen. Make sure"—he grew sober and drilled Cassak with a stare—"make sure the Eramites know this is not a raiding party. It's a sweep of the south desert, nothing more. I don't trust Sucrow to get that across. And bring me the amulet."

"Amulet?" Cassak made a face.

"I'll explain it later. No, I'm not getting suspicious on you. Hurry or you'll miss them."

His captain saluted and raced off. Marak watched him go. There was still the immediate matter of Darsal being alive when she was supposed to be dead.

"Now what?" she asked.

He started back toward the village. "We come up with a story to tell Sucrow."

twenty-five

The idea of going anywhere with a brood of the priest's throaters galled Johnis. But he needed Sucrow's cooperation more than he needed to be stubborn on the point. And Shaeda willed it so.

Therefore, so be it.

Johnis resisted the urge to strike Warryn right off his horse. Or find out what Shaeda's power could really do. He had yet to tap into that.

Tempting.

"Patience, my pet . . ."

This mental invasion was getting old.

"Yet you enjoy such . . ."

Johnis growled. "I don't."

Shaeda's mind flooded him.

Okay, so maybe he did.

They rode along the edge of a sharp cliff with even higher, more perilous verticals on his left and behind him. Rises that came to points so narrow and sharp that even if they could be scaled, no human could ever hope to stand at the pinnacle.

Before him: desert he'd crossed once before, once when it was yet uncharted, on a mission that really should have killed him right at the start.

Of course, that meant nothing.

"Trust runs both ways, boy," Warryn said.

"I never said I trusted you. I said your priest is a rock in my shoe." Johnis scanned the horizon again. Campfires dotted the rises well to their west, smoke curling.

"Eramites," the serpent warrior commented. "Blasphemous half-breeds."

Johnis gave a snort and went back to his horse. He mounted and looked at Silvie.

"To hell and back again?" he asked.

Their last quest had taken them west. But they prepared to go south, just as Shaeda had instructed him.

Retrieve the charm.

Prove Eclipse would work.

Conquer the Horde.

Get rid of Shaeda.

Keep her power.

Johnis winked at Silvie. Her lip curled into a smirk. "To hell and back again."

Warryn didn't have a clue. They were riding again, and Johnis enjoyed the opportunity to gloat. If this man knew half of what Johnis planned for his priest, he would run them through.

Or, at least, would try.

Johnis spurred his horse. A sharp curse and a thud. He spun back around.

Silvie had fallen off her horse. Warryn's right-hand man jumped down faster than she could recover and stomped a foot on her back. His sword pressed her throat.

He'd knocked her off.

Shaeda was oddly quiet. He should feel a surge of power. Instead he seemed more interested in leaving, in continuing on alone.

Leaving Silvie.

No. He would never leave Silvie.

Warryn laughed. Someone brought a torch forward, illuminating their faces in the night. "Didn't you hear, boy? I own hell."

"Hell is owned by your master," Johnis fired back. His heart pounded.

Shaeda, I need you. I need you now!

Shaeda wasn't giving him the clarity, the focus, the resolve he needed. No, no, now was not the time to be stuck in this lethargy!

Power. He needed her power.

No time.

The torch hovered over Silvie's bared skin. The throater licked his lips. "What red-blooded soul wouldn't want this pretty?"

Johnis snarled.

Think, think! You have to move! Shaeda!

But Shaeda couldn't hear or wasn't listening. Which made it possible for her to not always know his mind.

Maybe.

Later.

"What do you want?" he demanded, only to buy time while his mind and body caught up to themselves. He knew the answer.

"Don't touch her."

Warryn chuckled. He dropped down beside his men and crouched. Ran his hand along Silvie's body. "Tell me where we're going." The throater sniffed her skin.

"South of Natalga."

The claws and darkness punished him, tormented, even taunted him.

"Fail me not, my pet . . ."

Why won't you help me?

"Your lack of faith . . ."

Johnis started to shake, unable to throw off the internal vise on him, the one that demanded he leave them all and take off in a dead sprint to the canyon.

The one that said if he crossed these men, he would lose alliance with Sucrow. He couldn't give them the information. He couldn't give them Silvie.

Warryn's cackle swelled. Clearly, he misunderstood Johnis's plight. Silvie thrashed but couldn't free herself.

"Josef!"

Silvie's scream broke the stranglehold.

Johnis whipped his mount back across the twenty yards or so between them and jumped on the startled throater.

Shaeda blinded him completely. Sharp pain ripped through his mind, down his spine, down into his toes, into his hands.

"Do not betray me . . ."

You betrayed me!

Warryn tore at him. Johnis flung the stunned elite guard down and dug his knife against the serpent warrior's soft throat.

"Let her up," he snarled. "I swear I'll tear your leader to shreds and tell the priest it was his own doing."

The man didn't move. Johnis nicked Warryn and watched the blood trickle out. For a minute they remained at a stalemate. Evidently they had all expected two passive commoners, not two warriors.

Silvie broke loose and drove one of her knives into the man who'd pinned her down. "Kill him," she snapped.

"Not yet." Johnis dragged Warryn up. "Didn't you hear, throater? Thomas Hunter himself has sung our praises. Never forget that. The next stunt you pull, I run you through. I'm in command here, not you." He let go and remounted.

And he was reeling. He'd defied Shaeda. He'd defied Shaeda.

"You will pay for such, Chosen One . . ."

Silvie kept her hands close to her blades.

"I require a human, son of Tanis. Which I choose matters not. Remember such."

Johnis fought the heady, dizzy sensation. Was that really the key? Silvie meant more to him than anything. Than life itself. Than Shaeda's power. Her will.

Several seconds passed as he took in that thought. And Shaeda's chilling threat.

Reddish-purple haze overpowered him. Her eyes seeped into him. Razor-sharp vision cleared his mind.

The mission.

"Keep a sharp eye on the west," Johnis said. "I hope your boys are in for a hard ride."

Walking into a hidden Black Forest dead on his feet would be suicide. But stopping to rest would give Warryn and his men time to pull something.

His head was pounding, the migraine digging hard into his skull, tearing at his brains. Shaeda's eyes . . . the haunting eyes that forever watched him.

Through her eyes he saw desert. He saw the canyon.

"Come along, my pet . . ."

"We can't go on forever," Warryn said.

His mind was worn thin. He couldn't resist. No longer wanted to. Besides, Shaeda didn't care much for Warryn either.

"You may finish him in due time, my pet . . ."

He could live with that.

"Are you priests or warriors?" Johnis scoffed. "Warriors ride hard and fast, and they certainly don't talk like that."

He drove the horse faster, chuckled to himself when Warryn had to work to keep up.

CASSAK SQUINTED IN THE MOONLIGHT, WAITING FOR THE scout's report, watching the lone figure run over the dunes and toward his twenty-five warriors in black robes. All mounted, spread out far enough to be out of sight, but not signaling, range.

Twenty-five soldiers to make sure twenty-five serpent warriors didn't do anything foolish and start a war. Of course, the numbers were mostly for protection from Eram.

He'd sent a message out to the general, on Marak's order, so the man wouldn't think this was a war party. Not that he intended to be seen.

But Marak's head wasn't in the game. Not this time.

Apparently his quarry had earned the displeasure of the dark priest, who wanted the pair in custody badly enough to send out the throaters.

A lot of trouble for a piece of wood on a leather cord. They'd all gone insane.

"Bad enough they squabbled over a pack of albinos," Cassak muttered. "Now we get to squabble over a myth. Shataiki lair . . ."

What Marak didn't know was that Sucrow wanted the pair dead once he had the amulet. He suspected but didn't actually know.

"Captain." One of his men broke Cassak's thoughts.

"What?"

"About the general's slave . . ."

Oh. Right. The wench. That was another problem. She was supposed to be dead. And Cassak wasn't entirely convinced he was buying Marak's new sadistic streak.

The general hadn't been right since his family's death.

Since Cassak exposed them to Desecration.

Even albinos shouldn't scream like that. And then they'd stopped screaming.

"What about her?"

"Well, sir, she's . . . albino."

"Glad you noticed, fool. Get back to business and let the general handle his own." The man saluted and left without further protest. Cold, yes, but not something Cassak cared to deal with yet.

Two guards on watch stopped his scout at the front line and questioned him, then allowed him through. The little scout hurried over the sand and dropped to one knee before his captain.

"You've found them?" This was an unnecessary question. The scout would not have returned otherwise.

"They're almost into open desert, Captain." The scout rose. "Still headed south. I overheard part, sir. They're headed toward a canyon. If we press through the night we won't be far behind."

Cassak nodded. "We'll spread out farther and surround the canyon. Tell everyone to stay quiet or lose their heads. Borrow a horse and go."

MARAK RETREATED TO HIS ROOM AND PULLED OUT RONA'S leather journal. She'd started writing in it when they met, and when she became albino she sent it to him. His mind's eye could still imagine her strong, slender hand penning each page in her neat script.

But as he read, his mind also wandered. He'd barely spoken a word to Darsal since noon and finally sent her back to the house while he completed his work for the remainder of the day.

He shouldn't trust her. She wouldn't get far with her legs chained and his men all over Middle. Sucrow would know he hadn't killed the wench. Then there was the search party in the south desert. Tempting the rebels to arms.

Cassak would keep the peace. He had to trust his captain.

He'd come home to a clean, mostly dark house complete with a candlelit dinner. Darsal hadn't said a word, and he didn't comment on it. After the meal he'd put her in the study and had told her to stay there. His only means of being alone right now.

Darsal.

After today there could be no more touching. Marak grumbled to himself and stood. He wanted a dip in the lake.

Darsal's silhouette was in the doorway, watching him.

"May I come in?"

He grunted and stepped past her. "I'm going to the lake to bathe."

"Why do you bathe in the lake?"

The question surprised him. Marak didn't respond.

"Middle Lake won't heal if you bathe in it. And it isn't red, so you can't drown. Why bathe in a muddy lake?"

"What kind of question is that?" He didn't know if he should be offended or not. It was an odd question. A direct, personal question.

"An honest one."

"You should know the answer."

"I've been away a long time. I don't know what's happened here in the last five years. And five years ago you wouldn't have done a ritual bathing, muddy water or not."

Marak frowned. He knew the answer but didn't like the idea of her making him explain it. "I think you should stop asking questions."

"I have a lot to catch up on. Humor me."

After trying to kill her, why not?

"After the drowning, when we took Middle, many of the albinos came over to us because they refused to drown. It became permanent. Some of them continued the ritual bathing out of habit, as tribute to Elyon. The few who still believe such a person exists."

"I thought you couldn't change."

She didn't say Scab. Interesting.

"Since the drowning, that's true."

"And you bathe?"

His jaw tightened. True, that was one ritual he adopted. But the cool water felt good on his skin. It was only the red water that was dangerous.

This question-and-answer session was over.

Marak started to leave. "Stay here and try not to get into any trouble."

"I've been through worse."

He swerved. "You understand what happens when Sucrow hears this, don't you? Do you have any idea—"

"My life is already forfeit." Darsal spoke softly. It was that very look that had spared her life in the dungeons. The dark hair, the wide eyes. The defiance, even when staring death in the face.

"So you're determined to bring me to death with you? Is that it?"

"No."

"Darsal, do you have any idea what Sucrow can do to an albino?"

"Yes. I'm well aware of what the Dark Priest can do."

Moonlight streamed from the bedroom window through the door and lit her face, pronounced her scar. Her eyes were glossy in the silver beams striking against her long black hair.

She was gorgeous. Darsal had bathed and put on a floral-scented morst spiced with citrus, and a simple, light-colored nightdress she'd made from an old tunic of his. A sash belted it around her slim waist.

Shake it off, Marak. She's albino. She's an enslaved albino condemned to death. Shake it off.

That careless touch changed everything.

All the emotions he'd had for Rona were now directed toward

this diseased woman who could fight like a man and who carelessly threw her life away for a fool's notion of Elyon "curing" him.

"Why did you come back, after all of that? You would have escaped. You would be safe and at home with family by now. Surely your scouts would have . . ."

Darsal's head lowered.

"Would have . . ." Marak trailed off, watched her cover her face with both hands.

His blood ran cold. "Your family is gone, aren't they?"

Darsal didn't answer right away. Her breath came in short, forced spurts. "My story is a long one, Marak. I didn't drown until the day you took me for your slave."

Jordan. It had to be Jordan and Grandfather. They'd made another one sick. But how? How had she . . . ?

"My parents died when I was a child," she continued. "I was raised by an uncle who was a drunk." Her voice caught, and she took several moments to compose herself. "If you call that being raised."

Quiet.

"You don't have to tell me."

Darsal gave a soft smile.

Rona, coming close for a kiss.

Marak slammed the thought back. He was not falling for another condemned, diseased woman! Period!

"You told me," she said. "It's all right." She went on to tell him about a boy who'd started watching out for her and eventually stopped the abuse by killing her uncle and leaving with her. How they'd fallen in love.

She told him everything, beginning with the challenge that went out from the Forest Guard to the books to how she'd spent ten years in another world. To her return to a world gone mad.

"It was like trading one version of hell for another."

"No wonder you were curled up under that cloak like that." He sighed.

Darsal managed a smile. "I thought you were gloating." She sniffed and looked down at him. "I see now you were only angry."

She had no idea how angry he'd been. Heat tinged his face and neck.

Qurong. Sucrow. A botched albino hunt. Eram's rebellion.

Jordan's classic obstinacy.

"I was ready to wring his neck. I was angry with him. With me. With . . . everyone." Marak rubbed his temples. "I thought you were an albino spy."

"Maybe in another lifetime I would have been. But in that one I wouldn't have come into the presence of the mighty general of Qurong."

He allowed himself a small smile. "So . . . why did you come back?"

She sat with him, leaned against the opposite wall in the hallway, shackles clinking, and told him about her time with her cellmates. How they convinced her to escape. Marak noticed she left out anything that might give him direction to the pool's location.

Her description of the actual drowning was mesmerizing and terrifying at the same time.

Darsal came alive. Even in the pale light, her eyes brightened and her whole face took on another dimension. She went up on her knees, using hands and arms and sound effects to demonstrate.

The tale left Marak a little breathless.

What amazed him even more was how naive she was.

Jordan and Marak had both been present when the lakes turned to red, when the beautiful waters were defiled with blood.

Darsal clearly hadn't.

Marak knew at least the account, though he didn't believe all the rumors, nor that anything was to be gained by trying to drown oneself in the poisoned water.

Darsal trailed off. "What?"

A thought escaped before Marak could rein it in. "You. You are completely different from anyone I have ever met."

Liar, the inner voice rebuked. *You were betrothed to Rona.*

Darsal was so much like Rona . . .

She hesitated. "I'm glad you think that, General. I really am."

Marak tensed. This wasn't right. If he showed any sympathy toward her at all, he would die with her. That would not happen. He wasn't Jordan. He wasn't throwing his life away.

Strengthening his resolve, he moved to stand.

"May I ask you something?"

The floral and citrus overpowered the smell of her skin.

He should deny her request.

Rona's eyes stared back at him.

"What?"

"What was between you and Jordan?"

His heart lurched, his throat constricting. "I will not discuss that." He clenched his teeth and choked down the surge of emotion that swept over him.

Silence. "I understand."

"No," he said flatly. "You don't."

Darsal turned and looked straight into his eyes. "I understand, Marak. More than you realize."

He shut his mouth. Yes, she had told him all of that, hadn't she? The loss had turned her bitter and spiteful for a decade. Marak could only nod.

More silence.

Darsal got up. "Come on. You wanted to bathe, and I've kept you."

Marak rose more slowly. Then a thought came to mind.

Rona.

Sucrow's rituals.

"Darsal, I need you to hear me on this one thing. Can you do that?"

She looked up with dark eyes. "Maybe."

"What happened today can never be repeated, do you understand? Sucrow would love to find a way to kill both of us. I don't play by his rules. I don't ask my men to play by his rules or adhere to his religion. I won't put it past him to spy on us. You have to be careful. If you can't do this, it's over."

"Marak . . ."

"Do this my way, Darsal. Do this my way, and it might not come to that. Can you do that, Darsal? Can you trust a Scab general?"

"Sucrow would—"

"Sucrow takes albinos and tortures them, Rona. He does unspeakable things to them on the altar." Marak's jaw tightened.

Darsal's face went stoic. For a second they froze.

He'd called her Rona again.

It wouldn't take her long to put the pieces together. He'd let Sucrow do whatever he wanted to his own lover.

Sweat beaded on his skin.

"And Sucrow makes the rules," she said.

He didn't respond. The unspoken question lingered. Darsal spoke first.

"Go. I'll mind the house."

She was gone.

Marak stared. Only when she had all but vanished around the corner did he snap out of his trance. "Darsal . . ." But she was gone.

He put on his boots and cloak and left with a heavy heart.

twenty-six

Shaeda's lingering presence did not easily forgive. The darkness that gripped him now chewed at his flesh and mind like a pack of ravenous jackals, consuming him.

"Do not linger long, my pet . . ."

He couldn't think. The siren song, the overbearing power, the haunting eyes and seductive voice . . .

Each second attempt to overthrow her was met with invisible teeth and claws and oppressive fog. He still had to make the throaters stay behind.

Thus far the unwanted escort had behaved. The lead serpent warrior would be dead if he touched Silvie again. Really, he was lucky to be breathing now. Only the need for Sucrow's alliance kept the fool alive.

Pink and red light streamed across the desert. Even this small thing added to what felt like the throbbing in his skull. Johnis wasn't sure how far they'd ridden.

This was much farther south than he'd been before. And the ever-present serpent warriors only added to his unease. They needed to be rid of the vermin. Soon.

"Any sign of the canyon?" Silvie asked.

Shaeda's multicolored gaze bore down on him. It allowed him to see the canyon in the west. The desert rippled, shimmered.

His mind focused.

"Come here, my Johnis . . ."

The entity was allowing her pet a little freedom. And her pet he would remain if he didn't break this noose about his neck once and for all.

"Obey me, Johnisss . . ."

Invisible teeth sank into his neck.

He could not let her have the amulet. Take the Horde for himself.

Keep the amulet. Kill the Horde. Lose the Leedhan.

If he didn't, he would lose himself to the Leedhan. Forever.

But her power, her eyes . . . her strength . . .

"Johnis." Silvie spoke sharply.

His Leedhan-eye view of the canyon was still before him. He saw nothing else. Shaeda's siren song called to him.

"No. It's got to be coming up soon. Or we could have missed it."

"How do twenty-seven people miss a canyon, Johnis?"

"It's always possible."

"Are you sure you're all right?"

"It's . . . Shaeda . . ." He'd told Silvie what he'd done. They'd been ecstatic until the penalties set in.

Johnis couldn't eat. He would throw it up.

He couldn't drink. He couldn't sleep.

There was the mission and the mission alone.

The horses slowed to a walk, weary and white-flanked from the night's hard ride. No one had attacked them.

Still, ambush could happen.

The Eramites were out there, somewhere.

He would have to rely on Shaeda's power to survive if they attacked.

"They won't," Warryn assured. "Eram's too afraid of Marak."

"Not too afraid to defy him," Johnis pointed out. He half-ignored them and focused on his plan, considering the lethargy that only seemed to leave him be when he did Shaeda's bidding.

Shaeda and the intoxicating power she gave him. Shaeda, his muse to invoke at will, the source of his strength. Part of him could give himself to her, just to keep what she had to offer.

That had to end. He wouldn't stay on her leash forever.

No, no. Together they would rid the Horde of their greatest enemy. Rid the world of the Horde with the same Leedhan power.

And then he would rid himself of the Leedhan.

"What if Shaeda lied?" Silvie asked. "What if there is no canyon?"

"You better pray not," Warryn growled.

Sunlight reflected off his mother's ring, now on his little finger.

"She didn't lie."

They rode for another half hour, saddle sore and fatigued. The horses couldn't run, and the riders no longer forced them. The night chill faded like mist, warming the ground and their tired bodies.

Just as Johnis started to doubt himself, they came up a steep rise.

Silvie sped up. "Johnis, look!" He did.

He could see the faint, curving, jagged lip of a canyon breaking the western horizon. The same from Shaeda's vision.

The teardrop canyon . . . in which lay a million invisible Shataiki.

CASSAK LAY FLAT ON HIS STOMACH, A WARRIOR ON EITHER side, and stared out through his spyglass over the next rise and set of dunes at the black and purple–robed throaters and the two youths with them.

Impressive, they'd gotten the drop on Warryn. Amusing watching the pup take down Sucrow's favorite . . .

After Rona and Jordan, Cassak could only sneer. He'd sent a scout back to Marak to tell the general just that. Marak would appreciate the personal note. *Oh, by the way . . .*

Small favors. Sometimes justice did prevail.

Cassak already knew the canyon ridge in the distance was the Teardrop. He'd sent four scouts during the night and promised them rewards for finding it before the throaters did. And they had.

"The scouts saw nothing?"

"Eram's curious, Captain." A small band of rebels had evidently ventured south to see what their former comrades-in-arms were really up to.

"He'd laugh his bloody head off if he knew," Cassak muttered.

Eram already scoffed at the idea of fixating on albinos that fled like startled rabbits into the desert.

The laugh was a quiet one.

Thomas Hunter was renowned for his prowess in a fight. The albinos weren't fighting because they couldn't.

They simply didn't want to.

"What, lieutenant?" the man on Cassak's other side quipped. "You don't think racing through the desert chasing mythological monsters and bits of driftwood is laughable, do you?"

"It's embarrassing," Cassak growled. "That's what it is. Now shut up and pay attention. The men are in place? I want a net around this crew. Eram better not be dagger happy today."

Grown men chasing a legend.

"Marak's right."

"About what, sir?"

"Nothing."

"I didn't sign up to sit in the desert babysitting throaters."

"The Eramites are over that rise, Lieutenant," Cassak growled. "See how far you get before I run you through."

The second silenced himself. Cassak had no time for traitors.

Their prey had stopped at the lip of the Teardrop Canyon.

Cassak summoned a major. "Head out. Once they go down, I want this rim covered. Whatever the pup brings out is mine."

"Alive or dead, sir?"

Cassak grunted. "Alive, for now."

JOHNIS CHARGED DOWN THE FAR SIDE OF THE RISE AND galloped southwest toward the lip of the canyon. Horse hooves drummed in his ears. Johnis tucked himself into the horse's neck, gave him full head, and made himself as small as possible.

Silvie flew past him.

He kicked the horse's ribs and slapped its flank, urging the beast on. Of course, she was smaller, lighter, and therefore less of a burden.

He caught up and passed her. Warryn and the throaters were right at his heels, but he no longer cared.

Let them. They'd stew enough when he made them stay behind. Shaeda wanted it that way. He wanted it that way. They didn't have any business being down there.

Unless they wanted to be Shataiki food. Or Leedhan, for that matter.

Now that was a strange thought.

A few breathless minutes later, Silvie overtook him again. Then they raced neck and neck for about a mile. Another steep rise slowed them. Silvie pulled up first, right at the peak of the rise, and looked down. Johnis jogged after and felt the breath rush out of him.

Teardrop Canyon.

"Ye of little faith . . ." Shaeda chuckled.

He was understanding now. Shaeda needed the amulet as badly as he did. Needed to control this particular queen even more than he did.

She had managed to conceal her reasons why, though.

But the canyon was here. It was theirs and it was stunning. Red-washed walls formed the boundary of the canyon, roughly a mile wide on the north end, like Shaeda said, and probably at least as deep.

"Trust me now, my pet . . ."

Warryn came next, flanked by his men. They made a crescent, looking down into the Teardrop.

Beautiful, but the stark kind of beauty that only the desert can create. Ribbons of purple, orange, gold, and brown made long bands around the canyon walls. Brush, cacti, and open-throated desert flowers colored the floor. As it narrowed, flora and rock grew so densely they formed a canopy. He couldn't see what treasures lay within.

"Don't forget"—Johnis broke the silence first—"it's a Black Forest. That place is swarming with the bats. We just can't see them yet."

"Bats." Warryn eyed him. "Down there?"

"Yes. But you aren't going down there."

Warryn stiffened. "What?"

"Ever had your face ripped off by one?" Johnis demanded.

Shaeda's reddish-purple sight and dark presence bore down on him. Enveloped him. He welcomed her.

If the throaters went down there, he and Silvie were dead.

And death was counter to the mission. Period.

"Ever been tortured by Teeleh and live to tell the tale?" Johnis was inches from Warryn's nose.

"How many times have you been in Teeleh's private lair? In the abode of one of his queens? How many have you killed?"

The throater scowled.

"I didn't think so. Now I don't need you running off like cowards when this thing goes down. So here's what you're going to do: you're going to sit down and wait until Arya and I come back with the medallion, and then we'll go back to your Dark Priest. Understand?"

Warryn drew his sword. "Who are you to me, pup?"

Silvie's knives were in both hands.

Johnis smashed his fist into the serpent warrior's face. Felt the bone snap.

Warryn staggered backward and barely caught himself. His hands were at his bloodied nose.

Johnis wiped the sticky crimson off his knuckles.

"You'll wait here an hour. If we aren't back then, come down after us. It's a box canyon. Figure it out."

He remounted. Silvie turned her horse.

"Let's ride," he snapped.

CASSAK TOOK HIS MEN CLOSER AND HAD THEM FAN OUT around the canyon, spread evenly. The scouts had seen the Eramites, intrigued by the skirmish at the rim, start to move.

A runner from Marak. The general had not appreciated the attempted humor. Of course, the general had a lot on his mind.

Cassak made a mental note to remind Marak that his albino pet was going to have to be dealt with.

Something had the general in a foul mood. The message was short: Keep Warryn in line. Get the amulet. Don't provoke Eram.

Thanks, Marak. Please get over your dead brother and focus. Desecration, General. Desecration. Remember? Kill all albinos? Your job?

Cassak shook it off. He'd never say any of that. Marak would be over it by the time his captain returned. The general always bounced back.

Sucrow just should have known to leave well enough alone.

"Captain."

Cassak snapped his head up. A scout knelt before him.

"You might want to go over there. Sucrow's men spotted Eramites."

The captain swore and mounted up. "Hurry. The last thing we need is a war on two fronts."

DOWN, DOWN THEY WENT, FOLLOWING A MUD-STREAKED path and a narrow ledge barely wide enough for the horses. The path grew steeper.

Johnis leaned back in the saddle until his upper body was completely vertical with the canyon floor.

Shaeda's gaze showed him the winding path through the canyon, the graves . . . the lair . . . the medallion . . .

They were deep within.

He pulled out the harach.

The way was steep, and time was ticking.

Neither said a word until they reached the bottom, more than a mile later. Stiff and nervous, Johnis slid off and stretched his bowed legs until he could feel them again. Silvie did the same, staring up along the rim far above them.

"You're sure this is a Black Forest?" Silvie asked.

"Yes, I'm sure."

Shaeda's heightened senses were killing him right now. Her potency overloaded his brain. He could smell mangy fur and decaying flesh. Feel the presence.

The bats surrounded them.

Derias. The mangy beast was close. So close. Dark thoughts seeped in, the desire to kill this pureblood tyrant who had caused so much pain to his people. His blood would run red before this ended. He would lick it up himself. He would . . .

The thoughts shut off again.

Was Shaeda trying to hide something from him?

He tried to shake off the eerie feeling creeping up his spine.

"Let's get under cover," he suggested. "We're too exposed out here. A million Shataiki."

"Try not to think about it."

"I can sense them, Silvie. It's her. Her magic."

Silvie eyed him. "Are you all right?"

He shuddered. Didn't answer. Shaeda's mesmerizing gaze held fast. Too much, more than he could hope to explain.

Johnis could see everything.

"The path here runs through the middle of the canyon," he tried to explain. "We can't just leave it. We can let the horses rest in the shade. Carry only what we can."

They brought the horses in until the brush grew thick and tethered them in the shade with some of the water. The sun was now directly overhead and beating down on them. Johnis and Silvie took two water bottles apiece.

"How's your head?"

"Trapped in a shaking rain stick."

Their only company was snakes and lizards and the occasional vulture. And Shaeda's thoughts, mingling with his own.

The canyon not only narrowed, but rose up and dropped off into a second, much larger round depression that looked like an emptied lakebed. The rocks in the bottom looked like moss-eaten headstones, a sunken, flooded graveyard.

Would they be able to read the names?

"Some of them, my Johnis."

Johnis mopped sweat from his forehead and neck and resisted the urge to guzzle his water bottle or pour it on his head. It had to last.

His mind could focus on three things: Silvie's voice. Shaeda's voice. The Horde.

Otherwise it meandered where it willed.

Resolve. He needed resolve. And he needed clarity.

Shaeda's will brought him both. She'd promised him power, power he hadn't tapped into.

Blood always brought power. And the books.

Shaeda's prompting gaze directed his mind to something in his bag. Something he'd carried and forgotten.

"Remember your vows . . ."

She wanted him to help conquer the Horde.

Silvie wanted to kill the Horde.

Johnis's will was tearing in two.

He kicked mentally against Shaeda's stronghold. Her eyes overpowered his vision, swallowing him in her multicolored irises.

Silvie had a vow too. And her vow could be his vow.

"Do you remember your oath, Silvie?"

She smiled deviously. "Which one, my love?"

Johnis pulled out the Book of History. He'd almost forgotten it until now. He set it between them.

"Let's make an oath, Silvie, before we go down and get this medallion." He touched her hand. Her skin was hot.

"Let's vow to conquer the Horde."

She hesitated. "Johnis . . ."

"That is your vow. I just want to make it with you. I have to. It's the only vow that gets Shaeda out of my head. I can't be free of her, Silvie. Not without you."

Pause.

"All right."

They placed their hands over the book, then vowed. Nothing happened, as expected. No blood.

And it was done. They stood.

"We should continue down," Silvie said. "I don't want to be caught out here."

He started down the sloping fall with her. They fumbled and slid, tripped and swore, but finally reached the muddy lakebed. Mud but no water. And the mud was thick and brackish.

Unmoving.

"Invisible lake," Johnis muttered, half to Silvie, half to himself. He turned, looking for an entrance to the underground lair. He knew, because Shaeda knew. Her hold was growing. She became more dominant with each moment.

And she whispered in his ear again. His mouth spoke her words.

"Silvie, once we get the amulet, we can't let Warryn and his throaters have it. They'll take it and kill us."

"Likely. But like you said, it's a box canyon. We can't get out."

"The Shataiki can."

"And kill us too."

"Not necessarily. They don't like fire. And the healing water—"

"What healing water?"

"Water is water. And . . . I think . . . I think maybe Shaeda will help us."

"It's about time."

Shaeda led him along, though there was always a lapse between what his mind saw and what his eyes beheld.

But she kept them on track.

At the south end of the canyon the walls formed a kind of orb with a roundish hole carved out—an oval-shaped doorway with no corners. A six-foot overhang draped the entrance.

"Enter, Mighty Chosen One . . ."

"Silvie, I think . . . I think this could be it."

He started into the cave. Immediately the air became muggy and dense. Water dripped from somewhere deep within and echoed. Johnis marched on.

Silvie lit a torch and followed. They hadn't gone more than twenty feet when it snuffed out. Johnis turned.

"I don't know what happened," Silvie said to his unspoken question.

She tried lighting the torch again.

Nothing.

"This isn't normal, Johnis. I'm doing this right."

He barely heard her, compelled within.

"Johnis, something's wrong."

The shaft of light grew thinner and smaller, subdued by the bleak cave's gloom. Johnis could no longer see.

"Trust me, Johnis . . . Yield to me . . ."

He put his left palm against the wall and felt a familiar, slimy goo. He sniffed.

"Worm sludge."

The kind produced by Shataiki larvae.

Johnis grimaced. "I hate this stuff."

Silvie slid her hand into his. "How do we see to find anything?"

Johnis wiped his hand on his pant leg. "Just keep moving straight. Don't stop; don't turn right or left." He squeezed her hand. "We'll find it."

"We can't *see*, Johnis."

"Shaeda can, Silvie."

"The tart. Entity."

"We didn't come this far to get lost in a cave. We didn't."

Now if only he could feel as brave as he hoped he sounded.

Deeper into the tunnel they went, clammy, shaking hands clasped. Much time passed, lost deep within this unsettling blackness.

Shaeda's eyes proved to be their guiding light.

So did her hearing.

Soft squeaking sounds echoed off the cave walls and bounced around. Soon Johnis lost his sense of direction. Although there wasn't much direction other than forward and down.

The Leedhan's sense of smell was just as good as her hearing.

"You hear that?" Johnis asked.

"Dripping water."

"Bats. They're sleeping. Silvie . . . Silvie, there are probably millions of them. An eclipse of black bats."

Unease overtook him. The bats made Shaeda nervous.

Very nervous . . .

Derias was close. Whoever he was, he'd earned the fear and hate of Shaeda the Leedhan. And she would not suffer him much longer.

Shataiki surrounded him. Ordinary, small ones. Larger ones. The queen, one of those second only to Teeleh himself, who laid the larvae that spawned more of the beasts, was close.

Derias.

He had an enormous hive. And hated albinos even more than Shaeda did.

Shaeda withdrew her thoughts.

Concentrate.

"Think about it. How many does it take to blot out the sun?"

"Just remember this was your idea."

The air grew chilly. Long, unseen tentacles like icy fingers traced down Johnis's neck and spine. He could feel the hair on his neck and arms and legs stand straight up. Worse, a strange, sickly sweet smell tinged the air. More shivers through his raw, tormented nerves. He could taste the salt on his upper lip. The stiffness in his joints worsened. His skin flaked in chunks the size of maple leaves.

A red haze drifted up from the ground, curling around their legs and rising along their waists.

"Follow the light . . ."

Just enough to see by, winding around their cold bodies. Beckoning them to follow.

The walls and floor glistened with a thick layer of sludge.

Johnis drew a sharp breath and stared behind him down the tunnel, which had opened into a chamber where they now stood.

Four unlit torch stands surrounded the room like compass points. Or maybe they were lit. Maybe the red haze originated from these torches.

No . . .

"Silvie?" He wasn't sure why he was whispering. "Do you see the light?"

"I can't see anything."

Shaeda. Her eyes.

The walls within the cavern, from top to bottom, were made of some sort of black stone and covered in a greenish moss. Beneath their feet was a red-stained reed mat that was round and covered the entire floor.

In the center of the room was a four-foot stand made of ornately carved wood with a ram's horn on each corner and a hollowed-out top with a silver bowl inside. Nearby was a small silver gong and mallet.

The reddish mist grew up around the table but strayed from the gong. Shaeda was showing him something.

"I've never seen one like this before."

"We usually only see the library."

Now one rebel was dead, and the other one was probably wishing for death.

"I did nothing," Warryn protested. "They provoked me."

"Let them have their dead. We don't want a fight. Not now."

"You wish to know where their leader is, do you not?"

Cassak swore. He glanced at the rebel on the ground. "Take the body and go. This was not the doing of Marak of Southern."

But Warryn didn't release the tortured man.

"What are you going to do about it?" Warryn taunted. "Run back to your limp-wrist general and cry like a girl?"

He drew his sword.

"You'll lose that fight."

The captain bit back the desire to run this priest's jackal through.

"I said let them go, Throater. Your priest would not tolerate this insubordination. I don't care who's in command. You're dead."

An arrow fired down over Cassak's head. A warning shot.

Cassak held up his hand and swept the dunes for the archer.

"Come down!" he called. "This is not a war party!"

The rebel prisoner swore and coughed. "Could have fooled me."

Cassak scowled. "There's been a mistake," he called. "Hold your—"

A wave of Eramites crashed over the dunes, blades flashing in the sun.

Cassak drew his weapon.

"Take them alive," he ordered.

"Proceed, my Johnis . . . Brace yourself for my power . . . Fear not . . ."

He looked.

Just beyond them the cavern split into five openings, none more than four feet wide and six feet tall. Over each writhed the figure of a winged serpent with brilliant purple eyes that glittered in the unnatural light.

"Which way do we go?" Silvie whispered.

The serpents over the doors almost looked alive.

One actually flicked its tongue at him, scaly wings twitching.

"Hasten your steps . . ."

"More importantly, how long do you think it's been?"

Silvie didn't respond.

Johnis squeezed Silvie's hand and let go, then went to the silver bowl. He tried hard not to dwell on the throngs of slumbering, drugged bats. Nothing he was looking for.

"Choose wisely, my pet . . . Take the road farthest left."

A short tunnel brought him into a small room. He stepped inside.

More mist curling into his nostrils. More disturbingly sweet aroma.

Inside, the mist accumulated into a hearth. A heatless fire flickered over a metal grate. No logs. Two inches of ash filled the wall-length, low fireplace.

Atop a table stood a single golden pillar candle and two goblets, one containing water, the other a thick, red liquid. Too thick for wine.

Blood.

What in the world went on down here?

"Have no fear, my Johnis. Such is not intended for you."

Shaeda's assertion failed to soothe his unease. Equally unnerving was understanding that she concealed from him her knowledge of the chamber.

Her eyes drew him around the room. In the middle stood an altar made of the same wood as that in the main chamber but shaped like an enormous oval, horns on either end. Incense rose from the fire. The altar was empty. But completely soaked in blood.

A twelve-inch wooden knife with a painted hilt lay in the center. The blade was sharpened to a point. The edge could cut silk.

Johnis backed away. He bumped into the table in effort to get out of the room.

"De-dead end."

Something smacked into him. Johnis yelped and heard Silvie yelp with him, her knife at his throat.

They stared at each other, unmoving. Silvie's dull eyes looked like clouds reflecting moonlight on a dark evening.

She let him go.

"These two are sealed off, but I can hear scratching if I press my ear to it. The fourth is a library, but it looks as if someone stole everything out of it. The shelves are empty. The desk has only parchment and quills."

Johnis told her about the altar room.

"I want out of here."

"You're sure nothing was in the library?"

She nodded.

"It's usually the library. But I guess that makes sense. Wh hide something where we would think to go first?" He headed fc the cavern on the far right, Silvie in tow. He rubbed her hand wit his thumb.

"It can't be much farther. If it isn't here, we'll have to breal in—"

The ground gave way to open air beneath Johnis's feet.

He fell into an abyss and struck something hard. Silvi screamed after him.

All went black.

"STAND DOWN," CASSAK WARNED, APPROACHING THE throaters and Eramite captives at the canyon mouth slowly. He didn't look for his men. They would be in position.

No one was to make a move but by his word.

"Cassak," Warryn growled.

He and his men had taken positions along the canyon, too, but they had chosen too close to the edge and were now trapped. Perhaps Sucrow would have expected Marak's captain to follow.

His chief serpent warrior hadn't. These men were torturers, not warriors. They were lesser beings.

Two Eramites had gotten captured, and Warryn grew bored.

twenty-seven

A frantic Silvie knelt over Johnis, shaking him. He covered his face with his hands and pulled away, sat up. Sore and bruised all over, he could feel a headache coming on.

Concussion?

"I'm awake! I'm awake!"

The shaking stopped.

Johnis stood, feeling his body for any injuries.

A wet spot oozed at the back of his head. He stared at his bloody hand for a minute, made stranger by the mist that still clung to the air.

"Are you all right?"

They'd fallen about ten feet into a shaft that narrowed as it spiraled down and out of sight, dim save for the never-ending vapor.

How had he survived the fall? Shaeda's gentle laugh answered.

So he couldn't die unless she wished, either. The gift of life. Or death.

Perception . . .

Shaeda's eyes commanded his attention. Johnis took in his surroundings. Now they were on a small landing that gave way to a descending staircase. High above, even beyond the entrance they had walked into, were torn pulleys and shredded cords.

"You broke my fall." Silvie pointed to his skinned legs, bleeding at the knees and shins, and matching arms. "We fell down a lift." She tore off part of his tunic and wiped blood off his skin.

"How long have we been out?"

"I didn't pass out. Only a minute or two."

"We have to hurry."

The stair treads were narrow and close together. Johnis tested his weight.

It might hold him after all.

The passage shrank the farther he went. He started counting steps.

By fifty he was tired and cold.

By 136, he and Silvie were both getting winded.

Worse, the stairwell not only shrank in width, but in height, until Johnis was bent into a crouch just to fit.

Soon Silvie, too, slouched her way along, hand on the wall.

No railing, just slippery little steps and a rising sense of claustrophobia.

"Maybe you were right," he finally admitted.

"Should have listened."

Shaeda's claws twisted at him. Johnis stifled a cry.

The mission. Retrieve the medallion. Return to do the ceremony with Sucrow. Then kill him.

Shaeda's light chuckle. *"You learn quickly, my pet . . ."*

He had to get rid of the Leedhan, this entity. But her commanding eyes pulled him along. Like a dog on a leash.

The end of the staircase was so small, its ceiling so low, that they both ended up on hands and knees, crawling face first in sludge.

They reached the bottom. A metal grate blocked their exit. Johnis took his knife and pried at it. The metal gave, and he crawled through into an open room.

No red haze.

He blinked in the unexpected torchlight while his eyes adjusted.

Shaeda's sixth sense spiked. Her sudden terror gripped him.

Slumbering black bats lined the entire room, dangling upside down, licking up worm sludge from larvae crawling along the walls. The long, thin worms shrieked occasionally. Copper filled his mouth. Johnis licked his lips.

Shaeda directed his eyes.

Near the far wall smoke and flames curled from a bowl-shaped stand. Silvie crawled through and walked past him into the room.

Leathery wings rustled overhead.

More dark stone walls and slimy, moss-covered rock. An empty hearth. A wooden altar with an open book across it.

Atop the book lay something round with a leather string dangling off one side.

Silvie hurried to him to look at it as well. She snatched up the torch.

The medallion was the size of his hand, of a reddish wood he'd never seen before, the kind described only in tales of the legendary Colored Forest. A ring was painted on it, and a setting made of slate with a gold center, almost like an eye.

"This is it, Silvie. This is really it."

His hand closed around the medallion.

Silvie thrust the torch like a club. Her eyes were wide and round, staring past his shoulders. "Back!"

He turned. Then backed up into her.

Before them stood an oversized, mangy, black-furred bat, easily nine feet tall, with beady red eyes and long claws. A fly buzzed around its ear. The lips parted in a wicked grin.

Shataiki.

The Shataiki queen.

Derias.

Shaeda's teeth bared. A ruse. She was only half-Shataiki. The other half was abhorrently human.

Silvie raised the torch over the book. "Stay back," she warned the Shataiki.

The room was filled with the beasts.

"I knew there was a catch," Silvie snarled.

"Well, what is this, breaking into my home?" Derias sneered

as he eyed the medallion. "I would suggest you return that if you are to leave in the same condition in which you came." He outstretched a claw.

Razor-sharp, purple vision honed in on the bat.

Shaeda's instinct was to run. Copper and salt flooded his mouth. Johnis half lunged.

Wait!

"Not so fast. You can't use it. I can."

"Not if you're dead." The queen's lips pulled back in a fierce sneer. Amulet guardian he was, to be feared. "Of course, there are other arrangements. I see you've met Shaeda. Abhorrent little vampire, isn't she?"

Shaeda bristled. The hair on the back of Johnis's neck stood up.

He could feel her starting to dominate him.

Johnis pulled the medallion away from the beast, draped it over his neck. His heart began to race again.

He had to think. Outsmart this creature. Get them both out of here.

"Fly, you fool!"

Wait, wait!

He growled.

Human patience now surpassed Leedhan patience.

Silvie held the torch aloft. It was turning her skin red, but she didn't seem to care. The bats kept away from the fire.

"I'll torch us with it if I have to," she warned.

"Take us out," Johnis said. "I'll tell you the entity's plans and let you feast on the Horde instead. What do you think of that?"

The Leedhan had coiled up like a snake. She hissed. Johnis hissed.

"Amusing, pup." Again the Shataiki opened its palm, came forward several steps. "You will unleash more than you can imagine, and you will defy that which you do not wish to defy."

"I don't recall a Shataiki ever telling me the truth."

"Are you certain of what you know?" The bat paused, waited expectantly. "Or are you judging me by my fur?" He smiled, a yawning, jeering expression.

Johnis's mind warred between hatred and fear.

The beast grinned and raised a wing, drawing their attention toward the rafters. A dozen smaller bats clung upside down, their jaws dripping with a glistening gel. Some of the viscous liquid dripped down on Johnis's head.

Shaeda snarled.

"Let me take the amulet," Johnis said. "The entity holds me prisoner. Help me trick her and take her powers, and once the Circle is dead and we have the Horde, I will betray her to you. Think on this, Queen. Shaeda, the mate of the Leedhan chieftain."

Johnis glanced at the medallion around his neck. The necklace. It made them visible.

Leedhan magic channeled through the medallion and did what it willed.

The Shataiki guardian hissed. "Return it to me, and I will allow you to leave alive."

"I don't think I can do that . . ."

His mind was changing, slipping. His skin turned translucent white.

Through one eye he saw blue, through one he saw purple. Together he saw red haze washing over everything.

He gave himself to the Leedhan's impulses. His mind raced faster. His focus quickened. His senses razor sharp. Resolve steeled. Sharper his senses and more steeled his resolve.

Shaeda rushed through him, flooded him heart, mind, and soul. His thoughts were her thoughts. His will hers.

Silvie gaped at him. "Johnis . . ."

Purplish-red colored the Shataiki and Silvie.

The queen threw back his head and roared. The Shataiki all came to life.

Silvie set the book ablaze and flung it at the queen. He jumped away from the blaze. His minions took flight. The whole chamber swarmed, tearing and clawing through the air. Many tore through a shaft above and through the one by which Johnis and Silvie had entered. Their shrieks mingled with those of the worms. Sludge dripped everywhere.

"You fight well, for a vampire's pet," the queen jeered, "If you survive, I will trade you freedom for the vampire's blood and for her power over the Horde."

A loan on the amulet?

But . . . that did mean he could be rid of Shaeda. But a Shataiki was worse than a Leedhan. He well remembered Alucard and Teeleh.

The queen flung back his head and roared. They dove for the exit.

Silvie kept her grip on the torch and slung the rest of the water. Now awakened and angry, facing enslavement to two humans, the Shataiki were a boiling cauldron.

Johnis twisted through. Silvie scrambled over his legs and up his back, set fire to the entrance. He bent his knees. She slammed the grate on a Shataiki's snout and made it scream louder.

"Hurry!"

Johnis sped after her. Behind, the bats flung their bodies at the grate and cursed each other until it came open. They reached the top of the staircase, right where they had fallen earlier. Smoke and flames licked at their heels.

Shaeda's presence settled on him.

Her hazy eyes became his.

Her strength, his.

Her ancestors, her history, her hate . . .

All his.

"Now what?" Silvie asked.

He whipped his head around, lip curled. "Can you jump that far?"

"No!"

"Silvie—"

The bats were on them, snapping, clawing, and beating them with enormous wings and deafening shrieks. They would circle high and swoop down on Johnis and Silvie's heads, always attacking from above.

Only Silvie's torch offered any protection. That and Shaeda's phenomenal strength.

Johnis managed to strike a second and used that to keep them back. The torches went between their teeth every time they had to climb. Blood poured from open wounds. First: get out alive.

"Grab!" Johnis latched onto a bat right as it headed toward the top. It jerked under his weight. A second and third joined the fray. Johnis swung out and broke loose of the bat's leg, barely catching the edge.

The harach. He didn't dare lose it.

They craved human flesh. And Leedhan blood.

He hoisted himself over the lip of the floor, rolled, and reached down for Silvie. "Jump! Jump!"

She screamed again, so loud he thought she was dead. Then her hands slapped his. Johnis grabbed her fingers and pulled. She scrambled over him.

"Come on!"

They tore through the tunnel with its claustrophobic darkness and sped through the labyrinth with giant bats latched onto their backs, teeth digging into their flesh. Several pulled him down and tore a chunk out of him.

Silvie beat them off and half dragged him, flying down the

dark tunnel. Johnis staggered into a wall. Silvie tripped and nearly landed in worm sludge. Together they staggered like two drunks with one leg, back through the overhang and into the lakebed.

"What happened back there? Your eyes—"

"What about them?"

"They looked like Shaeda's."

"I think they were."

Bats were pouring out of the lair. The stark Black Forest surrounded them. The trees were laden in Shataiki so thick he couldn't see the sun.

Black wood, black dirt.

The muddy graveyard they had stood in was now full of murky water. The same raunchy substance flowed over the fall.

They were both losing blood, but they dared not rest, dared not stop. Where were Warryn and his men? More than an hour had to have passed.

The Shataiki queen's voice roared from somewhere within. Johnis grabbed Silvie. Shaeda's will overran him once more. "We have to go!"

"He said if we got out alive, he'd—"

"Run!"

ARROWS AND SWORDS FLASHED BETWEEN ERAM'S MEN, Cassak's men, and Warryn's men. Despite Cassak's orders, bodies were falling, dying left and right. So far the Eramites suffered the worst—they would not allow the throaters to take them alive.

"Sanctuary to all who lay down their arms!" Cassak cried over the melee. "Lay down your arms! Lay down your arms! We didn't come here to fight!"

A few rebels submitted, down on their knees, hands behind their heads. Only those who would not yield to the throaters fell dead.

"Warryn! Call off your men! Call off—"

A loud screech took to the air, followed by a low boom—lower than a drum, barely audible, yet piercing the ears—and the earth shook.

The canyon transformed into the thick, broad-leafed Black Forest with trees that climbed several hundred feet into the air. And from its depths came a howling black thunderstorm that screeched into the sky, blacking out the sun.

Throaters, warriors, and rebels all went still. Cassak realized his mouth was open and shut it. The cloud came straight for them, and several of the men began to run.

Then it all vanished.

All was quiet on the edge of a canyon, where seconds ago a bloody skirmish took more than a dozen victims.

The Black Forest reappeared. Then was gone.

Seconds passed. They turned to minutes.

Cassak recovered from his stupor.

"Take the Eramites and the throaters." He put his sword at Warryn's throat before the serpent warrior could protest.

"We'll wait for the pup."

JOHNIS TUCKED THE MEDALLION INTO HIS SHIRT. DESERT and barren canyon met them once more. He drew it back out. Forest so thick it blotted out the sun enveloped them and the Shataiki swarming out of the cave.

"Johnis!"

He shoved it back into his shirt and they fled together, hearts pounding.

"What in the name of Elyon was that?"

Silvie didn't answer. They didn't stop until they reached where they had left the horses, right at the edge of the Black Forest, and stirred up a flock of vultures.

Both horses were dead, corpses feasted upon by the birds. Silvie screamed. The sound made Johnis jump. He fought the sick urge to retrieve the medallion again.

No, not yet.

Only now, staring at the dead horses, they both staggered to the ground. Shaeda's strength left. He collapsed. He'd lost so much blood, and Silvie too. Johnis closed his eyes, the amulet in hand.

He couldn't give up. Not now. He'd survived the queen's lair, survived his challenge. Bats liked playing with their prey. The

Shataiki hadn't expected the Leedhan to give Johnis that much power, enough to get out of the lair alive.

Merely a taste.

What else could the Leedhan . . . the Leedhan do . . . ?

His eyes started to close. Silvie said something, but he couldn't hear it.

Fog enveloped him. Shaeda, punishing him for succeeding, only to die of blood loss . . .

Horses and riders shuffled toward them. Johnis felt hands reach for him. He jumped and tried to wrestle free.

"Easy," said the Scab.

"That's a lot of—what happened down there?"

"Look at him, Cap'n. He's almost glowing. And his eyes . . ."

"Help the woman," the captain said. "Tie them up." He crouched and took the amulet from Johnis's hand. Johnis tried to struggle but couldn't.

Immediately the Black Forest returned.

The captain concealed the amulet. The forest disappeared behind the veil once more. "What in the name of Teeleh was that?"

"Black Forest. Shataiki," Johnis rasped. "I told Marak . . ."

"Sucrow is going to want that," another said.

"It's for General Marak to decide."

They were taken up the path to the rim of the canyon, this Teardrop from Hades. Johnis was placed on the ground, on his feet, wrists bound behind his back.

Before him were almost two dozen of Marak's men. Evidence

of a fight. Dead Eramites, mostly, it looked like. And a few throaters.

The dead Scabs would be left. Four rebels were bound and waiting. And Warryn and the remaining throaters were also under guard.

Johnis felt his mind tumble down the tunnel. Shaeda's presence enveloped him. He did not resist. She was truly an entity—lovely beyond comprehension.

And she was right. His amulet worked. Sucrow would believe now, now that all these men had seen, now that Marak's own captain had seen the eclipse.

Every last albino would die. Johnis's mind began to spin. Sucrow would kill him.

"Don't give it to the priest," he said to Cassak. He looked over at Silvie. Only then did he notice everyone was staring at him. "What now?"

The captain. "You, using an albino magic?"

"Are you a fool?"

"You're doing it again," Silvie said. "Your eyes . . . Your wounds . . . and mine too . . ."

The warrior holding him let him look down. Sure enough. The bites and scratches and wounds sustained in his battle with the Shataiki were . . .

Healing.

His mind sharpened.

Shaeda's thoughts interposed with his own, and he couldn't tell which was which. No longer cared. She made him invincible. Omnipotent. Tasted so good . . .

"Shaeda," he whispered.

Rough hands dragged him forward. "Let's hope you two haven't started a war," Cassak growled. "Move along. Marąk and the priest can sort this out."

twenty-eight

Sucrow lit the last of his candles and settled to read the old Leedhan legends. Ever since the boy and girl had come, his interest had been kindled. He'd poured over the account and learned much, studied the ceremony the boy Josef kept going on about.

And his plans for the female . . .

Sucrow sneered. She was a lovely little wench, wasn't she? A perfect specimen for the Great One, His Excellency, Teeleh. The greatest among the Dark Ones.

A knock at the door.

Sucrow looked up, scowling. "Enter," he snapped. The wretch obeyed and went to both knees, groveling. Sucrow circled the little fool. "I should let Marak hang you just for existing. You're late. Again."

"My priest, forgive . . . There was much to—"

"Raise your head, boy. At least pretend to have a spine." Sucrow dug his nails into the back of the servant's neck and drew blood. The servant shuddered but didn't cry out. Sucrow raked deep along the bloated, flaking, already pained flesh.

His servant cried out. "My lord . . . forgive me." He sat straight on his knees now, however. That was a beginning. Little weasel couldn't stand at attention correctly in the presence of Teeleh's high priest.

"Forgiveness is for the weak. I am disgusted at tolerating your incompetence. Why are you here, wretch?"

The servant was out of breath. Fresh from the desert. He held up a scroll with Warryn's mark on it.

"My lord."

"About time," Sucrow muttered. He tore it open and scanned it, reading everything that had taken place, including the skirmish between Eram, Cassak, and his serpent warriors.

"Cassak?" Sucrow swore. "Why was I not notified of this immediately? I am weary of that albino-loving general's defiance!"

"There is more, my lord."

"Well, out with it."

"As in the scroll, my lord, they have retrieved the amulet. Everyone present has seen the lair of these . . . Shataiki."

"Where is it now? The youths are dead, I presume."

The servant shook his head. "The general has all three, my lord."

"The general. Eram?"

"No, my lord, Marak."

"Order him to bring me the amulet and to kill the whelps. And take the fruit from the boy as well."

"Regrettably, my lord . . . Marak has refused."

Sucrow ground his teeth. "Stand up. Your groveling irritates me." He poured a glass of wine. "Tell him to obey my orders or I will see him tried for treason. I want that amulet."

"He . . . he said you would say that, my priest."

"Finish, fool. You try my patience."

"He said that because you have executed his family and not allowed him to execute vengeance in his own manner regarding the slave, he will not turn possession of the amulet over to you."

Sucrow slowly turned from the man, tracing one of his braids. So this was it. Out of nowhere had come this amulet and with it the power to make or destroy all that mattered.

Rage boiled through his blood.

He would crush Marak for this.

And Qurong, if he got in the way.

In a matter of days, he would rule the Horde, and every single albino in the land would be dead.

"We will see," he said softly. There was a tremor in his voice. "We will see."

to be continued . . .

If you started with LUNATIC . . .

The Lost Books

The Lost Books Graphic Novels

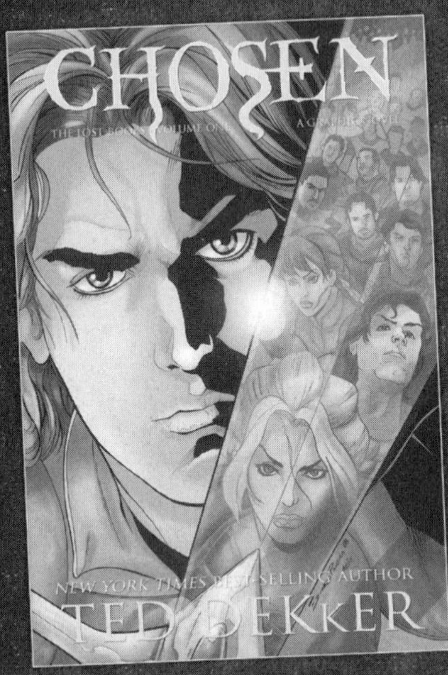

The Circle Series Graphic Novels

Available Now

FALLING.
EVER FALLING.
INTO AN ENDLESS WORLD OF WHITE.

ONE MINUTE, BILLOS WAS IN THE FOREST.
THE NEXT, HE FOUND HIMSELF IN THIS --
-- NOTHINGNESS.

HAD IT BEEN SECONDS? HOURS? DAYS?
THERE WAS NO WAY TO TELL.

WAS HE DEAD? ALIVE?
SOME STATE IN-BETWEEN?

WHETHER THIS WAS OF ELYON'S MAKING --
-- OR OF TEELEH, ONE THING WAS CERTAIN --
-- HE WAS GOING MAD -- OR, PERHAPS, ALREADY WAS.

ANOTHER THING HAD BECOME ALL TOO CLEAR TO BILLOS.
HE WAS UTTERLY --
ENTIRELY --
PAINFULLY --

-- ALONE.

ELSEWHERE, IN THE WORLD WHERE BILLOS WAS BORN --
WAIT!

YOU CAN'T TELL THE COMMANDER ABOUT THIS! YOU TOOK A VOW, DARSAL!
THOMAS MAY BE THE ONLY ONE WHO KNOWS WHAT HAPPENED TO BILLOS! HE'S THE ONLY ONE WHO'S BEEN BEYOND THIS WORLD!

THAT'S JUST A RUMOR!
PLEASE, DARSAL! YOU CAN'T TELL HIM ABOUT THE BOOKS -- OR BILLOS!
TRY AND STOP ME.

FINE!
UUUGH!

JOIN THE
CIRCLE

TED DEKKER is the *New York Times* best-selling author of more than twenty novels. He is known for stories that combine adrenaline-laced plots with incredible confrontations between good and evil. He lives in Texas with his wife and children.

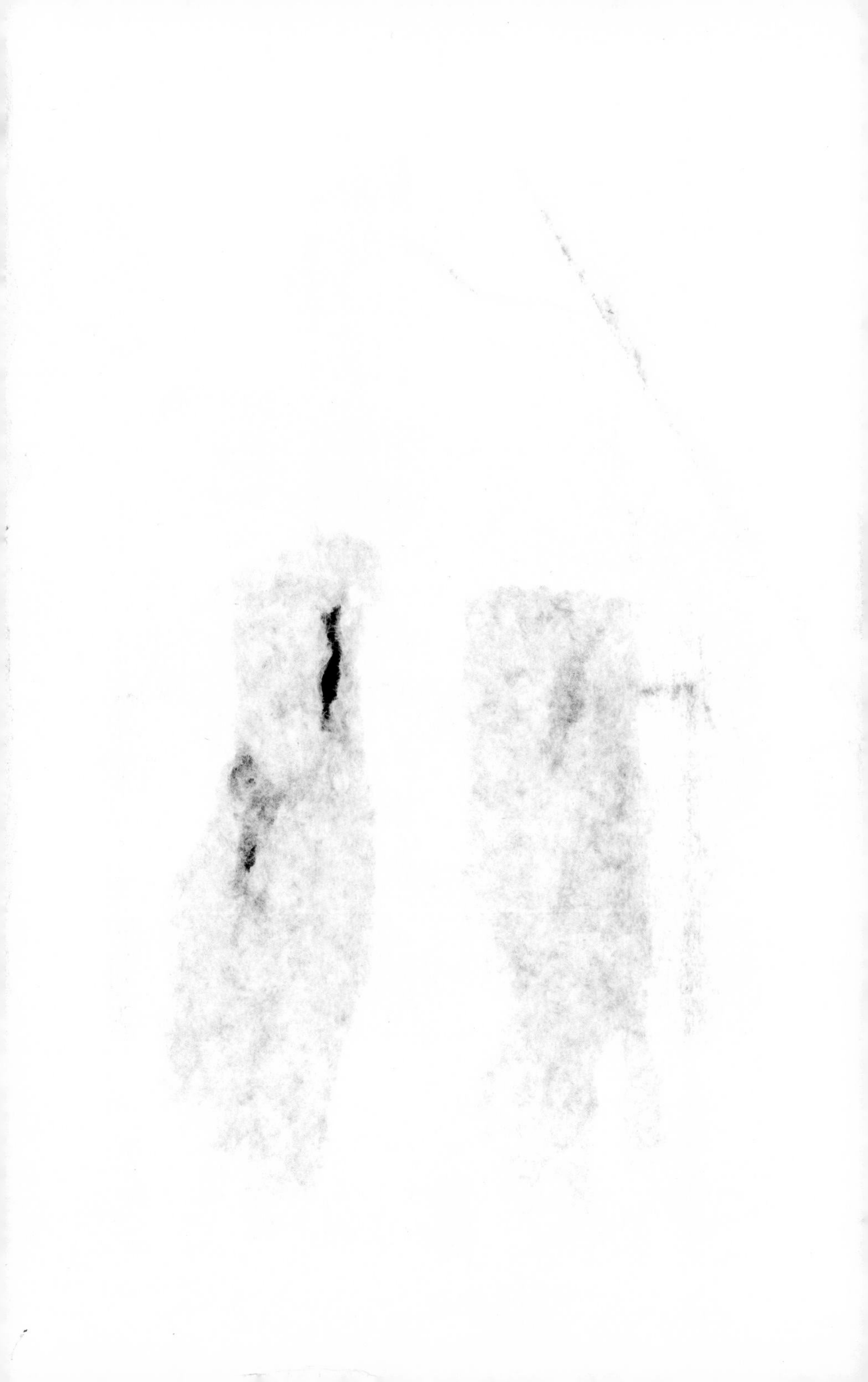

OTHER
EARTH
Black Forest
Western Forest
Desert